Arden House

BOOK 1 · FLIGHT
&
BOOK 2 · TOWN

by R. M. Bryan

illustrations by Ken Mabrey

Acknowledgments

I am forever thankful to my loving and tolerant family:
Dela, Katie, Sweetie, Dad, Dave, Mark, Rachel and Steve,
as well as Greg Schauer, my gifted editor,
my amazing beta-readers, led by Lindsay Harris-Friel,
and Cecilia Vore, my book designer.

In memory of Ryan Hall, Ronnie Powell, and her.

Dedication

Anyone who reads books in this age is either
Swimming against the tide or
Stuck on some kind of rock.
You are my people.
I wrote this book for us.

AUTHOR'S NOTE

This all happened in the year 2117. Some grim things must be said about what happened to the world before the beginning of this story. This is not a dark book, not really. Well, it is, yes, in a way.

It's a sorry shame, really, everything that went wrong. The systemic failures were so staggering and vast, they could fill many books, but not this book. To summarize, every complex system of the 20th century failed in the 21st.

Big banks, big pharma, big government, big oil, and big media all fell apart. We wasted our time and energy making everything "bigger and better". We might have done better to focus on making things "resilient" or "sustainable" but hey, who could have known? Who could have predicted? Where is the profit in being sustainable? Let's not dwell on beating ourselves up about it. We can't change the past.

Balances were pushed beyond tipping points. Reality responded the way it does. There were simplifications. Balances were restored. A global flu pandemic, the financial system collapsed, the oil market imploded, climate variability, a mutated hantavirus… they all blossomed into full flower, did their damage, then faded away. It was not an orderly or tidy process. It was a long, grinding nightmare. There was a lot of pain and more death.

Okay, so that's the bad news. The good news is that a few of us were left at the end to start something new and different. Not many.

Few.

How few? Of course nobody knew for sure, but let me put it this way… the state of New Jersey, which had about 9 million people in 2013, had about 5000 people in 2117.

It was not really much of a "state" anymore, just "some places." When our story begins, there are no cars, televisions, computers, internet, law enforcement, or practical currency. We had learned how to run small farms again. We re-learned to do without many things we rightly needed. We learned how to help each other again, to relate to each other and we knew again why that's vital.

We began to knit our little communities back together. We salvaged what we could from the old world and went on living.

The cheerful news for you, dear reader, is that these agonizing losses and painful horrors took place long before any of the people in this story were conceived.

Book One · Flight

CHAPTER 1

Latin hunched over a slender lawnmower blade by the flickering light of the woodstove. He buffed the razor-sharp edge with a fine canvas strop.

"What time is it?" asked Grandpa, knowing very well what time it was.

"Eight fifteen," Latin said, touching the face of his father's watch as he checked it.

"What time are you going to leave for market in the morning?" asked Grandpa.

"Dawn is at six eighteen tomorrow. I'd like to start walking well before then."

"Have you thought about getting to bed soon?"

"I wouldn't sleep—too excited. Besides, I want to hone the edge on that scythe, and I need to oil the shavers one last time."

"Mind if I have a look at your arrows?" Grandpa asked.

"Please do. I like the way they came out. I'm looking forward to testing them out tomorrow along the way to market. I finished the edges the way we talked about, with a low bevel and the edges flared out slightly at ends."

Latin wrapped the mower blade in an old, soft cloth and set it beside the other packages he would bundle together with twine. He lifted the scythe by the handle and admired his work by twisting the curved blade slowly in the firelight. He focused his eyes intensely, scanning the glistening edge for any nicks or pits. Finding no flaws, his eyes softened into a contented smile.

Latin plucked one of his longest brown hairs from the very top of his head. Holding the hair lightly between the thumb and pointer finger of his right hand, he tapped the hair against the blade. The hair sliced effortlessly in two. Latin slid the scythe carefully into its hard leather sheath. He put the scythe next to the mower blade.

"These arrows are fine," Grandpa said. "Highest quality. Not only the arrowheads, but also the shafts and the fletching. This is impressive craftsmanship. This is quite an accomplishment. I am very proud of your work."

Latin smiled up at him and winked. Grandpa nodded approval.

Latin started checking the dozen shavers he had given fresh edges for market customers. With slow care, he scanned those glistening edges in the firelight and tested them with hairs. When he found spots that were rough or dull, Latin worked them gently and patiently with his finest, black sharpening stone and heavy leather strop. When satisfied, he drew two drops of oil from a glass bottle with an eyedropper, dropped the oil onto the blade and rubbed the oil in with a soft cotton cloth. Finally, he wrapped each shaver in a cloth bundle and set it on the table for packing.

Latin stood, stretching. "Okay, I'll get some rest."

"Have you decided about carrying camping gear with you tomorrow?"

"I don't think I'm going to have room in the pack. Even if I did have room, the extra weight would be too much. If I take the camping gear, there's no chance that I'll make it there and back in one day."

"That's probably true. It's at least 10 miles each way, maybe a little more."

"I'm going to leave the camping things here. I'll just take it slow on the way back. I'll make it."

"It's a risk. It might be safer to take a sleeping bag, at least. It can get quite cold, you know."

"I know. The bag is so heavy, though. Over that much distance, if I'm going to take anything extra, I might as well plan on spending the night in the woods and take a tent and everything."

"I see your point. It's up to you, of course. I'm sure you'll be fine." Grandpa said, nodding encouragement.

Latin stepped into his moccasins. He pushed through a heavy door into the cold back room of their long Quonset hut for firewood. He shuffled past the apple press and the shelves loaded with jars of vegetables, crushed tomatoes, and applesauce. He loaded the rolling cart with split wood, wheeled it into the front room, filled the stove, set the rest of the logs in the wooden box beside it, and returned the cart. Latin went outside to brush his teeth and check the weather.

"Very cold?" Grandpa asked when he returned.

"Yes. Forty-three, it says. I wrote it in the weather log. This March has been just a few degrees colder than last year, on average. It keeps getting colder and colder," Latin replied. "Grandma's late getting back," he added.

"She'll be along. You know how those ladies like to talk on when they get the chance," said Grandpa.

"Maybe there's news?"

"News?"

"Maybe news of Ma and Pa?"

The sounds hurt Latin's throat to say. Their faces came fresh into his mind. He slouched from the fresh pain of their long absence.

Grandpa shook his head slowly and said, "If there were news, she would have run home as quickly as she could to tell you, I'm afraid."

With a heavy spirit, Latin changed into his nightclothes and filled a wooden cup with water from the bucket. He put the cup on the bench near his bed and said, "Goodnight, Grandpa."

"Goodnight, Latin."

Later, after Latin had been asleep for hours, his grandmother crept silently through the door, pulled in the latchstring, and put one last log in the woodstove before going to bed herself.

CHAPTER 2

Latin lay in bed, awake. His thoughts raced with eagerness, fear, anxious expectation, and excitement. He gave up on trying to go back to sleep. His father's watch on the bench by the bed read three forty-five in the dim moonlight. Latin got up silently, filled the woodstove, opened the vent, and put the kettle on, then laced up his moccasins and went outside.

He stood outside for several minutes gazing deep into the woods and up into the stars. He whispered a prayer. It rose up into the sky in tumbling puffs of cloudy breath. He asked for a safe journey, for square trades, and for his parents to return. When he felt the cold sink through to his bones, he went back inside. He undressed and put on his wool thermals, canvas work pants, and boots, and then he made a pot of tea and quietly packed his backpack.

"It's early," Grandma said softly from her bed.

"Four thirty," Latin admitted.

"Put the lamp on," she said.

Latin lit the oil lamp and drew the wick down until the glow was useful, but dim.

Grandma said, "I brought a letter from Miss Turner. It's for the widow Murphy. I left it on the table."

"I see it. I'll make sure I give it to her," said Latin, tucking the letter into the inside breast pocket of his vest.

"Enough water in the kettle for oats?" Grandma asked.

"Yes, plenty. I'll cook them. You stay in bed," Latin offered.

Grandpa rolled slowly in bed, putting his arm over Grandma. Quite loudly, he said, "Ooh...how about we let Grandma cook the oats this morning, right? Yes. I've had your cooking. You're a good man, but you cook like a bladesmith."

After eating, checking his backpack once more, and being reminded of the many barter requests from neighbors, Latin checked the watch.

"Five forty-five," he announced. "I need to be getting on the move."

"Would it help if I told you to be careful one more time?" Grandma asked, standing to hug him.

"It might," Latin said, hugging her.

Latin took a deep breath and then lifted his loaded backpack up from the chair and onto his back. He put his quiver of arrows over his left shoulder and his bow over his right. "That's heavier than I expected, even without any camping gear," Latin said with concern.

"You've decided not to take any gear?" Grandpa asked.

"I have the tarp for emergencies. Anything else would be just too heavy. I'll be fine. I can make do."

"Keep your eyes open," Grandpa said, shaking Latin's hand.

"I will. I expect it will be quite late when I get back," Latin said, pausing with his hand on the door.

"That's fine, we'll be right here."

CHAPTER 3

Latin took the first steps into the cold morning and then stopped to adjust the weight of his pack and let his eyes adjust to the darkness. He slowly followed the little trail through the woods toward the road, taking each step with care. Just before the road came into view, he stopped and listened for over a minute. As he crossed the road, he moved quickly and kept low.

He continued straight across the road, up a short gully on the other side, and down to another trail in the woods. After he had gone a few steps into the woods, he stopped and listened again. Hearing nothing, he took a deep breath and kept hiking into the growing dawn light.

He did not see anyone all morning. Everyone else going to market would travel by horse, on the roads. Latin's fear of horses was legendary. Horses had terrified him since his earliest memories. He did not understand why. Most of the others going to market had bulky trade goods like grain, wool, cheese, scrap metal, or vegetables that would have been impossible to carry on foot. Latin was fortunate that his goods were small enough to carry in a pack over distance.

There were eleven abandoned, burned-out houses along the way. Latin knew them well and counted them as landmarks. Long ago, Latin had walked the path to market with his Pa, who had to walk everywhere since he traded away their two horses when Latin was a toddler. To pass the time, Latin's Pa had told stories of the lives of families who used to live in the eleven houses along the way. Their roofs had all failed and rotted away years ago. Most of the buildings had fallen in on themselves and were being pulled back into the earth by weeds and small trees, but Latin remembered the names of the families in the stories. He retold them as he walked alone.

At ten forty-five, Latin finally reached the spot where he and his father had always stopped to rest. Latin grinned, planted his feet, drew his bow around in front of him, and whipped an arrow from his quiver. With his pack still on, he nocked the arrow, drew back, and shot his arrow across the clearing. It hissed in the air and smashed into the center of a massive oak. Bark flew off the tree in all directions.

Latin walked across the clearing toward the tree, set down his pack, and took a long drink of water from his canteen. Reverently, he approached the tree, bowing slightly in apology, and worked his arrow out of the bark.

He closed his eyes and ran his fingers along the mark the arrow had left in the tree. Quietly, he touched the other marks he had made with similar shots on previous trips. Finally, he reached up to the single notch in the tree his father had made on their last trip to market together nearly two years ago. Latin held his hand up over the mark, feeling the scar of it and trying to draw out something more.

He sat in the clearing, stretched his legs, and ate his salt pork, cheese, and carrots. As he was putting on his pack to go, Latin heard a horse approaching on the road just beyond the clearing. He slipped on his quiver and bow and went to see who it was. The dappled gray horse had come to a stop, and Latin recognized the rider immediately. "Hello, Mr. Fitch," Latin said as he stepped out of the brush into the road, waving.

"Latin! I thought you might be around here this morning. I wanted to come tell you that they've moved the market spot again this month."

"That was very kind of you, thank you so much for saving me the extra walking. Where is it today?"

"It's down the old railroad bed toward the pond."

"Nixon's Pond?" Latin asked.

"No, the other way, away from town, Pillar Pond," Mr. Fitch said.

"Any reason for moving it? Was there some threat?" Latin asked.

Mr. Fitch shifted on his horse. "No, I don't think so. I'm sure there's no cause for it except that Billy wants to make sure everybody understands that he's in charge around here and can do as he pleases."

"Okay, so nobody saw any—"

"No Skullers, nothing. No good reason at all, I'm sure. Just wanted to show he's boss now," Mr. Fitch said, leading his horse to take a step backward, away from Latin. "Am I getting the horse too close to you? Are you okay?" Mr. Fitch asked.

"I'm fine, that's good. Thanks for asking, and thanks again for coming all the way out here to save me the longer trip. I guess you won't be going to market yourself today?" Latin asked.

"Me? A simple farmer? Ha! I could never afford the price to get into market these days—not the way Billy keeps squeezing everyone. I am lucky to be able to trade with my own neighbors. My little vegetable crops could never bring enough for me to pay the entry fee. No, my market days are over. I do all my trading direct, but you…you've made quite a name for yourself, young man. You'll do well, I'm sure."

"Thanks again," Latin said with a slight bow.

CHAPTER 4

"Hey, it's Latin, last one to market," teased one of the two guards in brown leather vests blocking the dirt road.

"Day's almost over, Latin, you missed all the good stuff. Why so late?" asked the other.

"I'm always late. I have to walk ten miles to get here," Latin said with a sigh, setting down his pack.

"Why don't you just ride a horse like everyone else?" the guard on the right asked with a mocking sneer.

Latin nodded. "Yes. Good point. That would be easier."

"Whatever. Prices went up," said the guard on the left.

"Double," said the other.

Latin took a step back and rubbed his face. He squatted to stretch his aching legs. He considered his options. He could pay the price or carry his things all the way back home.

"Fine," he said quickly, pulling two arrows out of his quiver and handing one to each guard.

Latin walked into the bright clearing and smiled. A bustling crowd of seventy-five people chatted and traded in a huge circle, each person with their goods laid out in front of them. The sun had warmed the air, the ground was dry, and there were bright green buds hanging from the tips of every branch surrounding the clearing.

His eyes swept the market area looking for open space to sit down and rest. He saw Autumn, the pale herbalist, in her black dress, waving, smiling, and pointing to an open space beside her.

Latin winked at her as he walked over. Setting down his pack, he said, "Hey, Autumn. Good morning. How have you been? What's new?"

"Hi, Latin. I'm fine. Doing well. Good business. Glad to see you."

"Why is this space open next to you? Did someone set up here and leave already?"

Autumn made a quick movement with her head towards the two men standing in the tree line at the edge of the clearing.

Latin raised a hand to wave to the men, but they did not wave back. They were dressed in the brown leather vests of Billy's guards. "What's that all about?" Latin asked, sitting down and reclining to rest his head on the side of his backpack.

"Billy sent a couple of his guards to protect me," Autumn said, rolling her eyes.

"That's nice of him I guess," Latin said with a shrug.

"Excuse me, I'm so sorry to interrupt. I know you just arrived and haven't had a chance to set up yet, but…"

Latin looked up to see the widow Murphy. His eyebrows rose. She wore a graceful black dress. Her smile had such a sad and sweet quality; Latin was moved to tears just looking at her. He fought them back.

Latin stood slowly. "Oh, yes, hello. I'm very sorry to hear the news of your husband's passing," he said with a shaking voice, moving stiffly to shake her hand and then hold it as they spoke.

"Thank you," she said, nodding. Latin had to look away. The agonizing sorrow in her voice struck close to Latin's own loss.

The widow Murphy sensed what was happening for Latin and kindly gave him time to gather himself. "You know what my husband used to say?" she asked.

Latin nodded, unable to speak.

"My husband used to tell me, 'We give life everything we have to give. Then life asks for more, and we give that, too.'"

Latin frowned. "I'm just so sorry for your loss. Nothing seems to hurt so badly as the loss of someone you love. I'm so sorry."

"We go on," she said.

"Yes, I suppose we do. Grandma and Grandpa send their love and apologies. They said that if you need anything at all, just send word."

"You're very kind. That is a comfort, thank you. I need to get back to my place soon for some other things, so I'll need to be leaving…" she said, trailing off.

"Oh, yes, of course," Latin said, pulling the letter from his inside breast pocket. As the widow opened and read the letter, Latin dug through his backpack to find the shavers he had honed for the late Mr. Murphy. "Here they are," he said, offering the cloth bundle to Mrs. Murphy.

Looking up from the letter, Mrs. Murphy gasped, "Oh, his razors. I'd forgotten."

"When I heard the news, I oiled them and wrapped them all for storage. They'll keep like this for ages," Latin said.

"Latin?"

"Yes, Mrs. Murphy?"

"Could you…could you keep these for me? I'm not ready to have them yet…. Actually…"

"Yes, Mrs. Murphy?"

"Latin, would it be okay if I just gave these to you as a gift? You can have them. Trade them for whatever you like. I would rather that you had them."

"That's fine. Fine. Yes, thank you, Mrs. Murphy. I understand. Yes, certainly."

"Miss Turner will be expecting a reply from me. Would you mind delivering it?"

"Oh, Mrs. Murphy, it would be a pleasure, of course," Latin said, blushing. Autumn watched their quiet exchange with interest.

While Mrs. Murphy was writing her response, a squat, wrinkly man walked up and asked, "Latin, were you able to do anything with that rusty old fishing knife I left with you?"

"I was, yes. Let me get that for you," Latin said, excusing himself from Mrs. Murphy and rummaging through his bundles. "Here, what do you think?" Latin asked, letting the little man unwrap his knife and pull it from the new sheath Latin had made.

"Oh, heavens," the little man said with a gasp. "Are you sure this is the knife I brought you?"

Mrs. Murphy looked up from her letter and smiled.

Latin's shoulders drew back with pride as he said, "It is the same blade. I had to grind on it quite a bit to get through the rust, and I carved a new handle, because the old one was rotten. I wrapped the new handle with fresh leather. Of course, I made the sheath. That's new."

"It's beautiful, son. It's like a work of art. How did you get it to shine like this? And the leatherwork around the handle is first rate. You did this all yourself?"

"I did, yes. My grandpa and I did it together. He's a good teacher."

"Young man, I've seen your new axheads at work, so I knew you had some skill with a blade, but this—"

"Thank you, sir. So, you'll be interested in trading for the knife, then?" Latin asked, smiling.

"Oh, yes, of course—and more. I'll be back. Here, I'll leave the knife with you until I return. I have something very special that I'm pretty sure you'll like. I'll be back, thank you."

Immediately another man shook Latin's hand and said, "Hey, Latin, that sure is a fine-looking knife. Got my mower blade?"

Latin pulled a long, flat bundle out of his backpack and handed it to the man. "There you go," he said.

The man handed Latin a quart jug of clear liquid.

"You're not going to check it?" Latin asked with a smile.

"And nearly cut my finger off like last time?" The man laughed. "No, I'm sure it's plenty sharp. Tell your grandpa to enjoy the hooch."

"I will, thanks."

There was now a line in front of Latin.

The next man in line was the barber. He said, "I see you're busy. Can you let me have my shavers and my scissors now, then later you can come round for a haircut?"

"Sure thing," Latin said, handing over several bundles and shaking hands.

"You got my scythe?" asked the next man.

"I do, yes," Latin said, pulling a large, curved bundle from the bottom of his pack.

The man raised an eyebrow and drew the scythe from its sheath.

"Just don't check it with your finger, please," Latin warned.

"Son, I've been farming since before you were born. I've checked blades for shar—Ow! Damn!" yelped the man, jerking his bloody thumb away from the scythe.

"I'm sorry." Latin smiled sympathetically.

"Good Lord, son, where did you learn to set a blade like that?"

"It was handed down to me."

The man handed Latin a cured ham wrapped with string. "Good on you. That set us square?" he asked, huffing.

"Oh, more than square. Yes, sir. For this, I'll sharpen it for you three times more for nothing extra. This is a very nice ham. Thank you. Sorry about your thumb."

"My fault. It'll heal," the man said, walking away and shaking his head at the scythe blade as he put it back into the sheath with great care.

Walt the massive lumberjack was next. There was no one behind him. Latin and Walt shook hands forcefully. "Good to see you, Latin," Walt said, knocking Latin playfully on the shoulder.

Latin staggered sideways and steadied himself playfully by grabbing Walt's shirt. Autumn giggled.

Latin said, "Walt, I got your splitting maul here, and your two saws and the new axhead you asked for."

Walt smiled. He rolled the heavy splitting maul head around like a pebble in his enormous hands "That's a heap of work, all of it top notch, and I still haven't given you anything from all the work you did back in February, either. Latin, we're a far sight from square," Walt said. "Sure you don't need any firewood?"

"Sorry, Walt. We've got a full year of wood under cover and two more years' worth already split, outside curing."

"Care to walk around with me? Quite a few folks around the market owe me a little, and my credit is good with most. Maybe you could find some things you need, and that could help set us square?" Walt asked.

"Sure. I need to get a quick haircut, too. Autumn, could you please watch my bag? Do you need anything?" Latin asked.

Autumn waved him away. She said, "I'm fine. You go get what you need."

Just as he was leaving with Walt, Mrs. Murphy said, "Latin, before you go, can I give you this note? Could you please see that it gets to Miss Turner? I need to be getting back."

Latin folded the letter and put it in the inside breast pocket of his coat. "I will make sure she gets it, of course, and please do let us know if there's anything we can help with."

The widow Murphy smiled at Latin, Walt, and Autumn as she left.

After Latin's haircut, Walt said, "Now, look, Latin. I've got my cart here, and I owe you for a heap of work, and you do top notch, which I very much appreciate, so don't worry about asking for too much, okay? I want you sharpening my axes, knives, and saws for a long time to come, so I want to make sure we get good and square. Understood?"

Latin said, "Okay, we're squaring up on…let's see, the new splitting ax from last month, resetting the edge on the maul, the little saw that had the rust, the big saw from two months ago, two sheath knives, those planer blades that had all the nicks, that rusty froe, and the adze with the broken blade. Right? Is that it?"

"Sounds right," Walt said. "You just go around and get whatever you need, put it in my cart, and I'll make sure that it all gets to your place, seeing as you're…well, you know…not a horse person."

As they went around the clearing together, Latin got a large bag of dried apple slices, a corked bottle of sunflower-seed oil, two quarts of jarred peach preserves, a pound bag of sea salt, a quart of lamp oil, two pounds of brown sugar, three yards of cotton broadcloth, six flannel handkerchiefs, and a quart jar of honey.

"How are we doing?" Latin asked.

"Getting close, but keep going," Walt said, nodding.

From the sheep farmer selling wool and mutton, Latin picked up three dull knives and two sheep shears that he would sharpen. Then, with other merchants, Latin traded on Walt's credit for a large sack of roasted peanuts, a fine pair of leather work gloves, and a large bundle of dry scrap cloth. "I

feel we're getting close to being square," Latin said.

"Agreed," Walt said. "Close enough for me. I've got a two-man saw and two handsaws that need work. I'll come around to your pack in a bit and pick up any other things you need hauled back, then drop all this by your place this afternoon. Sound fair?"

Latin and Walt shook hands. "Thank you," Latin said.

"Likewise, and good luck with Autumn. I think she's sweet on you," Walt said with a grin.

Latin looked at the ground and asked, "What makes you think that?"

"Just the way she looks at you, plus I saw her turn away three different people who tried to set up in that spot where your things are now. She knew you were going to be late. She saved that spot for you. That's something. A girl that pretty saving a spot for you… you're a lucky young man."

"Aww, Walt. I don't think so. We're just friends. – Did she really save that spot for me?"

Walt nodded and smirked as he walked away.

Just as Latin made it back to his backpack, the little wrinkly man came up alongside him and said, "I got something really special that I think will set us square on that fine fishing knife you salvaged."

"Oh?" Latin asked with a curious lift of his voice.

"Yeah, smell this," he said, holding up a burlap sack.

Latin took a short sniff, then a great lungful. "Are you kidding me? Is that what I think it is?" Latin asked.

"What do you think it is?" the man asked.

Latin whispered, "Coffee? Is that real coffee?"

"It is. Would that set us square?" he asked.

"Where did you get this?" Latin asked with amazement.

"It came quite dear, I can tell you that. I want you to have it though."

"Oh, thank you. Of course, yes," Latin said, handing over the knife.

CHAPTER 5

"You've done well for yourself." Autumn said, raising her eyebrows in approval at Latin's heap of cargo.

"It is rather a lot. Do you need anything? Is there anything here that I can give you?" Latin asked, stretching his tired legs and sitting down on the ground next to Autumn.

"Is that moonshine?" Autumn said, looking at the clear jug.

"It is. You can have it."

"Mama and I could use that for birthing, anesthesia, and all kinds of things."

Latin handed it over. "You don't have to answer this, of course, but why is Billy sending his guards around with you?" he asked.

"I'm not sure," Autumn said, grinning. "Maybe he just wants to know I'm safe?"

Latin winced. "I doubt that's it."

The candlemaker approached Latin and held out a bone-handled hunting knife with a blade worn down to the sharpness of a butter knife.

"Your knife needs quite a bit of work," Latin said. "Looks like about 144 candles' worth to me."

The candlemaker whispered, "It's not my knife. A man I know heard about you and left this with me."

"What did the man offer in trade?" Latin asked.

"Fur. He's a trapper and a hunter," said the candlemaker.

"Okay, sure. I'll set a blade on it and bring it back next market."

They shook hands. Latin took the knife and set it with his pile of goods.

Autumn said, "Latin, do you need any medicines, herbs, tobacco?"

"Sure, thanks. I'll take some tobacco back to my grandpa."

Autumn made quick movements, untying a bag and scooping the dried leaves into a small sack. She tied it closed with a piece of twine. "That it? Nothing for you?"

A lean, bent lady who had been spinning wool into yarn approached Latin and Autumn with a burlap sack. "Excuse me, I'm sorry to interrupt."

Autumn said, "Hello, Rebecca, it's no interruption. How can I help you?"

"Oh, I don't need anything, I just brought you a bag of those Liverwort leaves you said you needed."

"Thank you, that's fantastic. What can I get you in trade? Do you need anything?"

"Oh, no. Nothing. Honestly, I don't know how I will ever be able to come square with you for saving young Edward's life last fall."

"You saved someone's life?" Latin asked.

"Oh, she did, yes. My young Edward is eight years old. He's a very healthy boy, but last fall, he had a toothache. I put clove oil on it because that's all I knew to do, but after a couple of days, he started running a terrible fever and sweating and screaming… oh, we had a devil of a time. It got to the point where I thought we might lose him, so I sent for Autumn's mother to help. She helped deliver him when I was pregnant, and I figured if anyone could do anything, she could. Autumn, is it okay for me to tell the story?"

"Sure, go on," Autumn said.

"Well, Autumn came herself in the middle of the night, and we thought she was too young to know any better, but we couldn't stop her. She jumped right in, opened up her little bag and just set up shop. I tell you what, I have never seen the likes of it in all my days. Her little hands were moving so fast, doing so many things at once, mixing medicines and poking here and there. It was more than I could bear to watch. I ran errands and brewed teas for her all night, and by morning, well, young Edward was far from working condition, but you could tell he was on the mend. His fever broke later on that day and about a week later, he was right as rain. I owe my son's life to this girl. She's a miracle. How many bags of leaves do you think I'd pick and bring to square up that kind of work? Young lady,

I'll bring you these leaves, and any others you ask for, as long as I'm able, and still feel like I owe you."

"I don't know what to say, except congratulations and thank you," Latin said as Rebecca walked back to her spinning wheel.

"These aren't Liverwort, by the way. They're Liverleaf, which is in an entirely different family and has an entirely different set of active compounds. The leaves she brought, Liverleaf, are somewhat rare, and quite useful. Liverwort is everywhere and basically useless." Autumn said, inspecting the bag. "I don't correct her, though. What would be the point? She could call them whatever she pleases, and they would work the same."

"Did you really save her son's life?"

"Probably. I mean, you never know if he would have died. I think he wouldn't have lasted much longer. His fever was quite high and his infection was going strong."

"How did you heal him?"

"It's complicated."

Latin looked around and nodded. He said, "What's going on with these guards behind us? It seems more like Billy is guarding what's his so that he keeps it his, more than he's guarding you to keep you safe, if you know what I mean."

"Maybe he thinks that," Autumn said with a flip of her hair.

A fat, loud man in overalls waddled up to Latin and said, "Howdy, neighbor."

"Hello, Mr. Connor," Latin said, standing and shaking hands. "Nice to see you all this way from home."

Mr. Connor said, "Latin, I was over at Walt's place the other day. He let me swing that new splitting ax you made for him. Latin, I've split wood off and on my whole life, and I have never seen anything that splits as well as that ax."

"Thank you. It's a family design. The splitting surface is of a particular shape," Latin said.

"I want one," said Mr. Connor.

"Well, they come pretty dear. I mean, I have to fire the forge for days and all the grinding…it is many days of work."

"What do you want, Latin? Name your price."

Latin said, "I don't know. Why don't I just make you one, and we'll figure out some way to get square over time?"

Mr. Connor said, "How about if I deliver a quart of fresh milk to your grandparents' front door? Wouldn't that be nice?"

Latin smiled, "Well, yes, Mr. Connor, but it—"

"How about a quart of fresh milk, delivered to your front door, three days a week all this spring?"

"I don't know," Latin said. "I've turned down offers that seemed quite a good deal richer than that."

"And fresh cheese once a week?"

"Honestly, Mr. Connor—and I don't want you to think I'm trying to drive an unfair deal or anything—but if I were going to make you one of the new axes, and carve the handle and everything, I'd want milk and cheese for a long time."

Mr. Connor put his hands on his hips. "How long?"

"First snowfall," said Latin.

Mr. Connor rocked back on his heels and whistled. "Really?"

"Please, don't agree if you think it's too much. I'm much more interested in having a neighbor I'm on good terms with than the sale of an ax. I'd very much like to make you an ax, but that's the price," Latin said.

"I think it's square. It's square, and I'll be glad to take you up on it," Mr. Connor said, shaking hands with Latin. "Hey, by the way, do you want a ride home? I know how you are with horses, but you could ride all the way in back of the wagon, far from the horse."

"Oh, no—no, thank you. You're kind, but I'll walk." Latin said.

"Well, at least let us take the heavy things back for you. We'll be glad to do it. We'll leave it all behind the rock at the head of the trail to your place."

"Well, Walt was going to make a special trip, but since you've got to go by our place anyway…yes, thank you, yes. That would really help me out," Latin said, putting together a load to carry to Mr. Connor's wagon.

After loading the wagon, Latin walked back into the market circle for one last look around. He wandered toward Autumn.

"What time is it?" she asked.

"Three fifteen."

"Your father's watch still keeps good time?"

"It does, yes, which is amazing, considering how old it is."

"How long did it take you to walk here?"

"Four hours and a quarter."

"You figure on five hours to get back?"

"Something like that," Latin said, sitting down next to her, closer than he had been before, "I have less to carry, but my legs are already tired. It will be dark when I get back home anyway, so I figure I might as well take my time."

They sat quietly for several minutes, watching the others finish their deals, pack up their goods, and say their good-byes. Latin checked to see that the two guards were still watching from behind them. They were. "Are Billy's men going to help you carry your things home?"

Autumn chuckled. "No. I don't expect so."

"I bet they would if you asked them."

"Perhaps. Here, take this," she said, handing Latin a small glass vial filled with a pale orange liquid.

Latin slipped the vial into his pocket. "Thank you. What is it?"

Autumn looked out into the clearing and said, "It will help you get home."

Latin looked at her, trying to look into her eyes, but Autumn pulled a wall of her long, straight black hair playfully across the side of her face, hiding behind it.

"What are you going to do about Billy?" he asked.

"What do you mean?"

"Well, I mean, if you let him send guards around with you, he might, you know, get ideas about how things are."

"That's my concern," Autumn said.

"It is, yes. I apologize, I just worry," Latin said.

A gentle smile rose in Autumn's eyes. Through her hair, Latin could see just enough of her face to know how she felt.

"You're kind to ask," she said.

"Well, I don't know what to say. Will you please let me know if there's anything I can do," Latin said.

Walt came over to them and said, "Sorry to interrupt. Latin, where's all your stuff? I came over to load up my cart."

"Oh, Walt. Thank you. I've sent it all home with Mr. Connor, our neighbor. I knew it was out of your way, so I sent it all with him, but I do appreciate your offering."

"You're a good man, Latin," he said, grinning at Autumn as he spoke.

"Thank you for saying so, Walt. Hope to see you again soon."

Walt left.

Latin stood, stretched, and lifted his pack, bow, and quiver onto his shoulders. "I don't want to go. I would much rather sit and visit, but if I don't leave now I won't make it home tonight. I didn't bring any camping gear, so I really must go."

"I know. Be safe," Autumn said.

CHAPTER 6

Latin checked the watch as he started walking home, slowly at first, then more quickly. After an hour, he took a five-minute break. He paced in small circles, stomping his feet to shake the stiffness out of his legs.

After a second hour, when he stopped to rest, he sat still with his back against a tree and stared out into the fading light of dusk. Latin rubbed at his legs, trying to loosen them, but stopped, as it was no help. His arms and hands were just as tired as his legs. When the watch said the break was over, he had to roll forward onto his knees first, then crawl up onto his feet, propping himself against the tree.

Latin struggled through the third hour, then rested, then started off again for home. After ten minutes of ragged staggering, Latin stopped. Now that the sun was completely gone, a damp spring chill rose up out of the ground all around him. The only light was the weak half moon, low in the sky behind him and sinking. Latin sat on a downed tree and started making plans for camping right where he was.

"First, a fire," he whispered to himself without moving. His shoulders sank as he thought of all the work to be done. His clothes were soaked with sweat. They would have to be dried on lines hung near the fire. There was wood to gather. Latin turned stiffly, squinting into the dark brush in all directions, looking for signs of a flat clearing.

Latin thought of his grandparents, worrying about him, watching out the window for his return. He started to think of his parents. He felt the hollow pain rising up inside. "No! Not now. Snap out of it," he said, smacking himself on the cheek. "One thing at a time. Build a fire."

Without standing, Latin started going through his pockets looking for his fire kit. Instead, he found the vial that Autumn had given him. "Oh, right…what's this?" he said. He pulled out the little wooden stopper and sniffed.

"Smells kinda like orange peel and…and what?" Latin wondered, drinking the whole vial at once. Once he drained it he declared, "Yuck," and drank half of the water in his canteen to rinse his mouth.

Fifteen minutes later, he was standing, stretching, feeling much better, and thinking of home. Very slowly at first, he started to walk along the path in the dark forest.

He settled into a steady pace, gentle and easy. Although it was slow, he could keep it going. He did not check the watch or stop to rest. He just kept shuffling along. When he came to the road crossings along the way, he just held his head low and kept walking. His mind wandered. He kept moving his feet and letting his thoughts drift.

Suddenly, Latin stumbled over a tree root, but recovered without falling completely, then froze in alarm. A bird call sounded very close to him. Latin dropped to the ground out of instinct and popped the button on his sheath knife. He heard the call again and immediately relaxed. It was his grandpa's chick-a-dee-dee-dee call.

"Grandpa?" Latin called.

"Are you okay, Latin?"

"Yes, am I home? Is it close?" Latin asked.

Grandpa walked out of the darkness, helped Latin up off the ground and hugged him. "I found a considerable stash of trade goods behind the rock. You had a very successful market. I've moved everything back into the house. It's all safe. Are you okay?"

"I'm beat," Latin replied with a sigh.

"I bet you are. Here, let me carry your things. Grandma sent me with a thermos of tea and some raisin bread. You're not far now. The fire is going, and I drew fresh water for the bath. It's all ready," said Grandpa with a warm smile of pride.

Latin drank the tea and ate the sweet bread, then followed Grandpa home, stumbling through the door already half asleep. After hugging and kissing Grandma, Latin staggered into the back of the hut, took off his clothes, and slid into the hot washtub. As his body warmed, Latin was so drowsy that he dozed briefly. Grandma woke him and helped him crawl out of the tub. Latin dried off, put on his nightclothes, and fell into bed.

CHAPTER 7

"Wake up. Someone is outside," Grandma whispered. Grandpa crept out of bed without a sound. He lifted the long shotgun down off its pegs. There was a loud, rapid knock at the door.

"Latin? Is this the right place? Hello? Latin?" cried a voice outside. "It's Autumn. I am in terrible trouble. I'm out here, hello?"

Grandpa opened the door and motioned with his head that she should come in quickly. He closed the door behind her and asked, "Were you followed?"

Autumn whispered, "Yes, but I don't think they saw me turn off the road. I sent my horse on up the road without me. I don't know what's happening out there. I'm so sorry…"

"Okay, don't worry, child. You talk to Grandma here. I'll stand watch outside. If you hear anything, come help. I'll be up in the look-out perch." Grandpa leaned the shotgun against the door, swung a heavy coat over his night clothes and picked up the shotgun. He took the rifle down from its pegs and walked out into the darkness with the shotgun in one hand and the rifle in the other.

Grandma put the kettle on for tea. "Catch your breath, dear," she said.

Autumn dropped her backpack by the door and shook off the cold. Latin slept soundly. Grandma added two small pieces of firewood to the woodstove and lit the oil lantern on the table. Despite the light and noise, Latin did not stir.

Grandma said calmly, "Okay, what's the trouble, dear? Are you hurt? How can we help? What do you need? Try to keep breathing."

Autumn flapped her hands around and took a big breath, letting it out slowly, then said, "There was a party at Billy's farm after the market closed down. His men, the guards who watched me all day at market, they gave me a ride over there. Billy, he…he…there was a lot of drinking. Things got loud and then we were alone. He asked me to marry him."

Latin shifted in bed, still asleep.

Grandma nodded and encouraged Autumn to continue.

"Of course I said no. He went just wild with anger. He threw a chair at me."

Latin rolled over and looked around the room through squinted eyes. Seeing Autumn, he asked, "What's wrong?"

Autumn said, "There was a fight. Billy got drunk and proposed marriage to me and I said no. He threw a fit and when I tried to run away, he grabbed my arm…there was a twisting. I kicked him hard in the shin."

Latin tried to get out of bed, but his legs were so stiff that he struggled to untangle them from the blankets.

Autumn continued, "He showed me a ring. He told me to take off the ring my mother gave me and wear his ring as a sign of, I don't know, something. I kicked him pretty hard. He screamed…"

Grandma moved toward Autumn slowly and put her hands on the girl's shoulders. "Take a breath, dear. You're okay now. Just give it time."

Autumn braced herself and continued, "Billy smashed up the room. As I ran out he just went into a raging fit and screamed to all of his men to catch me and hold me down until he got there. Of course I ran. I snuck out the kitchen door, there were many chickens in the yard…I stole a horse and rode here."

Grandma gave Autumn a hug, then sat her down and put a quilt over her shoulders. "They chased you all the way here?" Grandma asked.

Autumn said, "I heard them yelling. He sent everyone out, I'm sure. Twelve riders, at least. I know they were close. I just kept going. I didn't know where to go."

Latin stood slowly and shuffled unsteadily over to look out the door. "Where's Grandpa?"

Grandma said, "Perch."

Autumn said, "I'm so sorry to have come, to have brought my troubles to you. It seems so unfair. I just didn't know what else to do, where to go.

My mother isn't home. She's gone to deliver a baby down around Ludlum's Pond…. Someone will warn her, I'm sure…I hope. I just—"

Latin rubbed his face and said, "I'm sorry, excuse me. Can you back up? If he catches you, or one of his men catches you, whatever, what do you think he intends? I mean, why not just…? When he sobers up, what would happen, do you think? I'm sorry, I missed the first part of the story."

Autumn could not speak.

Grandma said, "Autumn, dear, you tell me if you think I'm wrong, but in Billy's mind, you would either be his wife or he would do you some great harm, yes?"

Autumn nodded.

Latin said, "What if you hide here tonight and go back tomorrow? He'll have sobered up. He'll see how things are, right? I mean, once he understands that you don't want to marry him, he knows he can't make you marry him."

Autumn and Grandma stared at Latin. With a small roll of her eyes, Grandma said, "Billy won't stop until he gets his way, one way or another…that's who he is. Everyone knows that."

Latin said, "Again, I'm sorry. Forgive me for being so dense, but… well, if you don't think he's going to cool down, then what are you here for?"

There was a long silence.

"What?" Latin finally asked.

Autumn lips twitched as she struggled to find words, but could not. Grandma finally said, "I believe she's here to ask you to help her, to go with her, to help her get far enough away that she's not in danger. Is that right, Autumn?"

Autumn nodded that it was, then closed her eyes tightly, struggling to keep in the tears.

Latin said, "Okay. Okay, I follow that. I see. Okay, but… go? Go where? Where would we go? What could we possibly do on our own? How would we live?"

Autumn shuddered and stood. "There's no time. I don't have time for this. I'm sorry. I should go."

Grandma stopped her. "Wait, Autumn. Here, have some tea. Latin needs a minute, darling. He's still mostly asleep. Give things a little time. Give it a chance."

Latin rubbed his eyes. "Okay, so… Billy asked you to marry him, and you said no. There was a fight?"

Autumn said, "Latin, he wasn't taking no for an answer. He intended to force me. I ran. He's got everyone from his farm—every farmhand, every guard is out hunting for me on horseback with orders to bind me and bring me back to Billy's farm."

Latin drank some tea.

Grandma continued, "She's come to us for help, Latin."

Latin nodded. "I get it. I know. I want to help. I understand that, but where would we go? There's nowhere we can hide where he won't find us or hear where we are. Anybody we would trade with would be at risk."

"That's right," Autumn said.

"So…what?" Latin asked.

Grandma said, "You would have to go far. You could get far enough by going North, toward whatever there is where New York City was, or west, across the Delaware River and on that way. It wouldn't be easy."

Latin sat down hard on his bed. He said, "But what's out there? I mean, there's nothing. We'd have nothing. All I know is here. This is the only way I know how to live. The only thing I know about New York City is the stories and rumors that it's full of Skullers and glows at night."

Grandma said, "West, then. Cross the Delaware. Get into Pennsylvania. Maybe go northwest, into the Alleghenies , or—" Grandma stopped as if interrupted by a thought.

Autumn asked, "Or what?"

"No, it's nothing…" Grandma dismissed.

"What?" Latin asked.

CHAPTER 8

Grandma said, "Well, I guess I might as well tell you. Latin, two years ago, when your parents, you know, disappeared, of course Grandpa and I asked everyone we knew if they'd heard anything or seen anything."

Latin said, "And…?"

Grandma continued, "Well, there were a lot of rumors, as you know, but nothing with evidence."

"Yes?"

Grandma said, "We never heard anything that we thought was reliable information about your parents, exactly, but we did learn that your father may have had a brother living in Delaware, and that he might have gone there for some reason."

Latin stood in agitated excitement. "What? Why didn't you tell me this before? You said there were no—"

Grandma interrupted him. "Stop. Sit back down."

Latin sat.

Grandma continued, "We didn't tell you because it didn't explain their disappearance. They never would have left you here, not for anything. If they had gone to see your uncle in Delaware, they would have told us. They would have come back, or sent word, or something. But they didn't. That's not what happened to them. They just went to market one Saturday and were never seen again. They left all their things here, and so forth, so the uncle in Delaware story didn't make sense, but—"

"But what?" Autumn asked, leaning forward.

"Something about the Delaware story seemed, I don't know, it just seemed right. The person who told me the story mentioned specifically that your uncle lived in a place called Arden."

"Yeah? And?" Latin asked.

"Well, your father told a story one time about his father—your other grandpa, Grandpa Tillich—having been a writer in Delaware back before the Reduction in a place called Arden, which seems too strange and specific to be a coincidence."

Latin said, "But…but that could mean nothing. We can't leave in the middle of the night and try to somehow cover that many miles on foot with people out hunting us, get across the Delaware River, alone, with me already too tired to really stand up straight. Plus, it could be nothing."

Grandma said, "Well, Latin, you're a good young man and I love you, but the simple truth is that if you stay here much longer, Billy's men are going to find Autumn. It's pretty clear what they intend for her. I don't think she's wrong to be afraid for her life. Latin, you're going to need to decide—and pretty quickly, I'm afraid. You're going to have to choose what you're going to do right now. I recommend that you start packing your things, so in case you decide to go, you'll be ready."

Latin pulled his backpack onto the bed and started packing while he said, "But everything I've ever known is here. I don't know anything about how to live out there. I don't even know what's out there."

Grandma said, "You know how to travel safely, you're an expert bladesmith, you know how to scavenge and glean, and you can take care of yourself. It doesn't matter. You know what you know, and you'll learn the rest as you go."

Latin said, "Learn the rest as I go? That's it? I like it here. I have things to do. I've got to fire up the smelter tomorrow. I got an order for a new axe head. There's a letter from the widow Murphy for Miss Taylor. I'm going to run the grinding stone.… I'll never make it out on the open road. I'm not a traveler. I don't know how anything works out there."

"This is pointless. I shouldn't have come. I'm sorry." Autumn said, picking up her pack and turning to leave.

"Wait," Latin said. "Wait, please. I'm sorry. Let me think. This is—"

Autumn said, "I'm not angry, Latin, but I don't have time. Billy's men are bound to come back here looking for me at some point soon, and I'm not going with them. I'm just not. I'll go on the road, as far as I have to… whatever. I'm not saying I have the greatest plan ever, but it's what I have, and I'm doing it. I'm going. I'm leaving in five minutes."

Latin looked at his grandmother, then into the fire. "What about Ma and Pa? If they come back, and I'm not here…how will they find—"

Grandma looked away. "Latin, I'm sorry to do it, but I must be clear. There is nothing on this earth that would keep them away from you if they were alive. They're dead."

Latin wobbled slightly. He tried to steady himself with a knee against his bed. His chest and shoulders shook as he tried to keep from crying. He reached out a hand to Autumn. She took his hand instantly and moved under his arm to hold him against her waist. Latin took deep breaths and fixed his eyes on a spot on the floor. Autumn held him up.

With tears streaming down his face, Latin packed what he could fit in his bag—food, water, a few supplies, his bow and quiver. "I don't know what to say," he said, hugging his grandmother and kissing her on the cheek. "I love you. You've been an amazing grandma. Thank you. Is this… I'm not going to be able to come back, am I?"

"Maybe you will be able to, someday. You're a good man, Latin. I'm proud of you. Your parents would be proud of you. Be careful. Take care of each other," Grandma said.

"See anything, Grandpa?" Latin asked from the base of the tree where his grandfather was keeping watch.

"One group of men on horse, moving quickly north, right after I got up here, maybe ten minutes ago, four or five men. I've got the .308 up here. If you stay along the tree line on the way out, I'll cover you until you get to the road," Grandpa said.

"Grandpa, I—" Latin started.

"I know, son. Look, I love you and all, but honestly, I think the best thing the two of you can do right now is to get out there, go as quickly and quietly as you can. Don't stop for at least three days. Did your grandma tell you about your Uncle Baskin who might live in Arden?"

"Yeah, but—what? Baskin?"

"Baskin Tillich, your father's brother. It could be nothing, could be something. Whatever, just go west and north, get across the Delaware River, and just go as best you can. Do your best."

CHAPTER 9

When they got to the road, Latin and Autumn turned and walked northward into the night.

Latin said, "Remember, if we hear anything or see anything, we both have to jump off the road in the same direction. If the cover is the same on both sides, we should go west if we can."

"How do we know which way is west before daylight?" Autumn asked.

"North Star," Latin said, pointing, "Just go left of the North Star."

The moon was gone. The sky was clear and cold. Their breath rose in steamy clouds trailing behind them. Every fifty paces, Latin turned to look behind them and checked his watch. "This is probably as cold as it's going to get tonight."

"Good thing we're moving," Autumn said.

"And there's not much wind."

They walked slowly.

"Will we hike after dawn?" Autumn asked.

Latin was about to answer when he heard horses coming up behind them at a full gallop. They both dove into the thick undergrowth of brambles and dried leaves. Latin cringed at the loud crash they made. Frozen thorns jabbed at their hands and legs. Autumn and Latin froze, side by side on their bellies, packs still on, feet toward the road.

"We were really loud, diving in here," Autumn whispered.

Latin replied, "Don't turn to look. Just listen to see if the horses slow down. If they do, well..."

"Well, what?"

Latin did not answer. The approaching clatter of the horses got louder.

"Those are not Billy's men," Latin whispered.

"What?"

"There are too many together in one group and they have metal tack. Billy's horses all have rope and leather tack."

"What?"

"These are Skullers," he whispered.

Autumn twisted back in a panic to face the road. Latin winced at her noise and movement, then relaxed and risked a look himself.

"They're not looking for us," he said softly into her ear as the sound of trampling hooves swelled around them. "They're racing to be somewhere before sunup. At the rate they're going, they couldn't possibly hear or see us in this darkness."

The gang of Skullers rode past at a full gallop, chains rattling and horses breathing hard. When they had sped past, Latin checked his father's watch and said, "Almost dawn. We need to find better cover for the day. This is no good here. Let's pick ourselves up out of these briars and get a move on."

They crawled out and got to their feet. "Are you badly hurt?" Autumn asked.

"No, just scratched up. You?"

"Just scratches," she said.

They brushed themselves off walked on though the last hour of night, looking for a good place to hide for the day. First light started to glow in the trees to their right.

Stopping to check behind them and take a quick drink from the canteen, Latin said, "We've got to get off the road soon, but all this undergrowth is no good for hiding. We'll leave a trail that anyone could follow."

Autumn said, "What about that little gully by the creek up there? It's hard to tell from here, but it looks like we could follow that far enough to be out of sight of the road, plus it looks to head due west."

"Yeah. Yes, that's good," Latin said, squinting. "It's uphill a bit, and we can probably walk on the rocks to keep from leaving prints."

They hurried to the gully. It looked promising. "Just hop the rocks all the way up?" Autumn asked.

Latin nodded. "Good plan. Let's get on with it. I am ready to be away from this road."

CHAPTER 10

They hopped from rock to rock until they were two hundred yards off the road. Latin stopped and said, "Okay, let's see. Is there a place here where we can set up camp and still see the road?"

Latin stood and looked while Autumn dropped her pack and scouted around. "There," she said, pointing to a large rock with a small, flat clearing just behind it.

"Oh, that's perfect," Latin said, walking over. "Indeed. We can see the road from here, but we still have excellent cover behind this rock. We're uphill, downwind—just perfect." He dropped his pack and took off his bow and quiver. "Good thing. I'm not sure how much longer I could have gone. I'm sorry to say this, Autumn, but you're going to have to take first watch shift. I'm just about asleep on my feet."

"I guess you are," Autumn said.

They both unpacked their sleeping gear. Latin wrapped up in his and curled into a ball against the base of the big rock.

Autumn put her blanket over Latin. "Do you want anything from my medicine kit for pain or to help you sleep?" she asked.

Latin did not answer. He was already asleep.

Autumn filled Latin's canteen from the creek. She settled into a perch behind the clearing that let her keep an eye on the road, Latin, and the creek all at once. She nibbled beef jerky and cornbread.

Autumn half-dozed in the warming sun when a movement along the road drew her attention. She squinted. There were two men on horses, moving at a steady walk. The men wore the brown vests of Billy's guards. She could not hear them at all. She watched them ride along the road until the trees of the gully blocked her view.

Autumn slipped from her hiding place and scampered quietly along a little path across the creek to the other side of the little stand of trees. Well inside the tree line, she found a spot where she could see the road on the other side. The two men on horseback were already there, still riding along the road away from them. Autumn let out a long breath.

"We should be watching the road from both directions," she whispered to herself as she crossed the creek again.

She moved to wake Latin and ask if he could stand watch with her so that they could cover the road from both directions, but when she saw his face, she stopped. Latin looked exhausted, even though he was asleep.

Autumn decided to let him rest. She stretched, jumped back up into her perch, and watched the road until she drifted into a nap.

CHAPTER 11

"You were asleep," Latin said, waking her.

"No," Autumn said, awakening. "Yes, I guess I was. I'm sorry."

"I don't think there's any harm done. Seems quiet. This is a great spot. There's a place over there you can see the road in the other direction," Latin said, pointing.

"Yes, I…I saw that."

"I think I woke up because I was hungry," Latin said, sitting in the clearing and pulling his bag of food from his pack. He brought bread and cheese and salt pork to Autumn in the perch. They ate together, sharing the canteen.

Latin said, "Well, I think we should wait until it's fully dark, head for the road along the tree line on the far side, then walk the back roads toward Millville. We should be able to make it almost all the way there before first light."

"You know the roads?" Autumn asked.

"No, but it's pretty simple. I don't know that it matters much which road we take. When we start to see more ruins, we'll know we're getting close. I think we should go south around Millville, then turn north and east tomorrow."

"Okay," Autumn said.

"I have to be honest, though, I don't really have a plan for what we're going to do. I don't know how we're going to get across the river."

"Thank you," she said.

"For what?"

"You didn't have to come with me, I know that. I'm sorry I had to come to your place like that, but I didn't know what else to do."

"Yeah, I think I understand," Latin said. "What about your mother? Does she know?"

"I don't know when she'll get home, but she knew about Billy and she made it clear that she expected problems, so it won't come as a surprise to her."

"He thought he was going to strong-arm you into marrying him? I mean, he thought that was going to work out well, I guess?"

Autumn rolled her eyes and said, "Who knows how he thinks? He's not right in the head, but you know, with things they way they are, that's not much of a burden to him. He does what he likes. He has enough people answering to him that he can make his own rules, pretty much. I thought I could..." she trailed off with a frown.

"Help him? Change him?" Latin prompted.

Autumn shrugged. "Cure him. I thought...I don't know, it sounds so silly now. I thought he...It's too embarrassing."

"What? Go on."

Autumn confessed, "I thought I could cure him. I thought he just needed good food and simple, wholesome living. Mama and I made some things, some medicines that we thought might set him right, but it didn't work."

Latin gasped, pointing at the road. "Skullers. Skullers on foot," he whispered. "Watch them. I'll pack everything up."

Latin raced around the clearing, jamming bedding and food back into their packs. "They're stopping," Autumn said quietly.

"Slowing or stopping?"

"Stopping."

CHAPTER 12

Latin grabbed his bow and quiver and slid them on, unleashing a flurry of questions at Autumn. "It's late afternoon, what are they doing? Are they out hunting? Why are they on foot? Are they on their way out for a night of raiding? Can you see their gear?" asked Latin, his voice rising.

"No, I can't tell anything from here," Autumn said.

Latin moved his head slightly. "They're definitely Skullers, though, right? I mean—"

"Yeah, they look like it, but they look…" Autumn hesitated.

"What?"

"They look lost. One of them just pointed this way," she said.

"They're starting to walk again," Latin said.

"How about I go over to the other side and watch?" Autumn asked.

"Yeah, okay. Take your pack," Latin said.

Latin watched the Skullers get closer until the trees of the gully blocked his view. As he crossed the stream to join Autumn, he stopped abruptly, right in the middle of the creek.

He scanned the ground from where they had camped to where Autumn was watching the road from the other side of the gully. "There's a path here. Why is there a path here? Oh. Oh, no. They camp here. This is their camp," he said to himself.

Latin sprinted to Autumn. "They're coming here. This is their camp. Look, a path. They keep lookout here, just like we were doing."

In one smooth and silent twist, Latin dropped his pack and slung his bow down off his shoulder into a position to draw. He flicked an arrow up out of his quiver and nocked it on the string. Latin took cover behind a tree, dropped to one knee, and pointed emphatically for Autumn to take cover behind a gray rock the size of a footstool.

They heard footsteps on rocks coming up the gully. Latin moved his head slightly from behind the tree, but still could not see the approaching movement.

After they had come quite close, the sound of the steps stopped suddenly. There was nothing. Latin waited.

He pulled his head back and glanced over at Autumn. She was pointing furiously back across the creek, her eyes filled with tears. Latin risked sticking his head out in front of the tree for a clearer view. He saw black leather and bald heads and guns.

While Latin maneuvered slowly behind the tree, trying to get into a better position to see and use his bow, Autumn jumped up suddenly and ran away from the creek, out of the gully toward the open field.

There was a gunshot.

Latin rose from behind the tree and drew his bow. He heard racing footsteps, but did not see any movement until a scrawny man with a bald head ran past, chasing Autumn.

Latin drew and let his arrow fly without hesitation. The arrow smashed through the man's back with a deep, wet crunch. The bald man turned to look at Latin, fired his pistol wildly into the air, then twisted, slumped forward, and collapsed awkwardly across a rock.

Latin flicked a second arrow from his quiver, nocked it, and drew. Before he could put another arrow into the fallen man, there was another gunshot from behind him, toward the creek.

Latin felt the bullet smack into the tree he had been using for cover. He shuddered. His neck stung. Turning toward the sound of the gunshot, Latin saw another bald man with a pistol. Latin let the arrow go. It raced from his bow, passed completely through the man's neck with an angry hiss, and skittered across the twigs and fallen pine needles on the forest floor. The wounded man dropped his pistol and grabbed his throat with both hands. Latin sent his next arrow on its way. It passed straight through the man's chest and out his back. He fell into the creek, motionless, dead.

Latin put the last arrow on his bowstring. Both the Skuller on the rock and the Skuller in the creek were dead. Latin saw a third Skuller, bald like the first two and also dressed in black leather, running away back toward the road. Latin watched him with his bow drawn until the man was out of sight.

Latin closed his eyes and leaned against the tree. His legs shook. He dropped his bow and held his head in his hands. Too dizzy to stand, he sat down hard and forced deep breaths.

CHAPTER 13

"Autumn?" he tried to say. His mouth was too cold and dry to move. "I…they…" he stammered, leaning his head back against the tree.

Autumn's voice called out from a distance, "Latin? Are you okay?"

"I'm here. There are two dead, um…men here. You can come out. It's over now, I think. Well, you know, but—I…they…we…what?" he muttered.

Autumn walked around the dead man on the rock and held her hand out to Latin. He took her hand and pulled her closer. "I need help," he said.

"Yes, I can see," she said, leaning in.

Latin said, "I don't feel well. What this is…I've done…I don't…and we can't stay here….my neck?"

"Okay, yes," Autumn said, putting her hand on Latin's head and bringing it gently toward her shoulder. She said, "You sit still. I am going to hold you now, until you let me know it's okay for me to go move around. Then I'm going to check you for wounds and patch you up the best I can. Then, I'm going to check these two men, make sure they're dead, get your arrows back, and see if they have anything on them that would be useful. After that, we're going to load up and move out—not toward the road, but back along this creek. We're going to go just a few miles tonight, not all night. We're going to find a very out-of-the-way place to make camp. I'm going to let you rest all day tomorrow."

Latin whimpered and let her hold him for a long while as the light of the afternoon faded around them. He fought to catch his breath. Suddenly, he pushed her away. Latin turned and threw up into the dirt. Autumn held his sides and sang an old nursery rhyme in low tones until his heaving was over.

"Am I badly hurt?" Latin asked, spitting to clear his mouth.

"I can't tell. The light is fading. Let me check you out. Does anything hurt besides your neck?"

"Just my neck, I think," Latin said.

Autumn took a quick look at Latin's neck. "That's…oh, yeah," she said.

"What? Is it bad? Am I going to die? If I'm going to die, just tell me," Latin asked.

"You're not going to die, not from this. It doesn't look bad to me, but we need to get it clean. You're in shock. Right now, your body is struggling to catch up with you. Plus, you're still exhausted. Even though you slept some, you need a great deal of rest, or you're likely to become quite ill, now that you're hurt. You need to get that neck cleaned out, maybe a couple of stitches, a fire, a warm meal, a decent bed, a good night of sleep, and a day or two where nothing happens."

Latin smiled, "Think there's any chance of any of those things happening?"

Autumn grinned, kissed him on the forehead, and went to check the bodies.

CHAPTER 14

She came back with two pistols, holding them at arm's length like dead mice. "Bring these with us?"

Latin nodded. "Yeah, I guess. Unload them and put them in my pack. I'll carry them. They'll be good for barter someday."

As she unloaded and stowed the pistols, Autumn said, "Those guys looked like they would have starved to death if you hadn't, you know..."

"My neck hurts," Latin said.

"Can you walk?" Autumn asked.

Autumn helped Latin get to his feet, then she helped him walk a few steps to a fallen tree, where she sat him down. She unpacked part of her medicine kit and soaked a white cloth with alcohol. "This is going to hurt," she said.

Latin did not flinch when she pressed the cloth into his wound.

"Clean it well," he said. "Don't worry about hurting me. An infection out here would be as bad as a bullet."

Autumn cleaned the cut three times, then packed it with a white cream and covered it with the cloth soaked in alcohol, wrapping a bandana loosely around his neck to hold it in place.

"It's not too bad. It's not good, but it's not too bad. I'll touch it up when I get a clean place to work. You'll live," Autumn said. She put two drops of a green tincture under his tongue with a glass eyedropper.

Latin retched, then forced himself to swallow. "What's that for?" Latin asked, cringing.

Autumn smiled and let out a happy little sound of confidence that things would be well again. "That's going to help you get your wits about you again."

"Tastes like moonshine and soap." Latin grimaced.

Autumn snickered. "It's not far off from that, actually, but it will help clear your head."

"I can't believe I just killed two men," Latin said. He shook his head and stared into the distance.

"Yeah," Autumn said, preparing a cloth bandage for his neck.

"What does it mean? I thought I was a nice guy. Now I've killed two people. For the rest of my life," Latin stammered, "I'm a killer?"

Autumn looked at him. "It doesn't mean anything. It means we get to live and they don't. It means you're crafty with that bow, and that you don't just carry it because it looks nice. You're the same person you were five minutes ago. You react quickly and intelligently in a crisis, and I'm very glad you're here with me."

Latin frowned. "I just…I didn't want to do that."

Autumn sat behind him on the fallen tree and held him, humming softly for a long while as night settled around them.

CHAPTER 15

The moon was dim and covered by passing clouds more often than it was visible. They started walking slowly. Autumn led and kept them in the woods. After an hour, she left Latin to rest while she went off to look for a place they could camp. After wandering around in the darkness and finding nothing, she said, "A little farther, let's go."

It started to rain. "Rain?" Latin asked. "Doesn't it feel too cold for rain?"

"Must be just above freezing," Autumn said.

After another hour, Autumn left Latin again to go look for somewhere they could stop. Latin sat on the ground with the tarp over his head in the rain.

"I can't see much, but I don't think there's anywhere around here that looks promising," Autumn said.

"No?" Latin asked from under the tarp.

"Let's keep moving. That will keep us warm. We'll find somewhere good soon."

"Is this what it's going to be like?" Latin said, folding up the wet tarp. "Diving into ditches, attacks from Skullers, fumbling around in the dark, frozen and soaked, hiding, hurt?"

Autumn smiled. "It won't seem so bad in the morning."

Latin said, "I just…it's more than that. It's just that…"

"What?"

Latin said, "One bow isn't going to be enough. They had us outnumbered three to two, with two guns, at least, against one bow. We got out of that one. Sooner or later, one bow isn't going to be enough."

Autumn smiled again and took Latin's hand. She said, "Shh, come on now. Let's keep moving, keep warm."

"Yeah," Latin said, sliding his pack up onto his shoulders.

After another agonizing stretch of slow walking in wet boots, Autumn went off to look for shelter. Latin was too tired to unpack the tarp. He just sat down in the freezing mud and held his head in his hands.

When she came back, Latin said, "I don't think I can go any farther. I'm really not feeling well."

Autumn picked up his pack and said, "You don't have to. We're here. I've found just the place. Get up. It's a five-minute walk. We're all set."

CHAPTER 16

By the time they got to the hiding place, Autumn was practically carrying Latin. She sat him down on the ground, covered him with all of their blankets, and put the tarp over him. She put his cooking kit under his head for a pillow and let him sleep.

While Latin slept, Autumn worked in the dark to clear the vines, leaves, and saplings from the mouth of the small cave she'd found. She cleared the ground inside and gathered a small pile of wet wood just outside the opening. Autumn slipped Latin's shiny steel Zippo lighter from his pocket as he slept. She cut a small pile of curled shavings from one of the wet logs and molded them into a little mound with her hands. She sprinkled on a few drops of clear moonshine to help get the fire started, then lit them and puffed gently until the little fire was going on its own.

She made a dry, cozy nest inside the cave warmed by the fire. She woke Latin, helped him into the cave, and took off his wet boots.

"Fire?" he asked, eyes still closed.

Autumn purred, "Yes. Warm fire, dry bed, cozy-cozy. Get all your wet things off."

She built the fire up with larger logs and put the lighter back in Latin's pants. She took off all of her own wet clothes and set them by the fire to begin drying. She climbed into the nest.

Latin was asleep. His skin was cold to the touch. "Oh, dear," Autumn said, moving close. He was cold all over.

She rubbed his back and legs to warm him. She held herself against him all night, except when she got up to put fresh logs on the fire. Eventually, Latin warmed up. Near dawn, his breathing slowed and deepened. Autumn relaxed, but did not sleep.

At first light, she crawled out of the little cocoon and stretched, looking around. "This could work," she said.

The rain had cleared, and the sun was up and warming the ground. She woke Latin.

"Latin? Latin. Good morning. Hey, you. All is well. How are you feeling?" she asked.

"Ugh…rough. Stiff. Sick. Neck hurts. Where are we?" Latin asked.

"Ah. Well, we're home. See if you can get up, stretch some. Have a look around at our new place." She grinned.

"We have a place? I don't remember…I'm alive?" Latin asked.

"You are," Autumn answered.

"I thought I was freezing in my sleep. I don't have a fever? I thought I had a fever," Latin said.

Autumn said, "You're fine. We found this place last night. Look, we're in the middle of a great forest with no footpaths and no roads. No ruins or anything that I can see. We can explore, but this place was covered with an overgrowth of vines and briars, so it has not been used in many years, if ever. We'll be out of the wind, and our fire will keep things warm. So far, it hasn't even blown much smoke in to the cave. The overhang keeps the little sleeping nest dry, and the whole thing is almost completely invisible from the outside."

Latin stood slowly and looked around, nodding. "This must have been a state park or something before the Reduction."

"I guess, yeah. Seems perfect for us. There's room for a little fire, and we can string the tarp up if it rains and blows really hard. Once we settle in there, nobody will know we're here."

"This is fantastic," Latin said, brightening.

"There's a little spring just up this rise. We can dry our clothes by the fire, and…well, what do you think?" Autumn asked.

"It's good. It's real good. We could stay here a while, no doubt. It seems safe. I like the look of it," Latin said, smiling. "Sure."

Autumn said, "The only thing we're short on is food. What we brought could last us a day or two, but we'll need to see to that. There is a lot of that garlic mustard around, and I saw some good mushrooms. There are lots of ramps and wild oats. Apparently, you're quite handy with the bow, and I expect there's some game about, so we could have meat, maybe?"

Latin walked a lap around the little cave, nodding his head in agreement. Autumn smiled brightly. "Yes," Latin said, "This is quite a find. How on earth did you see this last night in the dark and rain?"

Autumn grinned. "I'll start lashing together a rack to dry our clothes."

Latin said, "But…"

Autumn stopped. "But what?"

Latin said, "But then what? What after this? We can't live here, even if there's good hunting. I mean, this is a temporary thing, right? This is a place to rest and get our bearings and heal up, but we couldn't live here."

Autumn thought a moment, then said, "No, no, you're right. Yes. It's a place to rest, not a place to settle forever. Right now, we need rest. We need this."

Latin asked, "But what are we going to do after we're rested up? Are we going to stay here a couple of days? A week? A few weeks?"

Autumn smiled at him. "Let's not try to solve all of tomorrow's problems today, huh? Let's just do today. We have what we need right now. I can work on your neck after we get some water boiled and I get a chance to clean things up. We can eat. We can rest. We can dry our boots and stay warm by the fire all day and not walk. We'll deal with whatever's next after we've had a chance to think about it."

Latin smiled, too. "Good. Yes, that's good advice. Thank you, yes. This is what we need. Thank you. How can I help?"

CHAPTER 17

They spent the day gathering wood and washing their clothes, lashing together drying racks and cooking stands for the fire. Latin took short hikes to scout the area as well as several naps.

In the afternoon, Autumn started preparing to work on Latin's neck.

Latin awoke from a nap in the nest and turned to see Autumn cooking. "What are you cooking?"

"Thread."

"Why are you boiling thread?" he asked.

"This is the thread I'm going to stitch up your neck with," Autumn said calmly.

Latin sat up and reached for the bandage over the side of his neck. "Really? It's that bad? You can do that?"

"Sure," she said, raising an eyebrow at him. "You've sharpened my scalpels and put fine points on my needles. What did you think I used them for? It's not a very deep cut, but the neck is a difficult area to heal. It's hard to keep clean and it moves all the time, plus there's not a lot of flesh to work with, so I'll have to do very fine stitches, close to the surface. You'll need to be careful not to pull them out."

Latin squirmed. "It really doesn't hurt that much now. Why don't we just wait and see what happens?"

"Here, drink this," Autumn said, handing over a vial filled with green liquid.

"What is it?" Latin asked, smelling the cork as he pulled it out of the top of the vial.

"You'll like it. You won't feel a thing." She smiled.

"How are you feeling?" she asked after a while.

"Fine. Nice. Warm," Latin answered, flat on his back.

"Can you move?" she asked.

"Probably. Do you want me to?"

"Here. Sit up just enough to drink this tea if you can," she said.

"Okay," Latin said, smiling. He drank the tea in one swallow.

"Comfortable?" she asked, sliding a cloth bag full of leaves under his head as a pillow.

"Oh, very. Yes. Do you have a lot of that, whatever it was that you gave me before? The green goodness? Is there more of that somewhere?" Latin slurred.

Autumn smirked. "I'm going to start washing your neck with warm water, okay?"

Latin smiled, but did not answer.

She lit two candles and worked carefully. After fifteen minutes of cleaning and sterilizing , she was ready. She spent three minutes sewing the stitches in his neck, then thirty more minutes cleaning, sterilizing, and putting a sealed wet dressing on his wound. When she was done, she sat back against a rock, stared into the fire, and took a half dose of the green medicine herself.

CHAPTER 18

Latin woke first the next morning. He put wood on the fire and shuffled into the woods. When he came back, Autumn was awake.

"How are you feeling?" Autumn asked.

"I feel fine. Great, actually. The rest is doing wonders. I didn't realize how worn out I was," said Latin.

"How's your neck?"

"It's fine. It feels good. Did you put stitches in? I don't remember."

"No fever?" Autumn asked.

"No, I don't feel any."

Autumn said, "You've got nine stitches, quite small. I'll check them later. Hopefully, there won't be much of a scar."

"Thank you. I don't know…if you hadn't been there, after those men… and this place…" said Latin.

Autumn nodded, then stood and stretched. She walked off into the woods for a few minutes, and when she came back, Latin was making tea.

"So, we've had a little time to think and rest up," Latin said.

"Right. Let's talk about a plan while we eat," said Autumn.

Latin paused, then said, "I can't think of any good way to say this, so I'll just be honest. I wonder if maybe the best thing for us to do is go back to my place, with my grandparents."

Autumn stirred her tea.

Latin said, "We could hide you there, keep you safe. It's dry and warm and out of the weather, we could make you your own room…"

Autumn stared at the ground.

"Eventually, people could come over to us if they're sick. You could set up your herbalist shop at our place, in time, and make your medicines. I could build you a decent lab, maybe?"

Autumn clenched her teeth.

"Please, don't be angry," Latin said, "I'm only thinking. We should be able to talk about things. I'm not saying it's a great idea. It's just…I wanted to talk about it."

Autumn stood and said, "You have no idea. You don't get it. I should never have—" She threw her tea onto the ground and started jamming her blankets and clothes into her backpack.

Latin said, "Whoa, whoa! Autumn, I'm sorry. Let's talk. Can we talk? I don't get it, you're right. I'm not arguing. I'm sorry if I crossed a line by asking. Can we talk about this? "

Without turning to look at Latin, Autumn said, "If you want to go back, fine. Go. But don't you dare tell me I have to go back there. Don't tell me I have to hide. I won't hide. Nobody can tell me to hide. "

"Autumn? Autumn, look at me, please," Latin said, his voice shaky.

Autumn stood and turned, but did not look at Latin.

Latin stepped close in front of her and held both of her hands. He said, "Autumn, look at me."

She looked up at his face.

He said, "Autumn, you are the strongest, smartest, bravest, prettiest, most resilient girl I've ever met. You just sewed my neck back together, probably saved my life. The last thing, the absolute last thing I would ever do is try to tell you what to do. I would never want to do anything to put you in harm's way. I'm just trying to say, we're lost, Autumn. We don't know where we are. We don't know where we're going. We don't have any help. We're going to be out of food soon. I'm scared. I'm just reaching out, trying to make some kind of plan. I need your help with that. Your thoughts, your ideas, are probably going to be better than mine. We need that. I need that. We have to share what we have, even if it's not good. For that to work, we're going to have to learn to accept some things about each other. Not all of my ideas are great, or even good."

Autumn let out a long, slow breath and lowered her head.

Latin put his arms around Autumn and held her. He said, "Okay, so… we're not going back, at least not together. That's clear. Can we talk? Can we talk about what we can do, without, you know, either one of us blowing up and running off?"

"I need food," Autumn said.

Autumn made breakfast out all the beef jerky, dried apples, and cornbread crusts they had left. After they had eaten, Autumn said, "I understand. You can go back if you want."

Latin looked up from his breakfast. "What?"

Autumn said, "It was an emergency. I came in the middle of the night and you made a quick decision to come with me, to help me. You've done that. You've helped me get this far. Now it's not an emergency anymore, or not as much. You've had time to think about all that you're giving up by leaving."

"I hadn't thought of it quite like that," Latin said.

"You don't owe me anything."

"Okay, I don't think I felt like I owed you anything, but I understand. I hope you don't feel like you owe me anything, either," Latin said.

"Of course not," Autumn replied.

"Truth is," Latin said, "I like being out here. I like that we're together. There's certainly nobody else I'd rather be on the run with. It just…"

"What?" Autumn asked.

"I don't know how long we can keep it going, how long we can make it last," Latin said.

"Yeah. That is a concern," Autumn said.

They sat quietly in the chilly morning.

Latin said, "First things first. We have shelter. We've got water from the spring. We seem to be safe from Skullers and Billy and everything else here in our little cave in the middle of nowhere. That leaves food. As you said, I expect there are deer around, and I've got my bow, so let's make this a day for hunting."

"Good plan. How can I help?" Autumn asked.

CHAPTER 19

"We'll need a smoker. Have you ever built one?" Latin asked.

"No," Autumn replied, "but I've seen them. It's basically just a wooden pyramid over a fire, right?"

"That's exactly right. Six feet tall or so, and wide enough at the base that a small campfire can burn in the middle without catching the poles on fire. Lashed together at the top, the gaps between the big sticks filled in with leaves, smaller sticks, pine needles, mud, or whatever. Leave a flap somewhere so that we can reach in to hang the meat inside," Latin said.

"And then we just build a fire under it?" asked Autumn.

"That's about it. Build a fire, keep the fire going for two or three days, and we'll have smoked venison."

Autumn said, "I'll build the smoker while you go find us a deer, okay?"

Latin nodded and got to work putting together a light pack for hunting. Two of his arrows were nicked, but he did not take the time to grind them smooth. When he was ready to go, he practiced dropping his pack, swinging his bow around, and nocking an arrow. Then he practiced drawing the bow with his pack still on. Finally, he drew his bow and sent an arrow racing through the woods, smashing into a big poplar tree at chest height. Quickly, he put two more arrows into the same tree. His last arrow glanced off the side of the tree and stuck in the ground. "Good enough," he said to himself.

Latin worked the arrows out of the tree and picked up the one in the dirt. He dropped them all back into his quiver and went looking for Autumn. He found her gathering sticks and said, "I'm headed out."

"Neck feel okay when you do the thing with the bow?" Autumn asked with a smile.

"It does. It feels fine. Don't know how long this will take. I expect to be back tonight, deer or no. You'll be okay here by yourself?"

"Sure. Looks to be clouding up some and quite a bit colder. Will that be trouble for you?"

"No. I'll stay close."

"I'll work on the smoker, gather some garlic mustard and see what else I can find."

Latin said, "I feel like we should hug or something."

Autumn grinned, kissed Latin on the cheek and said, "Good hunting."

In the afternoon, there was a sharp drop in temperature as a solid blanket of dark clouds settled over the quiet woods.

"Oh, goody goody," Autumn chirped as she saw Latin coming toward their camp in late afternoon with a full pack. As he approached, she added wood to the cooking fire.

Latin warned her, "This is apt to be quite tough, as the deer are lean and hungry this time of year, but it's a big doe. I had to leave quite a bit of meat there because I couldn't carry it all, and it's too late and too far for a second trip, I'm afraid."

Autumn replied brightly, "I'm sure it'll be delicious. I've made six long skewers and a little stand to hold them over the fire, so we can cut cubes and skewer them between the fresh garlic and ramps I found. Tasty, tasty."

Latin dropped his pack and rubbed his shoulders. "I guess that's about fifty pounds of meat there."

"I'm starving," Autumn said, opening the pack.

"Does it feel like snow in the air to you?" Latin asked.

"It does, but it's the middle of March. I thought we were past the threat of snow," Autumn said, looking around.

"The sky is dark," Latin said.

Autumn shrugged. "How about I cook dinner while you spark up the smoker?" she asked.

Latin nodded, left a large cut of venison with Autumn, and headed over to the smoker with the contents of the pack. After he took a long look at the smoker Autumn had built, he checked the big pile of wood she'd gathered.

Instead of hanging the meat, he walked back to camp. "Hey, Autumn," he said.

She looked up from cutting meat into cubes and asked, "What? Is everything okay?"

Latin smiled. "That smoker is really top notch. I mean, really nice. And the stack of wood up there is perfect. That must have been quite a lot of dragging and carrying for you. Thank you. I really appreciate your attention to detail."

Autumn beamed. She wiped her hands clean on a handkerchief and walked toward Latin, smiling with pride. "You're welcome. It's no big deal," she said with a playful curtsy.

"Hey, no, it is a big deal. It's a very big deal. You could have just stacked some sticks together and thrown a little wood in a pile. You really worked at that and made it with quality. You didn't have to. That's something. That's important. It's important to me, anyway. It means that you're not just playing around."

Autumn's face lit from within. "Am I playing around?"

"No, you are not."

"No, I am not," Autumn confirmed.

She stood in front of him, smirked and held her hands together in front of her. "Go on now," she encouraged, batting her eyelashes playfully.

Latin's eyes glistened. "We've only been away from home a couple of days, and it looks like the world on the road is going to be a scary place. You know what I mean? It's just the two of us, and there's so much we don't know and there are so many dangers. Your smarts, your training, the way you go about things, the way we work together as a team, I am thankful for your… for you." Latin's voice wavered. He had to stop talking to keep from crying.

Autumn blushed. She reached out to hold Latin's hands.

After a few deep breaths, he continued. "Your work, your spirit about things, it makes me feel a … hope. Thank you."

Autumn's eyes were wet. A tear ran down Latin's cheek. "You're so sweet," Autumn said. They moved together.

Autumn pressed her forehead gently into Latin's chest. He put his arms around her. They held each other. Latin kissed the top of Autumn's head. She rose onto the balls of her feet and turned her face up to meet his. They kissed sweetly as snowflakes began to fall through the trees onto the forest floor in a whisper.

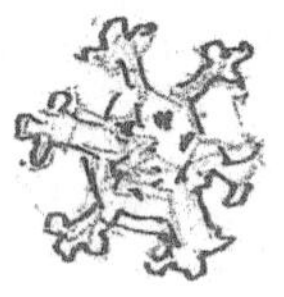

CHAPTER 20

They huddled together in the cave late into the night, watching snowflakes spiral down around the fire and eating venison steak.

"The flavor of the ramps and garlic blended so well with the venison. That was delicious, thank you," Latin said as he got up to walk to the smoker and put more wood on the fire smoldering within.

When he returned to camp, Autumn was asleep. Twice during the night, Latin crawled out of their cozy nest under the overhang of rock and added wood to both fires.

In the morning, the snow had stopped. There was half a foot of snow on the ground, but both fires were going strong. They had steak with garlic for breakfast.

They stayed snuggled in their dry, cozy nest all day, resting and telling stories. Their only trips out were to tend the fires and cook. They drank the last of their tea and then switched to hot water, which they called "diamond tea."

They lay on their sides, nested like spoons, both watching the campfire, when Latin said, "I'm ready to go."

"What? Where?" Autumn asked drowsily.

"I'm rested, my neck is fine. By the time the snow melts, the meat in the smoker will be done. We'll have venison jerky, garlic, and ramps to eat while we hike, and I'm ready to go on, to try to get to Arden, or to see, you know, whatever happens along the way. "

Autumn was quiet. When she did not respond, Latin asked, "Autumn, did you fall asleep?"

"You're ready?" she asked at last.

"If you're still interested in having me around, I would be very glad—

no, honored. I would feel honored if we could set out together. Is that okay? Are you ready to go? " Latin said.

Autumn did not respond.

Latin said, "Thank you for giving me some time to work things out for myself. It took me a while to accept that I'm ready—that we're ready—to be out on our own like this. Well, not ready, exactly. To be honest, I'm still quite scared, when I think of it. But, well…somehow, if we're together, I get stronger. You make me…more. I feel like, as long as we're together, I'll be okay—that we'll be okay. Does that make any sense?" Latin asked.

When Autumn still didn't answer, Latin propped himself up on one elbow and pulled Autumn toward him by her shoulder so that her could see her face. She was grinning, with a tear in her eye. She laughed and said, "I was just funning you. It's so cute when you get all nervous and try to talk."

They kissed.

Autumn smirked. "Why is it you're kissing me? I'm sorry. I fell asleep. Did you say something?"

Latin tickled her until she squealed.

CHAPTER 21

A warm rain melted nearly all of the snow in one day. They packed up at dawn the next morning and paused to take one last look around their camp before leaving.

"I like that we're leaving the smoker up," Latin said.

"Maybe someone else will be able to use it one day," Autumn suggested.

"I hope so. Maybe it will be us, who knows? Even if nobody uses it, it's just a sign, you know, that we were here."

"This has been a good place for us," Autumn said.

"It has. Let's go see what's next," Latin said, helping Autumn put on her pack.

They walked through the woods headed west-northwest at dawn. By ten, they had crossed six dirt roads, saplings growing up through most of them. No signs of recent use. They stopped, ate jerky, rested, filled canteens from a small creek, and continued on. At noon, they came to the end of the old woods. They looked out onto an intersection of two roads that had been paved once, but were now pitted with deep holes and washed out completely in many places.

"What do we do now?" Latin said, drinking from the canteen.

"We could rest until dark and travel the roads at night."

"I'd hate to lose the whole day. It's only noon."

"Are you in a hurry? It's bad enough travelling by road at night. During the day, we'll be ambushed for sure. We have to wait for dark."

"I guess you're right," Latin said with a sigh.

They made a quick camp hidden between two fallen trees. They could not build a fire, as the smoke would draw the attention of anyone passing on the road. They slept in shifts. There was no traffic on the road as they rested.

At dusk, Latin said, "Okay. That's good enough. Let's go."

"Why are you in such a big hurry? There's still light out there. We'll be safer if we wait longer."

"I just feel uncomfortable wasting time here. We're not doing anything. It feels like we should be doing something."

Autumn laughed.

"What?"

"That's funny. We are doing something. We're staying out of trouble."

"How do the stitches look? Are they okay? Do they need anything? Should there be a bandage on them?" Latin asked.

Autumn poked at them. She said, "They're fine. Don't need a bandage. It's better that they get air. Just rest. Relax. Try to take a nap." She rubbed his shoulders and neck until he relaxed, staring up into the fading light of the afternoon.

When it was finally dark, they set out on the road together. That night, they walked along the narrow roads in good spirits. They headed north and west along roads that were cluttered with potholes and fallen trees, but passable. At one point, the ground became too soggy and wet, so they turned back and went farther west. Latin kept their hourly rest breaks to exactly 5 minutes so their legs would not stiffen in the cold. In the middle of the night, they crossed a rusty bridge over two enormous roads with a row of trees between them. They continued on as the first light of day grew behind them and to their right.

Latin stopped walking suddenly.

"What?" Autumn whispered.

Latin held a finger to his mouth. He held her arm to keep her still and said, "Someone coming up behind us."

"Go!" Autumn whispered with alarm, hearing a horse's huff. "That's close."

"Quietly and quickly, just get off the side of the road and lie down, facedown." Latin said, pulling her down to the ground beside the road with him.

"Are you kidding? We're right out in the open, and the sun is coming up," Autumn protested as they settled into the leaves.

"There's no decent cover. Any better hiding will take too long and make too much noise," Latin said, taking one last look around before burying his face under his arms.

The sound of the horse's footsteps was steady and slow. Autumn tensed, getting ready to jump up and either make a stand or run away, but Latin hummed very low in his chest. The sound of it calmed Autumn and held her where she was.

With agonizing slowness, the horse passed within ten feet of them. It kept moving. Latin glanced up as soon as he dared. The brightness of the daylight startled him. In just the short time they had been covering their faces, the light from the sun had risen sharply. A stocky chestnut horse carried one of Billy's guards up the road. His lethal compound bow hung over his shoulder.

"How did he not see us?" Autumn whispered when the rider was nearly out of sight.

"Billy's still looking for us," Latin whispered.

"Of course. What did you expect? I said he'd never give up."

"I guess, I'd hoped," Latin admitted. "We have to get off the road right now."

"Let's wait until he's out of sight, at least," Autumn said, looking nervously behind them.

"This is a bad spot," Latin said. "All of these brambles and vines are going to make slow going and leave an obvious trail."

"Agreed, but if our other option is to stay out on the road, I think we'd be better off trying the woods. Let's be careful and try to cover our tracks, but we need to get out of the road as soon as possible."

Latin nodded. They set off, crashing through the overgrowth of briars. Latin did his best to cover their tracks by pulling the vines and broken branches back into place after they had gone through.

"How far should we go?" Autumn asked once they were out of sight of the road.

"Let's press on a bit. We're going to need water, and I suspect we'll come to a stream sooner or later if we keep going downhill."

After a while, they heard the trickle of running water. Soon after, they pushed through one last thick patch of briars to find a creek, bubbling with fresh, sweet water. On the other side of the creek, there was a cleared field, partially plowed.

"Whoa," Latin said.

Autumn gasped, "Crops."

"That field looks like it was plowed very recently," Latin said with excitement.

"Somebody lives around here," Autumn said, scanning the edges of the field.

Latin looked behind them and off to the sides to check for movement. There was none.

"Oh, that's a man, there," Autumn said, pointing across the field.

"Where?"

"Up the tree line on the other side of the field, there. See the path that goes off into the woods on the other side?" Autumn said, pointing with more emphasis.

"No," Latin said.

"Well, along the tree line to the right, about a hundred yards up, there's a man sitting on the ground with his back against a tree. It looks like he's smoking a pipe."

Latin squinted and moved his head slowly side-to-side. "I think I can see smoke," he lied.

Autumn giggled. "If I can see him, he can see us, especially if we start to move," she said.

"Can you tell if he's seen us already?"

"He's not moving. Beyond that, I just can't tell."

"Well, the only good place to hide is directly behind us. We could get water then back up into the brush and hide for the day."

Autumn said, "That sounds like a good plan. Let's go now."

Latin filled the canteens. Together, slowly and carefully, they backed up into the tangle of weeds a few yards until they were well out of sight from the field. They cleared a small spot of ground, unpacked and settled in to rest. "I'm exhausted, but I'm not comfortable sleeping during the day," Autumn said.

"I'll sleep first shift, then?" Latin volunteered.

"We'll take two hour shifts?"

"Yes please," Latin said, taking off his father's watch and handing it to Autumn.

"It's eight fifteen. I'll wake you at ten fifteen," Autumn said.

"Can't talk, sleeping," Latin said.

At ten thirty, Autumn poked Latin until he sat up. "All quiet. Shift change. My turn to sleep," she said.

"Did our friend across the field move?"

"I don't know. I didn't go look. Here's the watch. Wake me at noon," Autumn said, turning over and settling down into her sleeping bag.

"Not going to have trouble sleeping during the day?" asked Latin.

"Can't talk, sleeping," Autumn said.

At twelve thirty, Latin woke Autumn. He said, "Looks like a lunch of venison jerky and raw garlic mustard."

"Sounds good to me," Autumn said, gnawing on a piece of the hard meat. "Should we go see if the man across the field is still there?"

"That does seem prudent. I'll go check."

CHAPTER 22

Latin walked out of the brush to the little creek. Because he was looking at the other side of the field, he did not notice immediately that the short old man with a bright blue shirt, a bright red hat, and a cane was standing just on the other side of the creek, not ten feet away.

"My name is Thomas. I didn't want to scare you by coming through the brush, so I figured I'd just wait here. Pleased to make your acquaintance," he said with a polite bow.

Latin froze. His bow and quiver were back with Autumn, but he had his sheath knife strapped to his leg. Latin's hand crept just a fraction of an inch toward the handle of the knife.

Alert to Latin's movement, the little man said, "Look here, even amongst us common travelers, it's customary to exchange names on equal terms. I am unarmed, as you can see. Now, I've told you that my name is Thomas. By rights, you should give me your name, kind sir."

Latin did not want to tell the man his real name, but he and Autumn had not talked about using false names while travelling, so he decided to give his real name instead of lying and risking getting caught in that lie later. "Latin, sir. My name is Latin."

"That's a strange name. I've never heard of anyone with that name before," Thomas said.

Latin stepped forward across the creek and shook Thomas's hand. "Thomas, it is a pleasure to meet you. Is this your field?"

Before Thomas could answer, Autumn stepped out through the hole in the wall of brush. Latin stepped aside so that she could see Thomas, then said, "Autumn, I'd like to introduce Thomas, here. Thomas, this is my friend Autumn."

Autumn did a poor job of hiding her fear.

"Oh, I mean no harm, no harm," Thomas said with a bow. "I saw you here this morning and, well, I'm just a simple traveling man. I don't like to move about too much by daylight, you know how it is, so I thought I'd come over and introduce myself. I waited here by the creek because I didn't want to alarm you by crashing through the brush there, with my being a stranger and all."

Autumn stepped up next to Latin and shook Thomas's hand. "It's a pleasure to meet you, Thomas. My name is Autumn."

Thomas stammered, then bit his lip to keep himself from speaking.

"What is it?" Latin asked.

Thomas blushed and looked at the ground. Shyly, he said without looking up, "I always make trouble when I say things like this, but I just can't help myself. My goodness you are the most beautiful young lady I've ever seen. I'm just a simple old man. Please don't take offense. I don't mean anything by it."

Autumn smiled, which put Thomas at ease. "Are you a farmer?" she asked. "Is this your field?"

Thomas chuckled. "Ohh, no. No, I'm nothing. I'm just a—well, a traveler, I guess you'd say. Odd jobs, move about, help out here and there. How about you? How do you come to be here on this fine spring afternoon?"

"We're, well, I guess we're travelers much like yourself." Autumn explained.

Thomas brightened. "I have an idea," he said. "Let's have a spot of lunch together. I have some tea, some fresh greens, and a little bit of cornbread. It's not much, but I'll be glad to share. We could build just the tiniest little fire. I have a small kettle in my kit. What do you say?"

Autumn and Latin glanced at each other, unsure.

Thomas said, "Oh, I know. I see. I understand how it is. You're smart to be cautious. Yes. Let's not let fear keep us from enjoying a visit. Who knows what we'd learn from each other if we could talk, and we may never get the chance to talk again. Let me see... How can we make this work out? How about if I take my backpack and go just a few dozen yards down the field here, still well under cover, and set up a little fire, and put the tea kettle on. You two can go get your things and talk it over. If you choose to join me, that's splendid, just come down, bring whatever you're willing to share and we'll have a good little time. If you decide against it, my feelings will not be hurt in the slightest. You can just move on in any direction you'd like, whenever you choose, and if we meet later, it will be on good terms. Sound fair?"

Autumn and Latin looked at each other and nodded agreement. "Very good," Autumn said with a slight bow.

Thomas extended his hand to Latin and said, "It was very nice to meet you."

Latin said, "Peace be on you."

Thomas smiled and said, "And with you."

Thomas took several shuffling steps backward, picked up his backpack from behind a tree and started down along the edge of the field to where he would set up lunch.

Latin and Autumn hurried back to their little nest in the brush. All of their things were exactly as they'd left them. "We're going to need help sooner or later," Autumn said. "He probably knows the area. He might know who can help us."

Latin nodded agreement and said, "True. We are not likely to find our way across the Delaware River without help from anyone. Eventually, we're going to have to trust someone, at least a little bit."

Autumn said, "Indeed. I like the way Thomas thinks. He realizes we're skittish. He knows we haven't been out on the road for long because we're relatively clean and our clothes are in good condition. He's giving us the choice and letting us make the decision. We outnumber him and he doesn't look particularly strong or fast, so he's not as threatening as most of the other folks we're likely to run into."

Latin's lips turned up with a teasing grin.

Autumn smiled and punched him on the shoulder. She said, "And it's not just because he said nice things about how pretty I am."

Latin said, "I know, I know. It's okay. I agree. He seems like a good guy. He's charming and harmless. I agree we should go have lunch with him."

They packed up their things, crossed the stream and walked down to where Thomas had started a small fire.

"Oh, I'm so glad you've decided to join me. Here, you two can sit on this log and I'll use this rock. The fire is coming up slowly. All the tinder and kindling is wet. No matter. It'll be ready eventually. Sit, sit."

Autumn drew a bundle of long venison jerky strips from her pack. "We don't have much to offer, but we do have this venison jerky we made just a few days ago."

"That's fine. Splendid. I love venison. Oh, and you smoked it, too. That's my favorite. Much better than just drying it. May I try a piece?" Thomas asked.

"Of course," Autumn said, pulling one of the strips out of the bundle and handing it over to Thomas.

"Thank you," he said with a nod. Thomas pulled three hard biscuits out of his pack and set them on a flat rock beside his little kettle. He pulled three eggs out and put one on each biscuit. Then he pulled out a large sheaf of greens tied in a bundle with twine. "Swiss chard," he said. Finally, he pulled out a bundle of short, stubby carrots and put them across the greens. "Together with the tea and your venison, which, by the way, is delicious, we can have quite a feast," Thomas said with pride.

"How did you come by all this wonderful food?" Autumn asked.

"Well, that's a bit of a story. Until just this morning, I was staying with a family that lives near here, part of the group that tills and tends this field, actually. I had been sleeping in their barn and eating their leftovers for about two weeks doing odd jobs. I cooked for them some, cleaned a bit, pulled weeds, worked a hoe, planted some early peas, and so forth. They're an odd lot. Not bad people, just set in their ways. Anyway, they came into some bad luck and decided to send me on my way. They're superstitious people, believe in hexes and bad omens and such. I think that's all non-sense, of course, but they swear by it. Anyway, they blamed the rash of bad luck on me, so off I went. They gave me all of this from their pantry so that I wouldn't be angry and put a curse on them." Thomas laughed and bit into one of the carrots with gleeful defiance.

Latin chuckled and nodded in understanding.

Autumn asked, "What were the bad luck events? What happened?"

"Oh, it's nothing. Not interesting. Here, the fire is almost ready. Let's get this tea started. Do you two have cups?" Thomas asked.

Latin rummaged through his pack and handed over his cup. Autumn did not move. "No, seriously. What was the bad luck? What made them think it was you?"

Thomas smiled. He said, "You don't believe in hexes and all, do you?"

Autumn said, "I am looking at a tasty pile of real food that sits as solid evidence that something very real happened back there. You did not trade or barter for all this, did you?"

"No."

"See, Thomas, when things of undeniable practical value change hands based on belief or faith, my ears start to itch. Do you know what I mean? That's an interesting situation. Why? It can't hurt to ask questions. Why did they think it was you? Did the unfortunate things start happening soon after you arrived? Were you always nearby when they happened? Was there some other common thread that made them suspect you? Did you want them to think it might be you?"

Latin stared at Autumn with one eyebrow raised dramatically.

"Are you serious?" Thomas asked.

"I am," Autumn confirmed.

"I didn't have anything to do with it. Is that what you think?" Thomas asked with some offense.

Autumn nodded, "No. I don't think you did. Of course I don't know, but that's not what I think at all. I also don't think many things in this world happen by accident. I don't believe in coincidences either, so humor me. Tell me what made the people you were staying with think you were the cause of their bad luck."

Thomas grinned, "Okay, okay. I'll tell the story."

Thomas shot Latin a questioning look, as if to ask, "Is she always like this?"

Latin shrugged.

Thomas explained, "The first turn of bad luck did happen to fall on the very day I arrived, yes. Of course that's what got them thinking about me as the cause in the first place. We were out plowing a field with a team of two horses and an old single-row plow. Marlin, the eldest son, was running the plow. I was only there with him in the field to help. I'm not much use in the field, to be honest. I carried the seed bag and kept moving the water bucket as we went. Marlin hit a huge rock with the plow and cracked the blade. It was a deep, long crack. I told him to stop. I told him it could be fixed easily if he would just stop where it was. I told him it could be welded, but he didn't listen. He pressed on and snapped it clean in two. No way to fix that. Not without a proper smith, and there are none to handle that job around these parts."

Autumn and Latin shared a quick glance, but were careful not to reveal their excitement at the possibility that Latin's skills may be valuable in trade.

Autumn said, "That does sound unfortunate. I can understand how an unlucky turn of events like that could lead a naturally suspicious person to wonder if you had some kind of negative influence on things, even though it's clear that you had nothing to do with it. What happened next?"

Thomas pulled the kettle from the fire and poured the steaming water over the mound of tea leaves in his battered teapot. He said, "Marlin's uncle Horace... are you sure you want to hear about this?"

"Yes," Autumn and Latin said together.

"Horace runs one of the two little ferries that carry people back and forth across the Delaware River. Not the barge, Horace is not a part of that operation. He just runs a little raft back and forth for extra truck."

"Truck?" Latin asked.

"Trade goods," Thomas explained, "Anyway, he was ferrying a gypsy couple across the river. They paid with a gold coin, but then tried to rob him on the trip across. The way he told it, there was a terrible struggle. The gypsy man drew a knife. Horace wrestled him for a long while, as Horace tells it, and the gypsy cut him badly, but Horace managed to knock the gypsy off the raft and into the river. The gypsy woman jumped in after him. Horace paddled back to the New Jersey side. He was walking home when he realized that the gypsy woman had picked his pockets clean while he'd been wrestling her husband," Thomas said with a rascal's smile. "Those gypsies are something. If you see one, you might just as well hand over whatever you have. They're going to get it anyway."

Autumn was not smiling. She said, "His cuts are not healing well, are they?"

"Not cleanly, no," Thomas said, sobering quickly. "How did you guess that? Why?"

"They blamed the infection on you?"

"Sure," Thomas said. "They blamed me for the whole thing, gypsies and all."

Latin and Autumn nodded in empathy, straining to hide their excitement at learning of a possible use for Autumn's healing skills as well as a solution to their problem of crossing the river.

Thomas poured tea into Latin's cup. Autumn slipped her cup out of her pack and thanked Thomas as he poured tea for her. Thomas set the teapot down. Latin picked the teapot up and poured tea for Thomas. "Thank you," Thomas said.

The three of them dunked their biscuits in the tea and ate happily, without speaking. They divided the carrots and greens in equal shares and ate with their hands. Thomas put the fire out quickly by burying it with dirt. His careful method put the fire out with almost no smoke at all.

For dessert, they each peeled the shells off their eggs and ate them with little hums of pleasure.

"How did you two weather the snow we had?"

Autumn explained, "We found a nice little cave back in the woods on the other side of the big double road and just waited. We had the venison in the smoker, so we just kept dry and warm and waited. Seems strange to be so warm and pleasant now, so soon after so much snow."

Thomas said, "March can be like that. The weather is changing, too. Getting colder every year. A natural cycle, I suppose. You dropped the deer with your bow?" Thomas asked.

"I did, yes," Latin said.

"Good on you," Thomas said. "What's the bandage on your neck, if you don't mind my asking?"

Latin said, "Oh, that. It's a cut."

"Someone did some fine stitch craft on that cut. You're lucky," Thomas admired.

Autumn and Latin looked at each other with questions in their faces. "What?" Thomas asked.

Latin shrugged and said, "We might as well tell him. Maybe he can help?"

Autumn nodded in agreement.

"Tell me what?" Thomas asked, curious.

Autumn explained that she was an herbalist and a healer and apt to be of vital assistance to Horace with the cleaning and healing of his wound, which Autumn explained was probably infected and likely to get much worse if left untreated.

Thomas looked doubtful that Autumn had done the fine work on Latin's neck until Autumn pulled some of her medical supplies out of her bag and showed Thomas the needle and thread she'd used, as well as the tinctures and sterilizing agents she had in bottles. Finally, Thomas admitted that he believed maybe Autumn could be helpful to Horace. "They have all kinds of old medical supplies. They've got a whole attic full of first aid kits and salves and ointments and tinctures and bottles with long labels, but none of them know how to use any of it, so it just sits there."

Autumn's blood raced with excitement, but she did her best not to let it show.

Latin explained that he had considerable experience and skill with metal work. He proposed that he could build a small forge out of common bricks in one day and have the plow welded back together and working as well as new in three days. Thomas was incredulous. Autumn confirmed Latin's story, but it was Latin's sheath knife that really convinced Thomas.

"You made this?" Thomas asked.

"I did. You can see my initials there on the hilt. L.T."

Thomas shook his head in amazement.

Autumn said, "I don't know what Horace usually charges for a ferry ride across the river."

"They come quite dear," Thomas said.

"If I doctored Horace's leg and Latin fixed Marlin's plow, do you think that might get us a trip on the raft?"

Thomas spent most of the afternoon talking through dozens of complications and uncertainties before agreeing that there may be some merit to offering a trade of skills for ferry passage. Thomas explained that the family was distrustful of strangers, but that an introduction by Thomas, along with Autumn showing her medical kit and Latin showing his knife, might give them enough confidence to let Latin work on the plow. Thomas made it clear, repeated several times, that Autumn and Latin should expect nothing in advance, but if the plow could be fixed and Autumn could help with the cut, Thomas expected that the family would honor the agreement and give them safe passage on the raft.

"What do you get out of this?" Autumn asked.

Thomas said with a faint smile, "A wise question. I expect they'll let me stay as long as you do. I'll sleep in the barn, of course, and help with meals, if you know what I mean?"

Latin laughed and said, "Help cook or help eat?"

Autumn said, "I suppose the worst that could happen is I cure Horace's leg, Latin fixes Marlin's plow and they just send us on our way with nothing. At the very least, I'd be able to pick through their supplies."

Thomas nodded in agreement.

The three of them packed up and headed across the field. Thomas moved slowly, even with Latin carrying his pack for him. On the way, Thomas explained that, in addition to Horace the father and young Marlin, there was Bess, the mother and Jolene, Marlin's very young wife. "I'll have to go in first, of course," Thomas explained. "I'll tell them who you are and what you can do. If we're lucky, I'll convince them to let you in, and we'll just see how things go from there."

CHAPTER 23

The walk took until dusk because Thomas moved at such a slow pace. Eventually, they arrived at the massive, rambling old farmhouse at dusk. There was smoke coming from one of the many chimneys, and lanterns glowed in a few scattered downstairs windows.

Thomas said, "Now…I have to ask, and I apologize, but I have to ask that you two wait out here while I go in and explain things. I've just outstayed my welcome with them, remember, and they suspect me of bringing bad luck, so this will take some fancy talking on my part if they're even going to let you in."

"That's fine, we'll wait," Autumn said.

Thomas shuffled inside.

"This could be the break we've been looking for," Latin said, rubbing his hands together to warm them.

Autumn nodded eagerly. "I'm just worried that they won't let us in at all."

"You're not afraid they'll get us to do all the work and then not give us a ride?"

"It's a consideration. I didn't want to say anything in front of Thomas, but the medical supplies could actually be more valuable than even the ferry ride. I mean, depending on what they are. They could be priceless. Look at this place. It must have fifty rooms."

Latin said, "Looks like it's about to fall in on itself."

They heard a door slam, but they could see it had not been the front door. Latin noticed a flutter of motion in the darkness leave the house and go off into the woods. "Did you see that?" he asked Autumn.

"No, it's too dark, what?"

"Over behind the house…maybe someone ran into the woods," Latin said, puzzled.

"My apologies," Thomas called from the house. He stepped out of the front door onto the uneven porch and waved for them to come in. "Come in, friends. Sorry to make you wait out in the cold." As Latin and Autumn walked across the porch, Thomas said, "They've decided to let you in. In fact, they're going to invite you to dinner. They just sent little Jolene running to the neighbor for milk and cheese, a special treat for special guests. Come in, come in."

CHAPTER 24

Thomas showed them through several empty, unheated rooms into a dimly-lit dining room. The fireplace had a woodstove insert burning quite hot, making the room comfortably warm. Sitting around a long table were Horace, Bess, and Marlin.

Horace stood with a wince of pain and said, "Welcome, have a seat. We sent Jolene for milk and eggs. We'll cook up dinner in a bit. Have a seat."

Autumn and Latin sat next to each other. Thomas sat in Jolene's empty seat. "Thomas tells us that you're a doctor and he's a blacksmith?" Horace asked Autumn.

Autumn nodded. "Yes. I can do a fair bit of doctoring. I put those stitches in Latin's neck, for example. I've cleaned out quite a few infected cuts. I have a fair bit of experience, yes," Autumn said.

Latin continued by saying, "I've built several forges, melted quite a bit of iron and steel, some copper, a little brass. I've done some forge welding, which I believe could fix your plow, given a few days to work."

Horace said, "Thomas leads us to believe that you would expect passage across the Delaware on the ferry as payment. Is that right?"

Latin said, "Yes, that's right. If you see it as a square trade, that would be square for us."

Horace said, "I'm not sure. Let me see those stitches. My leg is hot, but how do I know you're not going to make it even worse?"

Latin walked around to Horace's seat and let him look at his stitches. "Those do look like they were done by a skilled hand. How do I know you did them?" he asked Autumn.

Autumn unpacked her medical kit and showed her bottles, tinctures, needles and thread. When she started to explain, Horace stopped her. He folded his hands in front of himself. He looked at Bess. She nodded silently. Horace said, "We feel that Thomas has brought some considerable bad luck to us here lately, but maybe this is his way of making things right. I feel like we can make a trade. You have my word, folks. If you can fix up my leg and Latin can fix the plow so that it's workable, I will take you on the raft across the Delaware and set you safely on the other side.

After a nod from Autumn, Latin stood and shook hands with Horace.

"Where do we start? With dinner, perhaps?" asked Thomas with a smile.

"You're predictable, if nothing else, Thomas," Horace said flatly.

"Actually, I believe we should start with your leg," Autumn said. "The sooner I can get some medicine on that, the better the healing will go. Where is the cut, exactly?"

Horace pointed and said, "Outside of my left leg, just above the knee. Cursed gypsies. I'll need to find a pair of shorts to put on so that you can look at it."

Autumn said, "That's fine. We can do it here by the fire. Thomas said that you had some medical supplies? Perhaps I could look at those while you're getting changed? In case there's anything useful there, I'll be able to get it on your cut right away."

Marlin said, "It's up in the attic. There's a whole room full of stuff. I can show you where it is."

Autumn was uneasy with the thought of being alone with Marlin. She didn't even try to hide her discomfort. "Actually," Horace suggested in response. "Thomas knows which room those things are in. He could show her the way."

"That would be fine, thank you," Autumn said, standing and grabbing her pack.

"I'll go along as well," Latin said, picking up his pack.

"Not much chance you'll need your bow," Marlin said.

"I always keep my things together, just a habit," Latin said.

"Of course. All good travelers do. Let's go," said Thomas, taking a small candle lantern and starting out one of the doors.

Thomas led Latin and Autumn through the dark and creaking house. They passed through a complex series of cold, decrepit rooms.

"I've never seen so many doors," Autumn whispered.

"It's a very old farmhouse. It was originally built, long before the Reduction, for a large farming family that, by the way the looks of things, expected to be rich for quite some time, in order to maintain all of this," Thomas explained. He led them through a low door in a short wall, down a hallway with no windows, through another door in the side of the hallway, up a long staircase, through two more doors, and down a hallway with three turns.

At the end of the attic hall was a massive door with double cross braces forming a gigantic "X" across the center. There were huge steel brackets on both sides, and the door was so heavy that Thomas asked Latin to hold the lantern so he could lean into it with both hands to get it moving. Once started, it swung just a few inches and stopped.

"How in the world did they ever get something this heavy up here? It's like a vault door," Latin said.

"So many unanswered questions about this house…" Thomas said, taking the lantern from Latin and squeezing inside. Autumn went in behind him. Latin had to turn sideways and take off his pack to fit through the opening. Thomas fumbled with the lantern and it went out, leaving them all standing in absolute darkness.

"Did you burn yourself?" Autumn asked.

"No, no. I'm sorry," Thomas said. "I'm just such a clumsy fool sometimes. Here, I've got a match…I'll get it lit again. So sorry."

In the darkness, there was a scuffle of quick footsteps.

The door slammed closed with a solid thud.

"Thomas?" Autumn cried.

Latin and Autumn heard a second deep thud from outside the door, as if a heavy bar had been slammed into place. They both jumped at the sound.

"Thomas?" Autumn asked again.

"This is bad." Latin moaned. They listened for footsteps, but did not hear any. Latin whispered, "He's locked us in."

"What?" Autumn asked, whispering curiously into the darkness.

"Thomas has barred the door. We're locked in here. I'm afraid we've fallen for some kind of trick," Latin replied.

"A trick? For what? Why?"

"Let me get a candle out of my pack. You think. Just try to stay calm and think."

Autumn sat down in the darkness. She whispered quietly, "What's going on? Why would anyone do this? This is a very strange house. Thomas—he…he's not what he said. He knows this house. He's not a traveler. There aren't medical supplies in this room. This doesn't fit together."

"We've been tricked. That's about all I'm sure about right now," Latin said, using his lighter to light a short candle pulled from his backpack.

Autumn mused, "Is this a closet? There's nothing here. This whole thing has been a trick from the beginning? When did it start? I need help."

"Actually, considering the heavy door, I'm starting to wonder if maybe this room was designed to be a kind of jail cell, which would be bad news for us," Latin said.

"What kind of house has a jail cell in it?" Autumn whispered.

"A very strange one," Latin replied, lighting the candle.

"What's this door go to?" Autumn said, getting up and opening a small door in the side of the room.

Latin held the candle up. "Bathroom, but the toilet and sink and bathtub are all gone."

"Is that a window?" Autumn asked, pointing up into the darkness in the bathroom.

"A narrow one, to let the steam out, I guess. Too small to fit through, even for you," Latin said.

They backed out of the bathroom.

"We have one chair? That's it?" Autumn said.

"He lied. Let's think and see what we can come up with," Latin said. "We have both of our packs and my bow. That's very good for us." Latin blew out the candle.

Autumn said, "But why? Why did he bar the door? Why is he holding us? None of this makes any sense. What good is your bow going to do us in here?"

Latin said, "I have a thought. You're not going to like it."

CHAPTER 25

They sat side by side on the floor with their legs crossed, knees touching. "What are you thinking?" Autumn said, leaning forward. Latin rubbed his chin. "I hope I'm wrong," he said.

"Do you think you are wrong?"

"No."

"Go ahead then."

"What if Billy sent all his riders out, not just to look for you, but also to offer a reward for your capture?"

"That does seem like something Billy would do, yes."

"And what if Thomas, Horace, or someone here in the house asked a lot of questions about us? What if they knew that I could work metal and that you were a healer?"

"And that we were traveling on foot," Autumn added.

"Right, yes. Thomas could have made up the whole story just to lure us in. He could have guessed, since we needed to get far away, that the one thing we really needed was passage across the Delaware River."

"But wait," Autumn said. "Billy could have sent his guards out with a reward for me, just me. Not you. Thomas, or whatever his real name is, told us that story about the broken plow, remember? That was part of the whole trap. That's what gave us the idea to come here in the first place, that you could fix the plow."

Latin rubbed his temples as he thought.

Autumn said, "Maybe Billy's men did go to your grandparents' place looking for me? Maybe they went there after we left? Maybe they figured out that you weren't there?"

Latin squirmed with worry. "Oh," he said. "Yeah, that could be." Latin turned in the darkness so that his face was directly in front of Autumn's. He leaned in slowly until their foreheads touched. They held hands. "It's our trouble now," Latin said.

"There are ways that Billy's men could find out that you're gone without anything bad happening to either of your grandparents," Autumn said.

"Perhaps, but it doesn't matter so much right now. We can't really do anything about it by worrying, especially being locked in here like this. We should try to focus on a plan."

"Yes. We have to get out of this room, out of this house and away from here," Autumn said.

"No."

"No?"

"That's not going to help us," Latin said. "Think about it. They've sent someone to tell Billy we're here. I saw someone run out of the house before we came in, so the word has already been sent. He will know that we were here tonight. There's nothing we can do to stop that. I don't know how long it will take him to get here, but when he does, even if we sneak out of the house somehow before then, he'll know we're close. We can run and hide more, but we're up against the river now, so we can't go west. We know everyone who lives around here will be looking for us. Even if we get out of the trap, we're still trapped."

Autumn let out a heavy sigh. They sat silently in the heavy darkness.

"What do we have with us?" Autumn asked.

"My pack, your pack, my bow, four arrows, quiver."

"And the chair," Autumn added.

"Yes, the chair."

"How far do you think we are from home, from Billy's, right now? How many miles?"

"Well, of course I don't know for sure, but we've come, what, forty miles? Fifty maybe?"

Autumn said, "If they send a fast rider, how fast can a horse go by road at night?"

"I have no idea. It would depend a great deal on the kind of horse and who the rider is, right?"

"If they found a good horse and a fit rider, how long do you think it would take them to get to Billy's? Two hours? Three hours?"

Latin said, "I don't know, Autumn. Forty miles is a long way. I don't think a horse could run that far without a break, but honestly, I have no idea."

Autumn said, "Let's say it's three hours. What time is it now?"

Latin flicked his lighter to check his father's watch. "Seven fifteen."

Autumn said, "It's been, what? Twenty or thirty minutes since we got here?"

"I guess," Latin said. "Maybe longer."

"So, seven, eight, nine, ten…the message could get to Billy's by ten tonight. He will know. Tonight, he'll know. His wild shouting will wake up the whole compound. He'll yell orders to move out immediately. He'll be crimson, screaming. Even with all the haste they can make, it will still take thirty minutes at least to rustle everyone awake, put on boots, pack the ammo, saddle up the horses, and go. Ten thirty, eleven, twelve, one thirty? He could be here with a significant force by one thirty," Autumn said, her voice rising.

"I guess that's possible," Latin said, shrugging.

"You have your sheath knife, right?" Autumn asked.

"Of course."

"Okay," said Autumn. "I think I have a plan."

CHAPTER 26

"How long do you think it would take you to cut your way through one of these walls with your knife?"

"What?"

"How long?"

"Autumn, I have no idea, but a long time. It's hard plaster and lathe."

"And which wall?" Autumn asked, spinning around to evaluate the possibilities. "Light the candle again, let's look."

"Autumn, I'm not sure that's a good direction to go with our planning."

"Yeah, we're probably too far off the ground to just drop straight down without damage, so…an interior wall. We need an interior wall. Those would be warmer, right? The wind on outside walls would cool them." Autumn started putting her hand flat on the walls at different heights. She said, "I'm feeling for differences in temperature. See if you can find a wall that's warmer than the others, even just a little bit."

Latin said, "Are you sure, Autumn? Are you sure about this?"

Autumn said, "Shhh. Get to work."

After several minutes of feeling around the walls, Latin said from inside the tiny bathroom, "Autumn, come here, feel this. Here, under where the sink was, between the sink and floor."

Autumn put her hand on the wall and said, "It's warm there. Why is it warm there?"

Latin said, "I have no idea. There are pipes in there, for sure, but there's no water in them. There hasn't been water in them for years, from the look of things. I have no idea, but that's a noticeable heat."

Autumn said, "Well, I'd say start there, right?"

"Start what?" Latin asked.

"Start cutting. Cut through the wall. We'll climb through, crawl out and escape."

While Latin was staring at Autumn, trying to figure out if she was serious, the candle flickered and burned out, leaving them in complete darkness.

Autumn said, "Gah, the candle is gone. I have others, but we'll need them later. Do you have anything else for light?"

Latin said, "No. That was all I brought. I have my lighter, but that's it."

Autumn said, "Can you work in the dark?"

Latin said, "Um, I guess, but won't they hear me carving a hole in their house? Won't that make a lot of noise?"

"I don't know. It's a big house. Maybe not? Maybe they will. Who can know? We're stuck. Do you have a better plan? I'm open to new ideas. Anything?"

"Well, no, except if we're planning to crawl through this hole, I shouldn't make it right where the pipes for the sink were, because then we'll also have to get through the pipes. Maybe just off to the side would be easier and quicker?"

"Sounds good. Let me know if there's anything I can do to help. Otherwise, I'll be in here doing my bit."

"Your bit? What's your bit?"

"My bit? The fire."

Into the darkness, Latin said, "Fire? Autumn?"

"Yes, fire. My intention is to burn this house to the ground," she said coldly.

"You don't sound like you're joking. Are you?"

"I am not."

"Isn't that a little severe? Everything we've discussed is just a theory. We could be wrong. Something else could be going on. Other things could be happening that we don't know about. Carving holes and setting fires are, you know, things we can't undo. Maybe these people don't really deserve to have their house burned down. Shouldn't we be more sure before we cause damage like that?" asked Latin.

With flat calm, Autumn said, "Latin, I have a purpose. I have things I am alive to do. I have intentions. No, that's not right. I don't have intentions, I am my intentions. I embody my intentions. Do you understand what I'm saying?"

"I think so. Probably not."

"I have a right to live, to exist. I have a right to realize my potential. When I act to defend my existence, I am obligated to do so with every last bit of my strength and every power I can muster to help me. Do you hear me? I do not fear dying. I don't fear pain. I don't even care about being right or wrong. None of that means anything. All I know is that I will not be captured. Not here, not by Billy, not on the road, not ever."

"Oh. I see. Clearly, you've thought about this before."

"You haven't?"

"Ummm… I'm thinking about it now."

"When Billy gets here, it will be too late for escape. Once he's here, it's a battle. He'll have at least fifteen men with guns. I don't like our odds. Let's not be here when he arrives, okay?"

Latin took a deep breath. Letting it out slowly, he said, "Did your mother teach you all this?"

"All what?"

"All this clarity and confidence about the morality of violent and aggressive self-preservation?"

"What? Morality? No. She taught me the science of nature. Life always defends life. Can we get to work? There is a great deal to be done."

"But why fire? Why does there have to be fire?"

"Well, like you said before, if we just escape, we're still trapped, because Billy will know we were here. He'll use his men to hunt us down. This way, he'll think we burned to death in the fire and he'll stop looking for us."

"I like the way you're thinking, but won't Thomas and the others smell the fire, come up, come through the door with guns drawn, see that we're not here, put out the fire, and find the hole in the wall? Won't they know we got out?"

"No. Not the way I'm going to do it. You'll see. Can we do more working and less talking, please? We're not going to talk our way out of here."

Latin started cutting into the wall with his knife. At first, after each cut, he heard a little dust fall to the floor. With more effort, small chunks of plaster fell away. He jabbed and carved and twisted and cut and pried away for several minutes with his right hand before it ached enough to make him switch to his left. Then he used both hands for a while, stabbing the point of the blade as deep into the plaster as possible, prying away as much material as he could.

He stopped for breath, then went back to hacking at the wall. When he stopped a second time, he said, "Autumn, I don't think this is going to work. My arms…I could go at this all night, I think, and not get through."

"That's nice, dear," Autumn said from the darkness in the other room. "Think whatever you like, just keep working. Also, I need the lighter, okay?"

Latin delivered the lighter and went back to work. Later, he chopped through to the thin wooden lathe boards in the center of the wall. He carved them out and started chipping away at the plaster on the other side. He stopped for jerky and water, then went back to work. Finally, at long last, he punched his knife all the way through to the other side of the wall. Latin put his face down to see if he could see anything through the hole. There was no light, but he felt a gentle breath of warm air.

"I've punched through," Latin whispered back to Autumn.

"Is there any air moving in or out of the hole?"

"Just a breath."

"Can you smell anything on the other side?"

"Well… no."

"Is the hole big enough to crawl though yet?" Autumn asked.

"No…not yet." Latin sighed. "How is it going in there, by the way? Would you like to come take a turn stabbing this wall?"

"No thanks, busy. Is your knife dulling?" Autumn asked.

"Yes," Latin replied, testing it with his finger.

"Maybe take a rest and sharpen it? You brought a stone, it's right here."

"Yeah, hey, good idea," Latin said.

"Here's your stone. I had to go through your pack and borrow a few things. I hope that's okay."

"Sure, of course, take whatever's helpful."

Once he'd sharpened the blade and caught his breath, Latin went back to carving away pieces of the wall. He kept working at the little hole until he could get his fist through, then his whole arm. Widening the hole progressed with agonizing slowness. The work was dark and tedious. Latin delivered thousands of strong punches with the knife he had made by hand.

Finally, the hole was just bigger than Latin's head.

"Can I borrow the lighter? I think I can see what's on the other side now."

Latin lit the lighter and glanced at his watch. "Twelve forty-five a.m.," he said. He put the lighter through the hole and then stuck his head in. After a quick look, he pulled his head back through the hole and closed the lighter.

"What's there?" Autumn asked, still working.

"Dusty boxes. It's an attic," Latin said.

"How much longer before it's big enough to climb through?"

"Um, let's see…that much took four, almost five hours. I'll sharpen the knife again. Maybe an hour?"

"Do be quick about it, please," Autumn said.

At two fifteen, Latin squeezed his shoulders through the hole in the wall and slithered into the dusty attic. "I don't like the idea of us splitting up just now. Why don't you come with me?" he whispered back through the hole.

"I'm not done in here yet. Also, the only way this is going to work is if we know exactly how we're going to get out. I can't light this up and then go wandering around. We need to light this and run. Go find us a way out," Autumn said from the darkness.

"But what if I get caught? What if I don't find a way out?"

"If you get caught, try to make a lot of noise. At least that way, I'll know you're caught."

"What if I don't find a way out?"

"Latin, I don't know what to say about that. It means everything. Find a way. Don't get caught."

"Should I take gear? My pack?"

"I've got it all torn apart in here. It'll just slow you down and make noise. You've got your sheath knife. That's probably all that's helpful at this point."

"Okay, right. I'll see you. I'll be back."

"Right," Autumn said, getting back to work.

Latin took a deep breath, rubbed at the soreness in his hands and arms, and began searching the cluttered attic for an exit. Dim starlight through a distant window gave a hint of light. Shuffling his feet a few inches forward with each step, Latin made his way toward the window. He stopped. Flicking the lighter on and holding it over his head, he tried to memorize the layout of the dozens of boxes and trash bags stacked and scattered in the dust. Once he had mapped the clearest, quietest route in his mind, he flicked the lighter off and crept forward.

Eventually, he reached the window and looked out above the porch at the front of the house. The stars were sparkling in the clear night sky. The moon was just rising, low and burnt orange over the treetops. The dirt road leading away from the house was shaded from the moonlight by tall trees on both sides.

Latin lit the lighter, mapped out a few steps in his mind, shuffled a bit, stopped and lit the lighter, again and again all the way around the attic. He found no doors. Back near the hole he had crawled through, Latin saw his footprints in the dust. Looking more closely, he saw other footprints, faded with time, leading away from the edge of the attic. He followed the old dust marks to a trap door in the center of the attic floor. He flicked the lighter on. A promising brass ring glittered at one end of the door. He pulled up on the ring. A heavy wooden trapdoor rose one creaking inch up out of the floor. Latin stooped down and turned his head for a look through the gap to see what was below.

There were stairs.

CHAPTER 27

Latin opened the door just enough to climb down through it. He inched his way down a few steps, then lowered the door closed very slowly, without sound. He froze there for a while, sitting on the steps, listening for movement below. Hearing none, he started moving slowly, keeping his feet at the sides of the steps to avoid making them creak.

After a dozen steps, there was a door, a turn and more steps down. Latin looked at the door. He looked down the steps. Which gave him the best chance? If he opened the door, it might make noise. There could be someone immediately on the other side. He would probably be on the second floor. Latin kept sneaking step by step, down the stairway. He checked every few steps to see if anyone had come through the door above him.

After twenty steps more, he came to a twist in the staircase with another door. When he stopped to listen, Latin heard voices and movement through that door. Latin kept on sneaking down the stairs, straining to be quiet and fast at the same time. He held his lighter, now hot and flickering, in front of him to light the way.

After many more steps down, he came to a very small door with an iron latch. Latin clenched his jaw and shivered with dread. There were no other choices. He had to go through the door. He recoiled at the thought of pushing himself forward into that mysterious space with no idea of what was on the other side.

He put his ear to the door and listened, but heard nothing. His body's instincts told him to run, to find some other way, to go back up to the attic, to try the other doors—anything but go forward through that door.

The lighter flickered one last time and went out for good. Out of oil. Latin closed the lid and slipped it back into his pocket.

He fought his instincts. There were no other options. His throat tightened. The despair of blackness without hope rose in his mind. His arms, aching from stabbing through the solid wall, fell to his sides. Hot tears sprung up in his chest. He did not fight them.

After standing quietly for one last moment, he drew his knife in front of him, took a series of short, sharp breaths, grabbed the iron latch, ripped it up and shoved the door forward. Racing into the darkness, he smashed his forehead into something agonizingly solid. He fell to the floor. It was dirt. He scrambled to his feet. Latin saw stars shimmering all around him. He closed his eyes, but the stars did not go away. Beyond the stars were steel pipes, old electrical wires, and wooden beams.

"Cellar?" he slurred, touching his forehead. He leaned forward and crawled for a bit, then stood in a crouch and wobbled around, steadying himself on pipes and beams that held up the floor above. "I'm going to pass out," he whispered to himself. He sat down with a thud. He lay flat on his back in the dirt and propped his feet up on a cracked cinder block.

In time, his breathing settled. His heartbeat returned to normal. Very slowly, he stood. His eyes had adjusted. Latin now saw that one end of the cellar was brighter than the other. He staggered toward that dim glow. Through a ragged hole ripped in the stone foundation of the house, Latin could see the light of the rising moon.

He pushed through the hole and looked up. He was under the front porch. The front stairs were directly in front of him. To his right, there was a wooden lattice with vines. To his left, there was no lattice, just an open hole, out from under the porch, across the small front yard, into the woods, and away.

CHAPTER 28

Latin retraced his steps back through the cellar, through the tiny door, up the long stairs to the attic, and back to the hole in the bathroom wall. "Autumn?" he whispered.

There was no answer.

"Autumn," Latin said loudly.

"Yes, yes. What took you so long? I almost came looking for you," she said.

"I've found a way out," Latin whispered through the wall.

"Any sign of Thomas or the others?" Autumn asked.

"I heard their voices. No sign of Billy yet. The lighter is shot. No more oil. Pass the packs through. You ready in there? Come on, let's go. Let's get out of here," Latin urged.

"What time is it?" Autumn asked.

"I can't tell. My lighter is shot."

"Here, use mine," Autumn said, flicking her lighter open and lighting it.

"You have a lighter?" Latin whispered through the hole in the wall.

"Of course."

"Why did you always borrow mine, then?"

"To make you feel good. You like being prepared. You enjoy thinking you're a provider. Anyway, what time is it?"

"Five after three. I feel tricked, by the way. "

"Billy isn't here yet?"

"I didn't see or hear any evidence of it. No horses. No men."

"Our estimations were off."

"You mean our completely wild guesses? I don't even remember what we came up with. Why does that matter?"

"We figured they'd be here by one thirty. It's after three."

"What difference does it make? Let's go."

"I don't know that it makes any difference. It's just interesting. I have a few things I have to do to finish up in here before we set that last bit into motion."

"Okay. How much time do you need?"

"Three minutes, maybe five, but once I light this thing, we've got to go. I mean, quick."

"Pass my bow, quiver, our packs, and everything through to me now. I'll get them all arranged by the trap door here in the attic. Then you finish up in there, light it, I'll pull you through the hole, we'll grab our stuff and make a run for it."

Autumn answered by shoving Latin's pack, bow, and quiver through the hole, then her own pack. Latin took it all to the trap door in one trip. "Okay, all ready to light things up in there?" he asked back through the hole.

"Yes."

CHAPTER 29

A few seconds later, Autumn reached both of her arms through the opening in the wall. "It's lit. Pull. Pull me through. Get me out of here right now," she barked.

Latin leaned back and yanked her all the way through in one motion. "Go, go, go," she said impatiently.

They raced across the attic, grabbed their things and shot through the trapdoor and down the steps. Latin was trying to go down the stairs quietly. Autumn shoved him in the back. "Go! Forget about being quiet now," she snapped.

They raced down the steps, through the tiny door into the cellar, and under the house to the spot under the front porch. Latin slung his bow and quiver over his shoulder. There was a commotion of men and horses breathing hard out in the yard.

Just above their heads on the porch, Thomas said, "They're up in the back room, it's quite secure. I expect to discuss payment once you've taken them."

Billy said, "Kill the boy. Bring the girl to me."

Autumn jabbed Latin with her elbow and gestured that he should cover his ears. He covered his ears with his hands.

First, there was a small pop. After a brief pause, the ground shook from the impact of a violent explosion, close and loud. The shock of it was sharper and more vicious than a thunderclap cracking overhead. Latin shook, struggling to catch his breath. Horses and men scattered in the yard, lit like day by the flames shooting up from the top of the house.

Autumn smiled and whispered, "It worked. That was a good one," into Latin's ear, but he was still deaf from the booming concussion. She gave

Latin a thumbs-up smile.

"My God, the house!" Thomas screamed.

"Run!" Billy shouted to his men. "Trap!"

When Latin turned to urge Autumn to run, she was already gone, slinging her pack onto her shoulders as she darted across the clearing and into the woods. Latin grabbed his things and ran after her.

Just as they entered the cover of the forest, Latin turned back to see the house. The back half was completely gone. Pillars of flame shot like gushing fountains from the ragged edges of the parts left standing. They ran through the woods in the darkness for quite a while. When they stopped to catch their breath, Latin said, "So, Autumn, remind me not to anger you, like, ever."

Autumn did not smile. "I meant what I said about defending myself," she said.

"I can see that."

"Am I playing around?" she asked, taking a drink from his canteen.

"No. You are not."

"No. I am not," she confirmed, moving on, leading the way through the dark forest.

CHAPTER 30

They hurried along through the woods until dawn, when they crawled into the burned-out ruins of a gas station to hide and sleep. It was the only building at an intersection of two small roads.

"What did you do to your forehead?" Autumn asked.

"Oh, just knocked it on a beam in the basement."

"Mind if I have a look?" Autumn asked.

Latin leaned forward. Autumn touched the edges of the welt gently with her fingers.

"Nice bruise," Autumn said. "I'll clean it up later; you'll be fine. Where do you think we are?" she asked, then took a few bites of smoked venison.

Latin shrugged. "I have no idea. I believe we went generally north from the house, but we didn't have long before the sun started up. We're lucky to find this place. Maybe an hour? Five miles at the absolute maximum, but probably no more than four. Not far."

Exhausted, they had both started to doze when Latin roused suddenly and said, "Autumn? How did you blow up that whole house with just some pieces of candle and a chair?"

Autumn grinned. "We should get some sleep while the sun is up. Two-hour shifts sound okay? I can stay awake for the first shift."

Latin nodded agreement, arranging his pack as a pillow and curling up. "Seriously, though," he asked again. "What was that?"

"How much chemistry have you studied?"

"Chemistry? Some, mostly for metal work."

Autumn said, "Well, it was a two-stage reaction. First, I mixed mineral oil with melted wax and shook that up well to get air bubbles in it. That was the primer. Then, I carved all the old glue out of the joints in that chair."

"You carved the glue out of the chair? Why?"

"It's a natural solvent and quite flammable. I didn't have anything else on hand. I also took apart two of the bullets from that Skuller's gun we found. I mixed the gunpowder, glue, mineral oil, and wax into a gel."

"And you lit the gel?"

"No, that wouldn't have done much of anything. I put the gel in a glass bottle with a good, tight-sealing lid. I used the broken-up wood from the chair, one of my old shirts, and some of your handkerchiefs, along with a little alcohol, to start a fire on the floor. I put the glass jar in the fire. That's when we left."

Latin stared at Autumn. "Did your mother teach you this?"

"The gel got hot, vaporized, and expanded, pressurizing in the jar until it shattered, which filled the whole room with an explosive mist of gunpowder and flammable glue. The fire detonated the mist, which pressurized the room, and, well, there it is." Autumn shrugged, a tired, proud smile on her face.

Latin nodded grimly. "You can be scary, you know? I thought you were an herbalist, a healer."

Autumn smiled and held her hand out for Latin's watch. "Just science," she said.

"Two hours, please," he said, handing her the watch and turning over to nap.

CHAPTER 31

Twenty minutes later, Autumn heard movement outside. She shook Latin, putting her finger over his lips to prevent him from speaking. She pointed to the intersection, then to her ears.

"That was quick," Latin mumbled.

Autumn pointed to the intersection again. Hearing movement, Latin awoke instantly.

There were many cracks in the crumbling walls to look though, but saplings and brush growing up around the outside blocked most views of the intersection. Latin and Autumn both moved around looking for a clear view of what was happening out there. Autumn found one and waved Latin over.

"Skullers," she whispered, eyes wide, pointing through the opening.

Latin put his eye against the crack in the wall and moved his head around. He shrugged. "They're on both sides of the crossroads, but they're facing the other way. I don't think they know we're here," he whispered.

Autumn looked through the crack. "Yeah. It looks like maybe eight or ten of them hiding on each side of the road. I don't see any horses, so they must be on foot. Why are they here, if not for us? It looks like they're waiting for someone to come down the road from the other direction. Feels like another trick."

"Sure," Latin whispered, "but they've got a couple of guns out there, lots of bows and arrows, and they outnumber us ten to one. If they knew we were in here, why the trickery? They could just bust in and open fire."

Latin picked up his bow and quiver.

Autumn whispered, "I'll get the pistol. We've only got two bullets left."

Latin nodded. They knelt and took turns looking through the crack in the wall. The Skullers crouched in their hiding places along the road, still and quiet, their backs to Latin and Autumn.

After about ten minutes, Latin whispered, "Maybe they are waiting for us, but they think we're going to be coming from that direction? It would make sense. We'd be headed west."

Autumn shrugged. She went back to looking. "Do you hear that?" she whispered.

"What? No. What is it?" Latin whispered back.

"Horses. Many, many horses."

As soon as she said it, Latin heard them. "Can you see them?" he whispered, moving his head frantically to get a look.

"No. Not yet. Wait, there. There they are. I… I've never seen anything like that in my life. It's an army," Autumn said, her eyes wide with panic.

Latin stood up straight and stuck his head out from behind the wall, exposing himself in exchange for a clear view. Dozens of enormous horses with uniformed riders in ornate blue vests and white leather riding boots were headed straight into a deadly Skuller ambush. Latin's mouth fell open in disbelief. The soldiers were trotting in precise formation down the edges of the road, carrying swords, pistols, crossbows, and pikes. In the center of the road were two massive wagons drawn by teams of horses wearing metal plate armor.

Latin realized two things very rapidly. First, that this many men with this much organization headed west, directly for the Delaware River, must have a way to cross the river when they got there. Second, that he was in a unique position to help them by exposing the ambush.

Without hesitation, Latin jumped out of the ruins of the gas station, waved his arms and screamed at the top of his lungs, "AMBUSH! Look out! Ambush!"

Chaotic screaming and vicious gunfire interrupted his second warning. The Skullers turned at once and opened fire on Latin. The cinder blocks of the gas station wall erupted like popcorn, spouting plumes of dust as dozens of Skuller bullets smacked into them. Autumn recoiled from her vantage point, then quickly returned to it once the firing had stopped.

Latin lay facedown on the floor, covering his head with his arms. "Are you hit?" Autumn asked.

"I don't think so," Latin cried. "Maybe."

"Get up and move. I think that wall might come down," Autumn warned.

Latin and Autumn clambered through the ruins of the gas station, out through a charred back doorway and into an overgrown patch of weeds. They turned back to see the intersection, now eerily quiet. Most of the Skullers lay sprawled on the ground with arrows and crossbow bolts through their bodies. The soldiers on horseback were finishing off the wounded and taking long-distance shots at Skullers fleeing down the road.

CHAPTER 32

"Hello?" Latin called from the bushes. "Hello…um, friends. Please, we are friendly. Please do not shoot us."

Two men from the center of the caravan rode up to the edge of the gas station and stopped. One of them said, "Friends, yes. We see you. Okay, you can come out. No weapons, if you please."

"I'm going to toss my pistol out into the grass," Autumn called out.

"Fine," said one of the men on horseback.

She threw the gun out.

Latin stood slowly and held his bow by the tip at arm's length, then squatted and set it down gently on the ground. Latin relaxed his shoulders when he looked up and saw that neither of the men who had approached them had drawn weapons.

One of the men, with what appeared to be an officer's insignia on his uniform, took off his helmet and asked, "Who are you?"

"My name is Latin Tillich. This is my friend Autumn. We are traveling."

The two men looked at each other. Their faces twisted in disbelief. "What did you say your name was?"

"Latin. Latin Tillich."

"And what is your destination, Mr. Tillich?"

"Well, to be honest, sir, we—" Latin hesitated and looked at Autumn.

Autumn shrugged and said, "Might as well tell him."

"We're headed for a place called Arden, sir, although neither of us has ever been there."

The two men looked at each other again. "Do you have family there?"

"I…I'm not certain. I think I may have an uncle that lives there or used to live there."

The other man on horseback smiled, leaned back and said, "Do you mean to tell me that Baskin Tillich is your uncle? You are Latin Tillich? Your father was William Tillich?"

Latin's face turned a pale gray. He staggered sideways. Autumn hurried over to his side to catch him in case he started to fall. "Yes," she answered for him.

"What are you doing here?" the man asked.

"It's complicated," Autumn said.

The officer jumped down from his horse and walked up to Latin with his hand out. Latin shook it.

"Master Tillich, I am Captain Lee Walsh of Belleview House. Your courageous act to warn us of the ambush helped us at considerable risk to yourself. Your actions bring even more honor to your family name, already so highly celebrated by all of the Five Houses."

Latin bowed slightly. "Thank you? You're welcome?" he said weakly.

"If you like, my team would consider it a privilege to provide you both with safe passage to Arden House. It is not far out of our way. We could have you there in time for lunch."

Latin tried to answer, but his voice would not cooperate. Autumn put an arm around him and said, "Yes. Yes, please. We both would be very grateful." Autumn leaned toward the officer and whispered, "Latin has a pathological fear of horses. He's quite brave, as you've seen, but horses terrify him. Of course we'll find a way to get him to go. Could we ride in one of the heavy wagons?"

Captain Walsh smiled and said, "Yes, of course, good." He made a gesture. Instantly, two men rode forward and collected the gun in the grass, the bow, the quiver and both packs. All the gear went into a wagon. They held the door open for Autumn and Latin to enter.

Captain Walsh leaned toward Autumn and whispered, "What are you going to do about getting Latin past the horses and into the wagon?"

Autumn smirked. She whispered, "I'm going to need some help carrying him, okay?"

"Yes, sure. Let me know how we can help."

Autumn walked up to Latin and said, "How are you holding up?"

Latin shook his head and said, "How am I going to get past the… horse…horses?"

Autumn smiled warm and sure. She hooked two fingers through the belt buckle on Latin's right hip and put her right hand in the hair on the back of his head. She held her face very close to his. With the sweetest, most generous and open smile her beautiful face could deliver, she said, "Latin Tillich, you are a brave and beautiful man, and I am going to love you until the day I die." She kissed him directly and passionately on the lips.

Latin fainted. Autumn, well prepared, held his weight by the belt buckle and supported his head as she turned with him and let him fall gently into the grass. Captain Walsh's men laughed and cheered, a few applauding. Two of them carried Latin into the wagon. They set him down gently on a row of wooden crates. Autumn jumped up, stepped in, lifted Latin's head onto her lap and sat down. "Thank you, gentlemen," she smiled.

Moments later, the whole formation started moving again, gradually building to a steady trot. Autumn held Latin's head in her lap and brushed his hair with her fingers. "What happened?" he asked, trying to sit up.

"Ohh, just you lie there and relax. You're fine. You fainted, is all. Do you remember anything?" Autumn asked, grinning.

"No. There were soldiers." Latin said, staring groggily up at Autumn.

"Probably just exhaustion. Low blood sugar, maybe," she smiled.

"Can I sit up now? We're moving, right?" Latin asked.

"Oh, no," Autumn said with a soothing lilt. "You just lay down right there and stay calm, take deep breaths and relax."

"We're surrounded by horses, aren't we?" Latin said, wincing.

"We are, yes."

CHAPTER 33

The caravan rolled out of the forest and slowed its pace at the edge of the Delaware River. The horses and heavy wagons went up a short ramp onto the deck of a long steel barge. Black smoke and steam rose up from the coal boiler welded onto a low platform at one edge of the deck. An old man with a humped back shoveled more coal into the boiler and pumped a bellows, sending even more smoke and more steam up into the clear sky.

When the last horse had climbed the ramp, a younger man at the rear of the boat turned the handles of a steel winch that released the ferry and sent it shuddering away from the shore and out into the river.

"Am I missing anything?" Latin asked, his eyes still closed.

Autumn was humming softly. She said, "Not really. We're taking a steam barge across the Delaware River, which is wider than I ever dreamed a river could be. A great team of armored men and heavy wagons surrounds us. Up the river, I can see the buildings that were Philadelphia. Two ferrymen wrestle a steering wheel to keep us from getting pushed down the river and out to sea."

Latin sighed. "Really? Are you making any of that up?"

Autumn whispered, "I'm not. It's happening all around us, but since you can't see it yourself, you'll just have to trust me."

"I do."

"That's good. You should."

"What's going to happen, Autumn? What will Arden be like?"

"I don't know, darling. We'll wait for it all to happen."

End of Book One

Book Two • Town

CHAPTER 1

Latin clenched himself into a tighter ball, jamming his head into the side of Autumn's lap, bracing against the jolts from the wagon's wheels, pitching them in all directions. He reached around her waist and grasped his left wrist with his right hand to keep from being torn away from her. He screamed out, "Autumn!"

"I can't hear you! Whatever you're saying!" she shouted back.

Dry heaves shook Latin's body as he shifted his weight into Autumn's lap to help keep them together, and to keep her from flying up off the seat between shocks. She held his head with both hands and tried to run her fingers through his hair, but managed only to bump him awkwardly behind the ear.

"What was that for?" Latin asked

"There, there. You be still now. Relax. Try to breathe." Autumn said, trying to soothe him.

"Breathe? Relax? Stop hitting me!" he yelled up into her armpit.

This went on for much of the afternoon. A light rain fell from the cold sky for a bit, then stopped. How far had they come? Were they being followed? Had they been right to trust these riders? What other choice did they have?

When the wagon slowed to a halt, Latin said, "Oh no. What now? What's happening?"

"I can't tell. We've stopped for something." Autumn said.

"What is it? Where are we? What do you see?" Latin said, excited again.

"Nothing, just ruins. This was probably a road at some point. It looks like we may be turning."

"Any sign of people living here?"

"Nothing, no. Houses all burned to some degree, and all the roofs are gone. Any useful salvage was done long ago. I don't even see any animal paths in the grass. It's all dead here, and been dead a long while, from the looks of it."

Latin continued to force deep breaths, and winced every time the horses stirred. Autumn held his shoulders humming one of her haunting little charms. A calm peace settled around them. The caravan of horses and carts started moving again, more slowly this time, now on a smoother road.

Looking out the hatch, Autumn said, "We've turned. We're on a smaller road. There is forest on both sides. The ruins here are farther from the road, some tucked into the woods. There are a few burnt car frames scattered around."

"Still no signs of anyone living here?" Latin asked.

"No…oh, wait. Here are some stumps, just off the side of the road. Those were cut down."

"By axe or saw?"

"Saw."

"Recently?"

"Not very recently."

The horses slowed to a walk as they climbed a long, steady hill. At the top, Autumn said, "We've reached the top. Now we're turning left and starting downhill again, hang on."

Autumn stuck her head out the side of the carriage just enough to catch a quick glance of the road ahead. "It gets steep," she said, quickly pulling her head back inside. "These drivers are doing a good job of keeping the horses slowed down."

The carriage sped up some, but the deep grinding of the brakes against the wheels kept them under control.

"Now we're going over a little bridge at the bottom of the hill and turning left into a little…oh…oh, Latin, oh!"

"What? What?"

"Sheep. Sheep! Sheep!" Autumn squealed, bouncing on the seat, knocking Latin sideways. "Ten of them, maybe twelve. Oh, Latin, they're beautiful. Scrawny, but beautiful. There are two little baby sheep! They're in a proper pen with a clearing in the trees. There's a strong little creek on the other side of the road here. Oh, oh! It's a place, Latin, a real place!"

"I smell wood smoke," Latin worried.

"Yes, there are wood fires and…people! Oh, Latin, it's a town. It's a little village. There's a yard with chickens. It's a little village hidden in the woods. The people are waving. They're stopping to wave."

"I smell wood smoke," Latin repeated, disoriented and pale.

"These houses are lived-in, most of them, some of them. Latin, it's… it's everything. It's alive. It's a living place. All of these little houses tucked in the woods…they're kept up. Kept! They're lived-in and cared for. The smoke you smell is from their chimneys. There's an arch over the road."

"Locked with a gate and security fence?"

"No, no. It's open. It's an open, wooden arch with the words, 'You Are Welcome Hither,' carved into the top."

"Are you kidding me? Are you making this up?"

"No, Latin. It's really here. It really says that."

"And it's just open?"

"Yes. It rained here earlier. Everything is washed, clean and fresh. We're coming to a clearing now and, ooooh, oh look."

"What? What!"

"There's a huge garden on the left side of the road now. It's the size of a whole field. It's set out in raised beds with paths, by a plan. A plan! Oh, Latin, they're planting mixed crops, and they have a well with a rope and a bucket!"

"Are we stopping?"

"No, it's just a tight little turn here at this strange intersection, just big enough for the team."

"Now what? What are we passing?"

"It's a magical little street with houses on both sides. There are tall trees and tended plants and window gardens and doors and windows and brooms, oh, handmade brooms. Also, cut bamboo stacked neatly there and clean shovels propped against the corners of that porch. Oh, wait."

"Wait? Wait for what? What?"

With a gasp, Autumn said, "We're pulling up to the front, or maybe the back, of the biggest house I've ever seen in my life."

"Bigger than Billy's father's farmhouse?" Latin asked, still hiding his face.

"Latin, it's three times that size, at least."

"It's a barn?"

"No, it's a proper stone house with four stories."

"And it's lived-in? It's kept up? It has a roof?"

"It's pristine. You'll see. We're stopping. This is it. We're getting out." Autumn lifted the brass latch and shoved open the heavy door with her shoulder.

CHAPTER 2

Latin choked. He strained to take a deep breath as his chest tightened. He whispered, "I'll shut my eyes if you can just lead me a safe distance away."

"I will. Yes. You'll be safe." Autumn took Latin's hand. "Step down, step. There, that's good."

Just as his feet touched the ground, one of the horses turned and snorted at Latin. The wet heat of the horse's breath was too much for him. His knees buckled as he tried to stagger through his panic, his face sweating, suddenly turned crimson. Autumn caught him under the armpits and dragged him away from the wagon. She pulled him around a large bush, where she gently laid him to rest on the damp ground.

She patted him on the shoulder, and then leapt up into the wagon and grabbed their packs, as well as Latin's bow and quiver.

"Thank you!" she called ahead to Captain Walsh with a flash of a smile. He and the other horsemen nodded back with grins and waves of their own.

When she got back behind the bush, Latin was bent over, holding on to his knees and working to slow his breath. Autumn leaned into him gently. She pressed her forehead against Latin's ribs and whispered reassurances to him, close and quiet.

A compact man shuffled from the gigantic house toward the front of the caravan. His clothes matched the simple design, mostly brown with deep red trim, that Autumn had seen on all of the townspeople working in the gardens. Extending his hand to the first rider, he said, "Captain Walsh, what an unexpected pleasure. Is all well? How can we be of assistance?"

Captain Walsh dismounted, shaking hands as he towered over the old man.

"Hello, thank you, Arthur. Yes, we are quite well, thank you. We are always glad to see Arden House. We've just come from trading up north, and we have a little, well…we have a special delivery for you." Latin vomited on the other side of the bush. A few of the horses stirred.

"He'll be fine." the captain said. "He's got a fear of horses. Once we're on our way, I expect he'll recover quickly. Arthur, these two…there's something special about them. By their quick thinking this morning, they saved Bellevue House from destruction at alarming personal risk. We're delivering them here because they said they were headed for Arden House, although they had no way to cross the river. If it's okay, we'll be going now so that young man can get his wits about himself again."

Arthur's eyes lit. "Yes, splendid! You've brought us visitors?"

Captain Walsh nodded, vaulted back up onto his horse, and led the caravan slowly down the street and away.

"Hello?" asked Arthur, making his way around the bush.

Autumn smiled, tilted her head with a bashful shrug and said, "Hi. Sorry about the mess."

"I feel better now. I'm quite well," Latin groaned, spitting and wiping his mouth with his handkerchief.

Arthur chuckled, "Oh heavens, what can we do to help? The horses have left. Could we help him over to the bench?"

Autumn nodded. She and Arthur got on either side of Latin and led him to a long bench on the ground-level porch of the great house.

Latin took several heaving breaths as Autumn sat with her arm around him and Arthur patted his knee. When he had collected himself, Latin, sweating in the cold, put his hand out shakily to Arthur and said, "Thank you for giving me a moment to collect myself. It's a pleasure to meet you. My name is Latin."

"Latin, welcome to Arden House. My name is Arthur, and I serve as the clerk here. You'll be glad to know that we have only a few horses here, but none of them are anywhere near us right now."

"That's nice. You're very kind. It's silly, I know, being scared of horses."

"Nonsense," Arthur said, putting his hand on Latin's knee. "I'm fairly certain there's a real reason for you to fear horses. You may not know the reason, but that is of little consequence, right?"

After a pause, Latin shrugged. "I wonder."

"My name is Autumn. It is a sincere pleasure to meet you, Arthur. Arden House looks like…well, to be honest, it looks like pure heaven. Thank you for welcoming us."

"Yes, yes. You look as if you've had a long journey. Perhaps there is time for a hot bath before dinner? You'll join us for dinner, yes? Would you like to come inside, perhaps we could find some tea?"

"Arthur, that sounds wonderful, but I feel I have to explain, before we go any further. I should let you know that my name is Latin Tillich, William Tillich is my father."

Arthur's eyebrows rose in surprise. "Really?" he asked with a nodding smile. "Yes, I believe I can see that in your face."

"It's true."

"That's fantastic!" Arthur said, shaking Latin's hand again. It's a pleasure to meet you, Latin Tillich. Is your father still alive?"

"I don't believe so, but I don't know. He's missing."

"I'm so sorry, Latin. We never heard anything of William after he left. Your uncle Baskin spoke highly of your father."

"My father told me many stories about Uncle Baskin. I don't understand why he never mentioned Arden House."

Arthur stood, "Well! Imagine that? You're family! Welcome! Welcome home to Arden House. How about that hot bath? We'll get you some clean clothes, a good meal, and very soon you'll be right as rain."

Autumn and Latin looked to each other in agreement. "Yes, that would be fantastic, thank you," said Latin.

Autumn helped Latin to his feet, steadying him more than necessary. She carried both packs. Latin carried his bow and quiver. Arthur led them through a plain, open room with several dozen simple, unfinished chairs in a circle and a massive stone fireplace that held a squat black woodstove.

"Our Peace Room."

They climbed a spiral staircase, simple and elegant, worn and pitted, but solid. They turned left at the top of the stairs and followed Arthur down a narrow hallway. He showed them into a room with a bed, pillows, folded sheets, a quilt, a dresser, a woodstove, a desk and a chair.

"Will this do? You can stay here until we've made other arrangements. The bathroom is just next door. Does this look okay?"

Latin could not speak.

"It's wonderful, thank you," Autumn said.

Arthur bowed slightly and said, "Rest a bit, start the fire if you like. I will send someone up with soap, a tank of hot water for the bath, and clean clothes. If you'd prefer to keep your own things, of course that's fine too. I just—you know, after a difficult journey, a hot bath and a fresh set of clothes can make quite a difference."

"Thank you so much. That would be wonderful," Autumn said, returning the bow.

She gave Arthur a quick hug, kissed him on the forehead and shook his hand.

Arthur blushed and smiled, shook Latin's hand again, and left.

Latin said, "Look, a bed," as he fell across it.

Autumn sat in the chair and started taking her boots off. "Can you believe all this? Can this be real?"

"I don't know," Latin said. "It's a dream. A wonderful dream."

Autumn kindled a fire in the woodstove while Latin lay on the bed, eyes closed.

As the fire rose, there were faint sounds of movement from the hallway, then a knock on the open door. Four tall, pale children stood in the hall. The oldest, a freckled girl whose round face was framed with bright red curls said, "Hello? Excuse us, Friends? We've brought bath water and fresh clothes."

Autumn said, "Yes, thank you. Hello. My name is Autumn and this is Latin."

The children all nodded with slight bows. A younger girl with the same curly red hair and freckles carried a folded stack of clothes under each arm. She put them on the bed. There were two pairs of socks, two pairs of cotton briefs, two pairs of pants, two undershirts, and two dark red and light brown shirts in each stack. These were not new, but they were clean and expertly patched.

While Autumn and Latin were admiring the clothes and thanking the girls, two boys pulled a cart with a copper tank of steaming hot water into the bathroom. Without speaking, the boys showed Autumn and Latin how the tank hung from hinges on the cart and tilted to pour hot water into the porcelain tub. The older girl left soap and towels on the sink and then explained how to adjust the temperature of the bath by pouring more hot water from the tank or adding more cold water from the tap.

Autumn and Latin both took steaming hot baths with strong soap and vigorous scrubbing. "How did those children get all this hot water upstairs?" Latin asked as he dried off.

Autumn shrugged. "I don't know, but these clothes fit. How did they manage that, I wonder?"

A bell rang outside. "That's the dinner bell," Arthur said from out in the hallway, before there was time to ask.

Looking into the room, he said, "Everything okay? Clothes fit? Hungry? Ready for dinner?"

Autumn said, "We are, yes. Thank you. Thank you so much for all of this. How did you come to have clothes on hand that fit us?"

"Our Craft Gild makes clothes for everyone in Arden House. We keep spares until someone grows into them. They're comfortable? I guessed at your sizes, of course," Arthur said.

Latin said, "They're quite comfortable. What's a Gild?"

"Oh, there will be plenty of time to explain all that later. First, let's eat."

Latin and Autumn started to follow Arthur. They both stopped at the same instant, unsure about leaving their packs. They didn't want to be rude by bringing their packs with them to dinner, but, at the same time, they didn't feel safe leaving them behind.

In an instant, Arthur knew what was worrying them. He smiled to put them at ease. "Oh, you can bring your things with you. That's best, yes, of course. You've been on the road. We can all imagine how it must be for you, away from home in a strange new place. Everyone will understand. Bring your things; it's fine."

They walked down the spiral stairs together and out through a heavy door to a covered pathway.

"So cold, too cold. We could do with more rain," Arthur muttered to himself as they walked.

The pathway led through a wall of bamboo to a great open space around a sprawling old barn. To their right, beside the barn, was a grass amphitheater with a brick stage. From all directions, people in dark-red and brown clothes were gathering, becoming groups and walking into the various doors around the barn.

Arthur said, "This is our Gild Hall. You'll learn your way around quickly, I'm sure. Although, learning names for everyone may take a while."

Autumn asked, "Everyone? How many people are here?"

"Counting you, we should have one hundred ninety-eight for dinner tonight. Last night, we were one hundred ninety-six. Although, I should say, we have two mothers-to-be. I don't believe either of them is ready just yet, but you never know."

CHAPTER 3

The double doors at the main entrance to the Gild Hall were carved in low relief with "You Are Welcome Hither" in an arching scroll across the top. The doors were too heavy for Arthur to open without help.

Inside, there was a warm entryway with dozens of identical, gray-wool sweaters hung in neat rows on wooden pegs. Through another set of double doors, they walked into the main room of the Gild Hall. An open fire burned in the giant stone fireplace just to the right of the door. A loose line of people in overlapping conversations curved between a few tables and down a narrow set of stairs. As the people in line saw their new guests, they waved and nodded in welcome.

Autumn and Latin nodded back, waved, and bowed as Arthur led them down the narrow stairs, bypassing the line.

At the front of the line, Arthur motioned for Autumn and Latin to lean in so that they could hear him. "I apologize in advance for the simplicity of our dinner tonight. Trade has been lean and our gardens haven't given us much yet this season. To be honest, we're living off the last of what we put away last fall. We don't make guests wait in line for meals, so we jump right to the front."

"You don't get to go to the front of the line for being clerk?"

"Oh, goodness no."

A hungry-looking girl held a rough earthenware bowl over a copper kettle of soup and her older brother ladled soup from the kettle into it. The girl leaned forward and reluctantly handed the bowl to Arthur with both hands. Arthur accepted the bowl, also with both hands. They bowed slightly to each other. A lady with only one arm handed Arthur a piece of cornbread. Latin and Autumn followed Arthur to receive their own bowls of soup and cornbread.

Arthur walked back up the stairs to the open room and sat at the corner of a table that looked out a large window onto the grassy amphitheater. Autumn and Latin set their packs in the corner and joined Arthur.

"You see, my friends, hunting has been poor so far this spring, and, though our livestock is generally healthy, there are just too few animals," Arthur explained. "The food, it's not enough, not nearly enough. We've eaten our way through nearly everything we put up last year. It's thin soup and stale grain for us until our gardens start to produce. It's hardest on the children and those Friends with hard, physical work to do. We try not to talk about it too much. Complaining is strictly taboo. You understand, I'm sure."

Immediately, Autumn said, "We have a few pounds of venison jerky. Would that be helpful? We'd be glad to contribute."

Latin's eyes flashed with shock, which he instantly tried to hide. Arthur was too quick and did not miss Latin's expression.

Arthur said, "Oh no, we couldn't. You've very kind to offer, but we…"

Autumn got her pack from the corner and started looking for the sack of jerky.

Latin said, "Arthur, I apologize for looking surprised when Autumn offered. Please understand that we've been on our own for a while. We're just not used to sharing and being shared with, that's all. Please let us give you what we have. We'd be honored. Please?"

"Of course, I understand," Arthur said with a nod, waving to a scrawny blond boy setting out spoons at another table.

"Yes, Arthur?" the boy asked.

"William, I'd like you to take this sack of jerky down to Miss Nancy in the kitchen, please."

William moved with the slow, slouched efficiency of a child accustomed to long days at difficult work.

"May we join you?" asked a tall lady with a bun of gray hair. She and a young couple sat down at the table.

"Autumn and Latin, this is my wife, Ruth," Arthur said. "Ruth, these are our guests, Autumn and Latin. Oh, and this handsome young couple, Susan and David…Tillich. Latin, these are your cousins!"

Susan and Autumn hugged and kissed cheeks.

"Cousins?" Latin asked as he shook hands with David.

David grinned and answered, "Baskin Tillich was my father, your father's brother. We're cousins for sure—look at us."

They shook hands a long time, finding shapes in each other that were familiar.

"It is a real pleasure to meet you, Cousin David."

"Same to you, Latin," Cousin David said.

Everyone ate soup and cornbread.

A quiet, older couple took the last two seats at the table.

Arthur said, "Autumn and Latin, this is our Doctor, Doctor Dash, and his wife Lucy. Doctor Dash, Lucy, these are our new friends, Autumn and Latin."

"We're very glad to have you with us," Lucy said, "If you'll forgive me for prying, can I ask if you're planning to stay with us for a while? Or are you just visiting on your way somewhere else?"

"Do you want to try answering this, or should I?" Autumn asked Latin.

"You go ahead. I'm curious about your answer myself," Latin answered.

"Well, I expect we'll stay for some time if that's okay. We can't go back where we came from, across the big river, and we don't really have anywhere else to go. To be honest, things are quite…? Latin, how would you describe it, the difference?"

"It's better here, much better all around. The conditions are much worse back home."

"Really? How so?" Cousin David asked.

"We didn't have a town where we came from. There were no towns. Just little homesteads tucked away here and there, out of sight of the roads, hiding."

"You have a lot of trouble with Gypsies?"

"Some Gypsies, yes, and others we call Skullers, but I think we're all talking about the same people. Swindlers and robbers, that kind of thing?"

Everyone at the table nodded, understanding.

Arthur said, "Yes. They're a problem. Captain Walsh from Bellevue House said when he dropped you off that you had been very brave and helped them a great deal."

"I'm not sure how brave it was," Latin confessed, shrugging.

"We made some bad choices and ran out of options," Autumn said in his defense.

"Isn't it curious how running out of safe options often comes to look a lot like bravery?" Ruth said.

The table sat in a reverent silence.

"So, what happened? Tell us the story," Cousin David asked.

"It's complicated," said Autumn.

Latin added, "We could write a whole book about it, I suppose."

"What's the short version?" Cousin David asked.

Latin shrugged to Autumn.

Autumn started slowly, "There was a bully. He took an interest in me that wasn't mutual. There was a confrontation. Things got physical. We decided to move on and try to find a better situation for ourselves. How did I do in summarizing things, Latin?"

"Close enough."

"How long have you two been together?" Cousin David asked.

"It's been, what, about three weeks?" Autumn asked.

Latin nodded, agreeing with her.

"Were you out traveling in that late, heavy snow we had?" Doctor Dash asked.

Autumn said, "Yes, we were in the woods during the worst of the storm. We had a nice little shelter, though, and a steady fire. We weren't uncomfortable. I mean, not as nice as being here or being home, but it was fine at the time."

"What did you do for food?"

"Latin took a deer with his bow and we built a smoker. That's how we made the venison jerky. I found some wild garlic and ramps. We made kebabs."

"Impressive. Resourceful and adaptable, the finest of qualities," Arthur said with a nod.

Gradually, the people who had eaten downstairs began to migrate upstairs, standing to fill in the gaps between the tables and along the edges of the big room. A jovial man with a great, black beard jumped up onto the stage and shouted, "Quiet down, you! Good evening, good evening, good evening!"

Arthur leaned over and said, "This is Brock. I'll introduce you later. He is our town crier, of sorts."

All of the conversations ended, and everyone turned to face the man on stage.

Brock shouted, "First of all, thanks again to the cooks for keeping all our bellies full. I think I speak for all of us when I say that you're doing a great job, but we're all looking forward to something different soon."

There were some groans mixed with a smattering of weak applause.

"A few of us at the end of the line did have delicious smoked venison this evening, courtesy of our guests. Stand up, folks. Arden House, our guests, Latin Tillich and Autumn…um…I'm sorry Autumn, what's your last name?"

Autumn stood and said, "My name is Autumn Rivers, and I want to thank every one of you for making Latin and me feel welcome and for sharing both your food and your hospitality with us. Thank you."

There was polite clapping as Autumn sat.

Brock continued, "Okay, what else? Let me see, I'm sure I forgot something. Oh, wait, I didn't say anything yet." He checked a notecard, "There will be a set of one-act plays up here after we clean up dinner. Tomorrow night is a dance. I'm sure we're all looking forward to that. I know I am. Katie, you have your fiddle all tuned up and ready to go?"

"Yes indeed!" answered a woman seated at a table near the stage.

"Fantastic. Okay, what else? Ruth, you have the work assignment clipboard for tomorrow?"

Ruth stood and held the wooden clipboard over her head. "For tomorrow, yes, and things are filling up quickly for Saturday morning as well.

Please see me after dinner if you have any work requests. Gild clerks need to have their plans for next week to me tonight, if at all possible, please?" she pleaded with a hint of humor in her voice.

"Thank you, Ruth. Did we thank the cooks?"

"Yes!" answered the crowd.

"Okay, okay, what else? I was asked to remind everyone that there are two openings for next Wednesday night's open stage. Talk to somebody if you would like to perform."

"Margret!" someone called from the back of the hall.

"Which Margret?" Brock asked.

"Young Margret!"

"Got it? Wednesday night, open stage, Young Margret. Is that it? Does anyone else have any announcements? Did I forget anything…any birthdays?"

The room was quiet.

"No? Okay, it's getting cold outside. Everybody stay warm, but not too warm, if you know what I mean! Thank you, folks, I'll talk to you all tomorrow night!"

There was a flurry of shaking hands and words of welcome for Autumn and Latin.

Cousin David kissed Autumn on the cheek and shook Latin's hand again, saying, "Susan and I want you to know, if there's anything we can do to help you get settled or if you need anything, please let us know. We're very much looking forward to getting to know you better."

Latin gave Cousin David another warm handshake and a quick hug. "Thank you," Latin whispered into his ear.

There was a natural crescendo as people started talking, moving chairs and clearing tables. Latin moved to help, but Arthur stopped him by holding his arm. Arthur nodded that Autumn and Latin should follow him. They grabbed their packs and followed Arthur out a side door onto a balcony that wrapped around the Gild Hall looking over the amphitheater.

"Let's go have a talk," Arthur said.

CHAPTER 4

Six candle sconces cast a dim glow about the Peace Room. Arthur, Autumn, and Latin arranged four chairs near the warm woodstove. Arthur added two pieces of firewood from the box beside the pile of kindling. He sat, then motioned for Autumn and Latin to sit beside him.

"Let's wait for Ruth," he said. "If you two haven't already figured this out, Ruth runs the place."

"She keeps track of who works on what?" Latin asked.

"Yes, and much more. It's complicated. I'll let her explain. Five days a week, we work in our Gilds, if we're in a Gild. If not, we work on whatever needs to be done. Saturday, we work on special projects. First Day, Sunday, we rest. Ruth coordinates…well, she coordinates everything, actually, and here she is."

"Thank you for waiting," Ruth said with unhurried grace. She put down her clipboard and books, kissed Arthur on the forehead, and sat down. She took a deep breath and closed her eyes.

Arthur said, "Latin, Autumn, as I've said, I serve Arden House as a clerk. Ruth is recording clerk. If you have any concerns or questions while you're here, please feel free to speak to either of us. We'll sort it out."

Autumn and Latin both nodded.

After a long pause, Ruth said, "First, let's start with your welcome packet. This used to be more elaborate, but, for now, it's just this rough map of the town and a chart of the Gilds. Arthur has mentioned the Gilds?"

"Yes."

"Each Gild is responsible for an array of related tasks. There are ten Gilds. Apprentices to Gilds are skilled, dedicated Friends, usually young and often with aspirations of being Gild members. Gild members are

Arden House
CREEK
Orchard
MILLER'S
Circle Lane
Lower Lane
GUILD HALL
The SWAMP
WOOD LOT
CRAFT SHED
INDIAN ROCKS
THE GREEN
WOODLAND
Orleans
Little Lane
S
E
W

expert craftspeople with years of training in their skill. Each Gild has one clerk who coordinates. We'll talk about all this in more detail some other time."

"Okay," Autumn said.

Ruth explained, "Here at Arden House, a person is allowed to make decisions about where they live, if they stay in school, and where they work once they reach their twelfth birthday. Once twelve, they can live where they like, make their own work requests, apply for apprenticeships, and so forth. Right now, the house has one hundred ninety-six members. One hundred twenty-three are adult. Ninety-one of the adults are either clerks, gild members, or apprentices. Gild membership is for life, although Friends will, from time to time, decide to surrender membership in one Gild and apply to join a different Gild."

Arthur said, "We have some older Friends who chose to give up their Gild status later in life to make room for younger Friends to take their place."

Ruth continued, "There are ten Gild clerks and each Gild has three members and seven apprentices, with a few exceptions. Simple enough?"

Autumn said, "Sure."

Ruth said, "Let's start with the three 'farming' gilds: Wood Gild, Garden Gild and Husbandry Gild. The Wood Gild is responsible for growing, tending, selecting, felling, chopping, curing, and delivering, on average, one full cord of wood every two days in the summer and two cords per day in the winter. Most of this is burned in the Gild Hall, of course, for cooking and heating, but our two other hot water systems, one here in Arden House and the other in the Craft Shop, require wood as well. The Clerk of the Wood Gild is Paul, and he leads the work of his three Gild members and seven apprentices.

"The Garden Gild plans and schedules crops for every growing bed in our two large plots. Last year, Katie, the Garden Gild clerk and our town fiddler, and her Gild planted, tended, weeded, harvested, and delivered forty tons of food. Obviously, as we're all feeling in our bellies right now, that wasn't enough. Not nearly enough. There are reasons. We grow vegetables in the gardens, as well as grains in the fields. We have berry patches, an apple orchard, beans, herbs, and spices. We have two large cotton fields on the other side of the creek. Right now, the Garden Gild is under a great deal of pressure to get food earlier than ever before because our stores are so low."

Latin interjected, "Excuse me, you said there were reasons for the shortage of food. What are they?"

Arthur elaborated, "There are several. First, the weather is changing, as I'm sure you've noticed. Winters are colder and longer, which gives us less time to grow food. Second, the well that was uphill from the gardens has failed. We have no way to get water from the creek or from the other wells to any of our crops except by carrying it uphill by hand, in buckets."

Latin cringed.

Ruth said, "And our size?"

"Yes. The town is shrinking," Arthur explained. "It has been for some time, which means fewer mouths to feed, of course, but also fewer hands to work. The smaller the town gets, the harder it is for the people who are left to produce enough food."

Latin and Autumn nodded.

Ruth continued, "The Husbandry Gild tends our chickens, cows, goats, alpacas, sheep, pigs, and horses. Latin, I hear you're not fond of horses. That shouldn't be too much of a bother, as we only have six now and they're used mostly to haul the wood. Mules? Do mules bother you?"

"I'll find a way. It's nothing. I'll be fine, thank you."

"Good. While the Husbandry Gild is focused on getting more production out of our livestock, the animals simply aren't mating and bearing as many healthy young as we need. The chickens are laying fewer eggs. The only thing prospering is our goat herd. We've plenty of goats."

Arthur said, "I hope you like goat cheese, goat milk, goat meat and goat butter."

"Of course," Autumn said with a shrug. "Who doesn't?"

Ruth continued, "So, those are the 'farming' gilds. Garden, Wood and Husbandry. Any questions?"

Autumn and Latin nodded; no questions.

"There are three 'craft' gilds. They are the Arden School, the Craft

Shop, and the Doctor. The Arden School works to raise and teach our children from when they leave their mothers to when they're ready to work. We focus on education, spirit, and craft. We teach all the arts and crafts, all the Gild skills, mathematics, reading, writing, history, science, philosophy, and civics. Nearly all of the younger children live in the school dormitory, although there are some exceptions. Jacob and Margret, Arthur's sister, have run the school together for nearly thirty years. They are raising their third generation of Arden children. Young Annette is their apprentice, and she has taken on many of the classroom teaching duties.

"Doctor Dash does his best to see to our sick. He works to heal our injuries, deals with our toothaches, and helps us through our births and deaths.

"The Craft Shop makes our furniture and does our weaving, mending, and spinning. They build and maintain our looms, sew our clothes as well as other fabric, and trade goods. They make our pottery. They weave our baskets, make our candles, and knit our sweaters. They tan our leather, make our shoes, cut our hair, and make toys for our boys and girls. They repair our houses and carts, maintain our tools, and shovel paths through the snow. The laundry is also part of the Craft Shop, although they work in different buildings."

Arthur said, "Three 'craft' gilds. Questions?"

"No," said Latin.

Ruth continued, "The last three are 'business' gilds. The Arden Store, Constable Pete, and Trader Jack. The Arden Store manages our storage and reserves. Much of this is kept in the basements and attics of Arden House and the Gild Hall. The shopkeeper and his Gild members are responsible for all town property. They keep the town's inventory and work out what's available to trade and what our most critical needs are. They also plan and lead the Arden Fair, which happens every fall. It would take far too long to explain the Fair right now. Later, you'll hear plenty about that, I'm sure. It's a year-round job.

"Trader Jack has, perhaps, the most important job in town. He travels to the other four houses, and beyond."

Seeing the confused looks on Autumn and Latin's faces, Ruth stopped.

"Has no one told you about the other houses?" Arthur asked.

Autumn said, "No."

Ruth explained, "Well, there used to be more than a dozen houses we traded with. Now there are four. Bellevue is the closest. They are a military house, and they conduct all of our long-distance trade via armored caravan like the one you arrived in. Next closest to us is Granogue house. Well, that's its real name—we all call it Granola House. It's a loose, no-rules, open-family type of house, if you know what I mean."

"I think I understand," Latin said.

Arthur joked, "They do, by the way, make excellent granola, although we're not able to trade for as much of it as we'd like."

Ruth continued, "Winterthur House is one of the two most prosperous houses. They're Bible-folk, Christians, and they have probably five hundred citizens or so now. They have huge fields, good soil, good wells, strong security, and a herd of cows you have to see to believe. Finally, the most prosperous house by far is Longwood House. It's a full day's walk from here, but they have everything you could ever want there. They grow food year-round in the greenhouses. They have a wonderful school, library, arts…Everything is first class there. And, the most important thing to know about them is that they have open immigration."

Latin asked, "Open immigration?"

Arthur explained, "Any citizen of any of the other four houses can show up, surrender their house citizenship in writing, ask to be accepted into Longwood House, and they will take them in and give them a place to stay, food and a job. We haven't lost too many Friends to Longwood yet, but some have gone, and it's a concern that we might start to lose more if things stay so lean."

Autumn asked, "Does Arden House have open immigration like that?"

Arthur said, "We have a Clearness process. So long as you are clear in why you want to live here, and you can work, you are free to become a member."

Ruth continued, "Anyway, Trader Jack goes to the other houses and sometimes beyond, bartering our trade goods, making deals with those that need what we have extra of, taking orders for our craftspeople, and bringing back what he can trade for. He travels by foot when he can and by horse when he has to. Day, night, rain, snow, you name it, he goes out and makes the deals that turn the things we have into the things we need.

"Constable Pete does our hunting, such as it is. He settles whatever arguments and gripes between Friends that we can't work out for ourselves. He goes out and looks for people who don't come back when they're expected and keeps a lookout for bandits and beggars. He deploys his three Gild members and seven apprentices to walk around the roads and fields at night to check that things stay quiet. They ring the alarm bell if there is trouble. He keeps our fire wagon in working condition and puts out fires, runs our defense drills, and keeps our armory. He keeps someone up in the fire lookout tower when conditions are dry like they are now."

"Well, that's a lot of information, and I know you've had a difficult day, so if you have any questions, of course, feel free to ask, but, if not, maybe you'd like some quiet time to wind down?"

Autumn said, "Thank you so much. If I remember correctly, you said there are ten Gilds. You've told us about nine. What's the tenth Gild?"

Ruth smiled, "Oh, I forgot the Folk Gild. I'm sorry, of course. Most nights after dinner and on some special occasions, we have concerts, short plays, dances, readings, and recitals. The Folk Gild runs all that. There's no clerk for the Folk Gild; they just sort of all do their own things."

Latin said, "And the uniforms? Does everyone in town have to wear them?"

Arthur said, "We call that "plain dress" and it's only tradition, not a rule. You're free to wear what you like. Plain dress keeps us near our call to simplicity. Also, it's the most efficient way for three people to make clothing for two hundred. Most Arden House Friends are children, growing quickly, and we need an easy way to make the best use of the town's clothing as the children grow through them. We live in hand-me-downs. We do our best to give each child some piece of new clothing that fits them for their birthday, but, lately, we haven't been able to manage even that in many cases."

Ruth began to arrange her things to leave. She said, "Let's leave it at that, Friends. I've asked to have the woodstove in your room tended, so it should be comfortable for sleeping. Feel free to open the windows or adjust the stove, as you like. Our room is just down the hall from yours, so, if you need anything at all, please just come down or call out. In the morning, we ring the rising bell at six. Perhaps we can meet down here at about six thirty, and we'll walk over to breakfast together?"

Autumn and Latin thanked Arthur and Ruth several times, hugged, and shook hands, then went up the spiral stairs to bed.

CHAPTER 5

Autumn and Latin washed their faces and changed into the fresh bedclothes that had been laid out for them. Latin refilled the woodstove and slid between clean sheets under heavy blankets.

"Quite a day," he said.

"I'm too tired to sleep," Autumn murmured.

"Has all of this happened? It feels unreal."

"What do you remember of it?" Autumn asked.

"Of the day?"

"Yeah."

Latin closed his eyes and said, "It all kind of blends together. We got trapped in a dark room, I cut through the wall with my knife, you blew up the house, and we ran all night and hid in a falling-down building. I jumped into a Skuller ambush to save a bunch of men on, well, you know. I fainted for some reason. There was a great deal of violent jostling. We landed in a town where everyone is friendly but starving, and they gave us a hot bath, a warm meal, a friendly conversation in front of a hot woodstove, and fresh bedclothes."

"Yes, that's what I remember, or close enough. Must not have been a dream."

"But this town...something doesn't quite seem right about it."

"Could we both be having the same dream?"

"I don't know, Autumn, it just seems too good to be true. I have a thousand questions. I'm not sure I trust these people. I don't think they're telling us the whole story."

"Not the same dream, exactly. Each would be in the other's dream."

"Don't you question all this?"

"I don't know, what's bothering you?"

Latin said, "What about, just, like, basic safety. They say some men walk around at night, but there are no fences. Why don't they have Skuller raids here?"

"I can't imagine."

"It feels strange to you, doesn't it?"

"Honestly, Latin, it doesn't. The way we lived back home—hiding and sneaking around, relying on Billy for 'protection'—that felt strange. Let's sleep on it and see if you still have the same questions in the morning."

Latin said, "Okay, good night."

"Good night, Latin."

After Autumn had drifted to sleep, Latin asked, "What do you think happened to my grandparents? Do you think they're okay?"

"I don't know, Latin. They're pretty good at taking care of themselves."

"It just hurts, is all, not knowing, wondering how they are."

"I suppose."

"What?"

"Didn't you always know you were going to leave home?" Autumn asked.

"I don't know. I'm not sure I did. Maybe, after my grandparents died, maybe I was going to leave then. Maybe. Not before, no."

"Yeah. I guess I always knew that Billy would wreck it for everyone one way or another."

"I agree. Ruin did seem to be at the core of his nature. I thought it would take longer."

"I wasn't going to marry him."

"Oh, that's clear; I don't question that decision at all, I just miss my grandparents."

"Do you wish I'd gone by myself? Do you resent my pulling you into it?"

Latin thought long enough for Autumn to fall asleep. "I do, and yet at the same time, I don't. Can both of those things be true at the same time? It feels like they're both true."

"I know what you mean, Latin. If that's the way it is, then it's so. Often, events and feelings don't make sense. Let's sleep."

After Autumn had fallen asleep again, Latin asked, "Aren't you worried about your mother?"

"No."

"Really, not at all?"

"Well, I miss her and I'm sad that we're not together, but I don't worry. It's not that way between us."

" 'Way between us'? What do you mean?"

"I don't want to talk about it because it's complicated and I'm mostly asleep."

"Do you think Billy is going to come looking for us?"

"Latin, I was asleep. No. I don't think so. The ferry costs a great deal, I'm sure, and nobody over here knows of Billy, so they're not scared of him. He'd have to bring a big crew. He doesn't know where we're headed and he doesn't have anywhere safe to stay over here, so I doubt we'll ever see him again."

"Do you think we'll stay?"

"I'm sorry, I'd fallen asleep, what?"

"Autumn, do you think we'll stay here in Arden House?"

Autumn slept.

CHAPTER 6

The rising bell woke Latin, but had no effect on Autumn. He slipped from the covers, quietly arranged fresh wood on top of the glowing coals in the woodstove, slipped his shaving kit from his pack, and shuffled into the bathroom. He looked out the window into the dim, frozen morning and lit a candle. He filled the pitcher with icy water from the bathtub faucet and poured it into the washbasin in the sink. He splashed water into his hair to mat it down, and then wet his shaving brush, worked it into his bar of soap, and spread the thin, freezing slurry into his chin and around his face. Eager to be done and dry off his face, Latin held the razor softly and deftly sliced off the longer hairs around his cheeks. He scraped once at the shorter ones on his chin, then shrugged. He dried off, slipped back into the bedroom, and changed into his Arden House clothes by the woodstove.

"Time to wake up, Autumn. Did you sleep well? Cheery morning!"

"I need more time," she said, burrowing deeper into the covers.

"Come on, sleepy-face. Up, up, up. Breakfast, let's go. The bell rang. I've been up and shaved; come on, let's go."

"Ugh," Autumn moaned, "I like this bed. I want to spend more time with it."

"Up and up!"

Autumn crawled to her feet and slouched into the bathroom, mumbling, "...you are annoying in the morning. My goodness...so cold... 'Cheery morning,' did he say that? Ugh."

"Where is everyone?" Latin asked Arthur as they walked into the basement of the Gild Hall for breakfast.

"Most Friends have already stopped in, eaten, and taken their packed lunches to work with them. Although we get more and more daylight every day, there is none to waste, even in the cold. Also, we ran out of tea last week, which has caused much hardship. Even thin, weak tea does a lot of good. There's not much complaining out loud, but I do see fewer people staying to eat breakfast and talk now that there's no tea at all. Some have a little tucked away for themselves, but the cook is out." Arthur paused and then smiled. "Plain dress suits you."

"Thank you. What's in the packed lunches?" Autumn asked.

"Well, usually there are fresh vegetables, apples, bread, and cheese, but, like I said, things are lean right now. We're down to potatoes and what we call 'Arden Mix.' It's usually dried, crushed oats, cracked wheat, toasted soybeans, dried apples, dried blueberries, and whatever we have on hand that won't spoil. At this point, it's basically just dried oats. In better times, there are fresh eggs that we hard-boil and pack into lunches, but not so much now. The few eggs we get, we give to the children."

Latin asked, "Any chance we'll be able to get to work today?"

Arthur nodded, "Yes, I have two things for us to do today. First, I'll give you a tour of town and we'll look into a few empty houses so you can start to think about what it might be like if you choose to stay. If there's time left, we'll look at the work list and let you choose your first jobs. I should mention before we look at houses that we tend to shift between houses often. I've heard visitors say they find it strange. I know it's a matter for much discussion in the other houses, but it's worked well for us for many years, so we stick with it. Our tradition is that anyone who wants to change who they're living with will simply move. Friends will move, go live by themselves for a time, then move again when they're ready. That's all there is to it. Nearly all married couples live apart for a time. We have several groups, mostly of younger Friends, that prefer to live as a group in one house. Many of the young Friends in the Wood Gild share a house, for example. After breakfast, we'll walk. One advantage of a declining population is ample housing."

Latin asked, "You all live, just, out in the open like this? No fences or anything? No locks on the doors? Don't you worry about theft or safety? I know you said you have Constable Pete, but, with everything open like this, I don't understand how that works."

Arthur nodded and said, "Oh, yes. I understand. There's not much concern with Friends taking things from each other since we all have essentially the same things. We used to have quite a bit of trouble with others, outsiders, but it's been quite a few years since that was a problem."

"What happened?" Latin asked.

"How do you mean?"

"If it was a problem, but now it isn't a problem, what changed?"

Arthur hesitated, then said, "We really should have tea for this kind of conversation. Latin, how much do you know about your uncle Baskin?"

Latin said, "Almost nothing. My father rarely spoke of him."

Arthur leaned back in his chair and crossed his legs. He said, "Many years ago, your father, your Uncle Baskin, and I used to fish together, down in the creek. I can take you there, if you like. Your father was quite a fine craftsman, even as a young man. He was a quiet man, but, when he spoke, he had something to say and he put it plainly. He was a respected man around here. I particularly admired how he defended your Uncle Baskin."

"Defended him?"

"Your Uncle Baskin, nobody speaks of it now, but there was a time when he was not well thought-of here. He had ideas that were difficult for many in town. He could be abrasive and confrontational. He had very little patience with anyone not quick enough to keep pace with the flow of his ideas in a conversation. He could be quite difficult, but your father always stood by him, even when Baskin was talking nonsense."

"Nonsense about what?"

"No topic was safe from Baskin Tillich: science, astronomy, physics, farming, banking, medicine, archery, cooking, sewing, you name it. Baskin thought he was an expert in everything."

"Uncle Baskin had something to do with what changed between outsiders and the security of Arden House?"

"Well, it's still a mystery, I have to say. I doubt anyone really knows exactly what happened, but I'll tell you what I know of the story. This happened maybe twelve or fifteen years ago. Some of the other old people around here might give you a different version, but this is how I remember it. We had trouble with outsiders from time to time, like anywhere. Then, the attacks got worse. Bald men in black leather…I like your word for them. You call them 'Skullers'?"

"We do."

"Skullers would ride into town in a big mob, kick everyone out of a house, take everything there, and move on to the next house until they had all they could carry on their horses; then they'd leave. We were terrified. They even took over Arden House once, I remember, long before I became clerk. They held it for two nights, emptying out the stores as quickly as they could until a regiment from Bellevue House came and helped us fight a fierce, two-day battle. As Quakers, pacifism is one of our core beliefs. We seek to live in a manner that removes the causes for war, but the sight of those men hauling away our food and our children's winter coats was more than some of us could bear. Several Arden House men, honest Quakers, fought ferociously in those horrific days and nights. Your uncle Baskin was one of the best of those men.

Latin said, "It's a wonder Bellevue came to fight for you. I mean, to put themselves at risk for another House like that."

Arthur nodded in agreement and said, "It's complicated. Of course, Bellevue House was a more frequent target of attacks because they have a much more valuable inventory, but there were also other considerations that are far too complex to explain now.

"Then, one day a few weeks later, a gang of Skullers rode in with guns and quickly surrounded a family working in the big garden. I watched helplessly from the street by the Craft Shop while they beat the father with clubs and a sword. Two of them held the mother down while the others took her little boy. They rode off with him screaming and howling. She staggered a few steps after them, then collapsed. It makes me sick to my stomach even to tell the story. That night, one of the Skullers rode up to the Gild Hall and walked right into dinner by himself. I was there. He had a pistol, but he never drew it. He stood up on the stage and announced, 'The boy is alive, although I won't say he's doing well. He will only stay alive as long as our demands are met.'

"They set up a drop-off spot in the woods by Naaman's Road. We were supposed to leave things for them at noon every day. They would leave a list of what they wanted next. This went on for about a week.

"Then Baskin Tillich stood up at dinner one night and made an announcement. He said he had an answer to our problem with the kidnappers, but he gave us no details. He had been drinking. I did not understand much of what he said, but he made it clear that nobody could talk him out of going and that it was likely he would not return. His son, your cousin David, was just a toddler, but Baskin was resolute."

"Oh my goodness," Autumn said with a gasp.

"Yes, indeed. Well, several Friends followed him, trying to talk him out of it. I'm not proud to say it, but I did not try to stop him. I don't know if I really thought he could change things, but I clearly recall being thankful that someone was willing to try something, even something senseless. He left that night. He shook hands with a few of us and left."

"Was my father here then?" Latin asked.

"No, your father had gone before this."

"So, what happened?"

"He left that night with a large backpack and two toolboxes. Nobody's seen him or heard from him since. The next morning, the kidnapped little boy walked into town. He found his mother. You can well imagine that scene. He was healthy, but didn't stop crying and clinging to his mother for a few days. He couldn't talk about it for a long time. Later, when he could talk about it, he didn't remember anything helpful to explain what happened. Since then we have not had a problem with Skullers. Not one. We've had wanderers, peaceful vagrants, hobos, and a traveling mystic maybe once or twice a year, but no Skullers."

"I wonder what happened?" Autumn asked.

"It is not ours to know," Arthur answered.

"You must have some theories, some guesses?"

"Your uncle sacrificed himself for what's been a long-lasting peace. That's all we know. I doubt there's a name in all of Arden House history more thankfully respected than Baskin Tillich."

"Can we see his house when we're out walking around?"

"Yes, your cousins live there."

CHAPTER 7

They walked out into the morning chill. Wisps of mist rose up out of the ground where the gardeners were already working in their raised beds. Arthur led them around a garden field he called, "The Pettit Green," then down a short, steep path to a one-room log cabin in the shade of a high tangle of weeds. They went inside. The floor was wet dirt with a rusted, freestanding woodstove in the center.

Arthur raised an eyebrow. "Okay, well…that's something. I didn't realize this little cabin had gotten so bad. I guess nobody's lived here for a while. Let's keep looking."

He led them back up the hill, around the other side of the garden, and back toward Arden House. There were tidy, well-kept houses to the right with windows looking out over the large garden. Arthur chatted away about who resided in each house at various times in the past and what Gilds they were in.

They passed Arden House on their left and came to a crooked intersection of paths where the huge garden spread off to the left. On the right, a lady waved to them from a flagstone walkway leading to a stone cottage beside a white dogwood tree. The lady motioned for them to come up the path.

Arthur said, "Latin, Autumn, this is Betsy. Betsy, I'm sure you've heard of our new Friends, Latin and Autumn."

Tall and angular, Betsy shook hands with both Latin and Autumn. "It's a pleasure to meet you both," she said. "You're looking for a house?"

"We are," Autumn answered, looking behind Betsy.

"Well, I wish you'd do me a favor," Betsy said.

"What is it?" Latin asked.

"I wish you'd take my house."

Latin and Autumn both dropped their packs and looked at the clean, well-tended, one-room stone house behind her. Their mouths opened slightly in wonder, but neither spoke.

"Oh, not this," Betsy said. "This is where I should be living. I come here almost every day, tend the garden, and enjoy the light. It's so bright here in the clearing. My house is down by the creek, in the woods, down the path. It's a fine house, really. Maybe you could come look at it?"

"I don't understand," Autumn asked. "Is someone else living in this house now?"

Betsy smiled and said, "No. Oh no, but this is no fit for you two. You'll want a family soon. This is only one room. This won't do at all, no. Please do come look at the house in the woods. I'll explain on the way? Grab your packs. Let's go."

"Sure," they said, following her down the path into the woods.

"I've been trying to talk Mara into moving for several months. We're both getting along in years. We get around fine now, but this path is poor passage in bad weather. If we moved up to the corner house, we'd be in the light, we could see the garden, and we would be closer to the Gild Hall for meals."

Latin, Autumn, and Arthur followed Betsy down the steep, rocky path into the woods.

"You're right about the light," Latin said.

"Oh, I know; this forest is so thick and tall. Almost no light gets through to the ground. It was fine at first. I liked it for a long time. There's a magic in these woods, you know. I loved it, but now I'm ready to be up by the garden. Mara built this little place in the woods almost all by herself, and it took her years. There were only ruins to start with. It just needs someone to live in it, that's all. If she knows that someone is living in it and taking care of it, she'll agree to move up to the garden. You'll see. I think she really wants to move as much as I do. I don't mean to pressure you. If you don't like it, that's fine."

Betsy stopped and said, "There it is."

Autumn and Latin looked up from the path. The creek was to their left. The cottage was built into a cluster of boulders uphill beyond a circular clearing. The stones in the walls were framed with red mud mortar. The roof was emerald moss.

"She built it into the shape of the rock outcropping that was already here," Betsy admired.

"That's amazing," Latin stammered.

"Come inside," Betsy said, opening the door.

Two glass windows facing the stream lit the sitting room, plainly set with a square table and four rough-hewn chairs. "The roof never leaks. She put plastic sheeting under the moss, so whatever doesn't get sucked up in the roots runs off the sides. She cut the hallway out of the rocks with a flat chisel, by hand."

Latin ran his hands over the walls of stone. "This is amazing work. It must have taken years."

Betsy nodded. "It really is a special place. The floor planks have mostly settled. There's a dry sink there and two fireplaces. We never use the fireplace up here in the sitting room, except when it's bitter cold. The room in the back has a woodstove. It heats the sleeping rooms. Come on back. Let me show you."

Autumn and Latin shared an excited grin as they followed Betsy down the short hall.

"There are actually three bedrooms, but one is tiny, it would work well as a nursery. The bedrooms all have glass skylights. They don't leak. Don't ask me how she did that."

A warm woodstove sat in the center of a shared space that opened into all three rooms. Betsy opened the woodstove and placed two split logs from a stack in the corner of the nursery.

"There's an outhouse back up the hill a bit. We get water straight from the creek. There's no well. It takes about five minutes to walk up the path to the Gild Hall, so it's not like you're out in the middle of nowhere, but it's quiet enough. We sleep on a bed with wooden slats, but of course you two could work out anything you like. We keep a cloth pinned up against the ceiling to keep the dust down and help reflect the light, so we have to keep the candles low. That's something you'll have to be careful of."

Arthur said, "And the creek rises, of course."

Betsy nodded, "Oh, yes. The creek used to get right up to the door after a heavy rain. Of course the creek is low now, but that could be a problem during a wet year. Mara built a special doorjamb, I don't know if you noticed it on the way in; let me show you."

They walked back down the hallway to the sitting room. Betsy lifted the bolt and opened the door. She pointed to a long pocket carved in the frame and a matching raised bead around the edge of the door. "Mara affirms it's waterproof, although the creek has never gotten high enough to test it, which is fine with me, of course."

"The windows?" Latin asked.

"If it gets up to the windows, we'll all have much bigger problems than water in the house," Autumn answered.

"Quite right," Betsy agreed.

"I've never seen anything like it," Latin said. "It's hard to imagine anyone wanting to leave."

Autumn sat down at the table and looked out the window toward the creek. "It's well hidden," she said with a meaningful look at Latin. "And out of the way."

There was a long silence.

"Yes," Latin finally said.

"You're quite sure you're ready to move?" Autumn asked.

"I am," Betsy confirmed.

"Is there anything we can do to help convince Mara?"

"You'd both like to stay here?"

"Yes, of course. It's a dream," Autumn responded.

"More than anything," Latin agreed.

"Okay, well then, let me go talk to Mara. She's working at the Craft Shop. You're more than welcome to wait here, if you like."

Twenty minutes later, Betsy walked back through the door holding hands with Mara, whose curly red hair was littered with curls of wood shavings. Her face was puffy and damp from recent crying.

"Oh, don't mind me. I cry at everything. It's good. We should be moving closer to…You'll take good care of the…Oh, Betsy, look at these two. They're such a perfect couple. They fit right in here. This feels right. Let's get our things out and let them settled in."

Arthur said, "Well, that was easy, excellent. Just in time for lunch. We'll eat with the children in the Gild Hall. Then we can check the work lists."

Arthur stopped a few steps out of the door when he realized that Autumn and Latin were not following. They were both stood frozen inside the house. "What?" he asked.

"What should we do with our packs," Latin said.

"Of course, you're welcome to leave them here. Mara and I will move our things out this afternoon. As you can see, we don't have much to move."

After a long pause, Autumn said, "I'm leaving mine. Yes. Thank you. It's heavy, I'm not going to need it, so I will leave it here."

Latin shook his head. "I'm sorry," he said. "I know I should. It's not because I don't trust you, believe me. I just can't leave it yet. I still don't feel right without it."

Everyone shrugged. "Sure, keep it with you, whatever. Let's go," Arthur said.

CHAPTER 8

A gaunt, serious young woman led a scraggly procession of thirty or so children into the Gild Hall basement for lunch.

"There seems to be quite a lot of children. I hadn't noticed so many last night, they blended in so well at dinner," Latin said.

Arthur said, "That's only half of them. My sister will be along with the others. Let me introduce you to our young teacher, Annette."

Annette's expression lightened as she shook hands with Autumn and Latin. She explained, "These are just the youngest children. We call this the Lower School, up to eight years old. When they turn nine, we send them along to Mr. and Mrs. Gerstein."

"You teach all of these children by yourself?" Autumn asked.

"In a way, I suppose," Annette answered. "Mostly, they teach each other."

"That's quite a gift," Latin said.

Annette's cheeks turned pink and she looked at her shoes, then hurried off to move the children toward the serving line for lunch.

Arthur sat down to his potato and leek soup and said, "Okay, let's see if we can find you some work for the afternoon. Here's the clipboard of job cards. Ruth takes the work requests from the clerks and writes a card for each request. Let's see…the Craft Shop needs a hand with laundry. They can always use the help, but that's not very interesting to either of you, is it?"

Autumn and Latin both shook their heads.

"They are also breaking down the broadcloth loom to switch over to summer-weight spindles. Either of you interested?"

Latin shrugged. Autumn said, "Keep going."

"The teachers always have their hands full and can use help."

Autumn said, "No chance."

Latin said, "Maybe, but keep going."

"Constable Pete has taken a rifle up to Wind Lane to see if he can rid us of the fox that has been getting into our chickens. He's not asking for help. I'm not sure why this card is on here. The Wood Gild is splitting and hauling cord wood to…"

"That's me. Sorry to interrupt, but I'd like to help with that if possible," Latin chimed in.

"Very well, that can be arranged. And what else, Doctor Dash is tending sick alpacas over by the barn."

"No need to go any further. I'll help Doctor Dash," Autumn said.

"Splendid. Well, okay, that's settled," Arthur said. "I'll ask Annette to have two of her students be your guides. I have other things I need to attend to this afternoon."

"Of course, you've been very kind. Thank you again," Autumn said.

"It's my pleasure. Now, I'm going to finish my lunch and be on my way before the older children come in." Arthur motioned for Annette to come join them. He said, "Annette, could you please have one of your students lead Latin to the east end of Indian Field? There is a wood splitting crew over there."

"Of course."

"And another to help Autumn get to the Barn to help Doctor Dash?"

CHAPTER 9

Latin shook hands with his guide, a blond boy with green eyes. "I'm Latin."

"William," he said, shoulders back, shaking hands.

"I believe we met last night at dinner. You carried our spare venison jerky to the kitchen."

"Yes," the boy said shyly.

"Did you get to eat any of it?"

"I did, yes."

"Did you like it?"

"It was okay."

"You know where we're headed this morning, William?"

"Near enough. We'll find 'em," he said, heading out the door. Latin slung his pack up onto his shoulders and hustled to catch up.

William led Latin beside Pettit Green, down a steep path in the woods, past a dark log cabin, then straight down a set of stairs made of squared timbers set in the ground. They crossed a rickety footbridge, turned left, and continued downhill until they reached the creek.

William stopped and looked at Latin with one eyebrow raised.

"What is it?" Latin asked.

"Do you want to stay on the path or go rock-hopping?"

"Are we going up that path over there, across the creek?"

"No, we're going down the creek that way."

"Where does the path across the creek lead?"

"Nowhere."

"Come on, William. It's a path. It must go somewhere. If there weren't anything there, there would not be a path."

"That path goes to Prisoner's Cave."

"Prisoner's Cave?"

"Yeah, we don't want to go down there. Trust me. We want to go either up this path or along the rocks. It's up to you."

"Oh, heavens. Rock-hopping, yes, definitely."

"Good. Race?" William asked with a glimmer.

Latin smiled. "Race? Now that's not fair. You know these rocks like the back of your hand."

"And you're twice my size!"

"What do we race to?"

"The old railroad bridge, up that way," William said, pointing.

"That's quite a long way to run hopping from rock to rock."

William shrugged.

"What do we race for?"

"You mean like betting? Oh, nothing. We don't bet. I don't have anything you'd want, anyway."

"Really? Try me. What would you bet with someone your own age?"

"I have a yo-yo, not with me—back in the dorm, but I'm not betting you that."

"Does it work?"

"Sure it works. It sleeps and everything. I just put a new string on it last week. It's my favorite, and I'm not giving it up. You'll probably win anyway."

Latin looked down the creek to the railroad bridge. "How about my... watch? Would you bet your yo-yo if I offered my watch if you win?"

"You're joking."

"I'm not. Here, look, it works perfectly. It belonged to my father."

"Omega?" William asked.

"It is. Who made your yo-yo?"

"I made it myself in the craft shop," William said.

"Okay, well, I really think having longer legs, I'll win, so I'll bet my watch against your yo-yo."

William shook his head in disbelief. "You're going to run with your pack on?"

"It won't slow me down. I'm used to it."

"Hey, if you're serious, you got it, Latin. Shake on it?"

Latin and William shook hands and walked across the rocks into the middle of the creek.

"You sure about this?"

Latin said, "You want to say, 'Go'?"

William shrugged and said, "You do it."

Latin said, "Ready…Set…Go."

William shot across the rock tops at a full sprint. Latin took three tentative steps, then stopped and watched in wonder.

Later, when Latin caught up with William, he was sitting with his back against a rock at the railroad bridge pretending to be asleep. Latin cleared his throat and William couldn't hold back a smile.

"You know," Latin said, sitting down next to him. "I don't think I could run in an open field as quickly as you run on those rocks."

"Maybe, but there are plenty in town faster on the rocks than I am."

"You all look so scrawny."

"We're strong from hard work."

Latin unclasped his watch and handed it to William.

"I can't take your watch, Latin. You keep it. It was your father's. Wouldn't be right."

"No, here. I'm serious. It's yours. Take it. That's amazing, what you did there."

"Really?"

"Yes, here."

William's hand shook as he took the watch. "I've never held a working watch before."

"You have to wind it every morning."

"How?"

Latin showed William how to turn the knob, how to wind the spring, and how to pull it out to set the time.

"Can I ask you one favor?" William asked.

"Sure."

"Don't tell anyone we bet. We're not supposed to bet. Can we just say you gave it to me?"

Latin thought. "I doubt anyone will believe that I just gave you my watch. Working watches are impossible to come by, as you know."

William thought. "You're right about that," he said.

"Hmmmmm," Latin hummed.

William's eyes brightened. "Hey, what if we make like it's a trade? I'll give you my yo-yo. It's not a fair trade or anything, but people might believe it, maybe?"

Latin agreed. "Fine by me."

They shook hands. William said, "Let's go. Do you want to keep your watch until I can give you my yo-yo?"

"No, you keep the watch. I'll get the yo-yo later."

They walked together along a narrow path through the woods. William checked the time every few steps.

CHAPTER 10

"What's your name?" Autumn asked after walking in silence with her sheepish guide.

"Emily," the girl mumbled into her chest.

Autumn followed Emily down a shaded lane, then along a worn footpath between houses.

"What's this big building?" Autumn asked as they passed a complex, three-story building on the corner facing the long garden green.

"Craft Shop."

"Who lives there?"

"Nobody lives there. It's the Craft Shop. They make furniture, fix things."

Emily turned left to cross the road, but Autumn stopped to watch the people working on the green.

"Is this the garden field we saw on the way into town on the heavy carriage?"

"I guess," Emily shrugged.

"They're working raised beds..." Autumn said to herself, wandering away toward the edge of the field.

Two lanky girls in their late teens saw Autumn and came to the end of the green to talk.

"Hi. I'm Autumn."

"Pleased to meet you. I'm Elsie. This is Esther. Welcome to Arden."

"Thank you. Are you twins?"

"Yes. Where are you headed?"

"Emily is leading me over to the Barn to see if I can help Doctor Dash tend livestock. Say, do you grow any medicinal herbs here? Echinacea, chamomile, ginger?"

The twins looked at each other, then Esther said, "No. There are some cooking herbs over in the Pettit Garden, but the rest is all vegetables and grain. These are all vegetables, here. The fields over on the other side of town by the barn…those are all grain."

"What are you planting now?"

"Oh, we're not planting; we're just hauling compost and mixing it into the beds, getting things ready."

"So, I get the feeling Emily doesn't want to go to the Barn. Do you know why that might be?"

Esther and Elsie shrugged and looked across the street at Emily. "She's probably just tired," one said.

"Emily, you can go back to school now if you like. We'll get Autumn over to the Barn," said one of the twins.

"Emily, you go on back to Teacher Annette. We'll make sure Autumn gets to the Barn," said the other.

Expressionless, Emily turned and dragged her feet back toward school.

"Poor little thing," Autumn said, frowning.

"It's not her fault. Everyone's been worn down by the hard winter, by all the work and fewer hands to do it, and by our food being so thin. The little ones take it hardest."

"Yes, Arthur mentioned things were lean."

Both twins nodded in agreement.

"I'm sorry, I forgot which of you is which."

"I'm Elsie, she's Esther. Plain dress compliments you."

"Thanks."

"Do you plan to stay with us?"

"Oh, yes. We're staying. We'll be in the little house down by the creek."

"Latin is staying?" Elsie blurted.

"Are you two married?" asked Esther.

Elsie blushed, then they all giggled.

"Not married, no," Autumn said with a smile.

"Does he shave every day? Do you mind me asking? He shaves, yes?"

Autumn thought. "I guess he shaves most days, why?"

"It's so handsome. Haven't you noticed? All the men here have beards?"

"They do?"

The twins nodded with wrinkled noses. "Did Arthur tell you about the dance tonight?"

"Dance? No. What dance?"

"Most Fridays we dance in the Gild Hall after dinner."

"Sounds like fun."

"We have a little band. Katie has a working fiddle. There are some guitars and we make drums from buckets. Different people sing. We hope you'll be there."

"What she means is that she hopes Latin will be there," Elsie corrected with a roll of her eyes.

"I'll do my best to get him to the dance," Autumn said. "Now, how do I get to the barn from here?"

The twins pointed. "Straight up that path. It's not far. It'll be on your left."

CHAPTER 11

William and Latin heard dull thuds from the Wood Gild crew long before they saw them. William called out, "Friends! I've brought help."

Three men, all older and taller than Latin, stopped, smiled, and loped forward to shake hands.

"Hey, Latin. Nice to meet you. I'm Danny. This is Mark and Tom."

"Danny. Mark. Tom," Latin said in turn as he shook hands with each of them.

Mark said, "We have two horses there, hitched to the cart. We heard you're skittish. Is this distance okay? Should we move them?"

Latin said, "Thanks for asking, this should be fine. I'm fine. It's a help to know that they're hitched."

Mark said, "We're glad to have an extra hand. You have experience with wood?"

Latin nodded and said, "I do. It's my favorite work. How can I help? What kind of gear do you use?"

William interrupted, "Latin, I'm going to leave you with these Friends and head back to school, okay?"

Latin and William shook hands. "Thank you very much. It's been fun."

William waved to the crew and headed back toward Arden House at a jog.

"Latin, you're just in time. We're sitting down to lunch. Come join us?"

"I ate, but I'll sit with you, sure."

The four sat on stumps around a wide disk of wood like a low table. Danny opened a canvas bag by untying the knot in the leather string that held it closed. He put a glass quart bottle of water out in the middle of the disk and threw burlap pouches to Mark and Tom. They all dug into their mix. Latin let them eat in silence.

When they had eaten, Mark said, "Is that all there is?"

"Afraid so," answered Danny, checking the bag.

Mark said, "Well, what's the plan?"

Danny stood up on his stump and looked around. "We've probably done all the sawing we need to do for the day. Let's see if we can get one load split, loaded, and sent back to Paul on the wagon by late afternoon. Tom and Mark, when we're done, you two can take the load back; Latin and I will stay and split until the light starts to go, then we'll walk home. That keeps Latin away from the horses and gives Mark a ride home to rest his ankle. Sound good?"

Everyone nodded.

Weary, hungry, and stiff, Mark stood and said, "Latin, where would you like to start, splitting or stacking?"

"Oh, I'll split if it's okay. What happened to your ankle?"

"I was stupid; a log rolled into it. I don't think it's broken."

"Did that happen this morning?"

"Yeah."

"Is there any ice? Have you put anything on it? Should you see the doctor?"

"Not worth risking a trip to the Doctor. I wrapped it. It'll be fine."

Mark handed his splitting maul to Latin.

"You guys have a sharpening stone or anything?" Latin asked.

Danny answered, "No, not out in the field. We have some back at the wood lot, but, as you can see from that maul, we don't sharpen often."

Latin said, "I've a sharpening kit in my pack. Is it okay if I take a few minutes to work on this before I start?"

Danny shrugged, and Mark said, "Suit yourself."

Latin pulled apart his pack, slid out his kit, and hunched over the rusty splitting maul. First, he scraped at it with a short file to knock the edge into rough shape, and then he used his stone to even out the bevel.

After a few minutes work, he said, "That's better. Good enough for now," and walked over to Danny.

"Ready?" Danny asked.

Latin nodded that he was.

"Why don't you go split one of those disks over there?" Danny said, pointing at a leaning clutter of disks that had been sawed from a large tree trunk and rolled onto each other.

Latin walked over to the disks slowly, gently swinging the maul around his shoulders, rolling the weight from side to side and to loosen his muscles.

"Let us know if you need any help moving those around," Danny called over to Latin.

Latin did not answer. His eyes were focused on the patterns in the grain of the wood around him. His hands were learning how the maul rotated, spun, and twisted. He planned his angles of attack. He climbed up and walked from disk to disk, checking which ones wobbled and which sat solidly. Latin stepped up to the leaning edge of the tallest standing disk and set the head of the maul down quietly, leaning the handle against his leg. He rubbed his hands together to warm them and help get a better grip on the handle.

Gathering his breath, he lifted the maul, then swung it around and up over his head. He let it fall and rise and fall in fluid sweeps, building momentum while he searched for the one spot on his target disk, well below him, where a swift strike would be most apt to force the disk to give way.

Finally, in a jumping twist, Latin leapt down to the disk he had been eying on the ground. His boots caught the edge of the disk perfectly and he swung the maul down around him, smashing through the disk with a cracking pop. Continuing the motion, Latin twisted the maul up away from the disk, this time looping it over his left shoulder and back down into one of the half-disks still wobbling from having been split. Without pause, he swung again and again, alternating shoulders as he went. His motion flowed. The head of the maul never stopped. His feet danced in short, fierce bursts, putting his shoulders where they needed to be to deliver each swing, recover, and prepare for the next. Right shoulder, left shoulder, right shoulder, left shoulder until the entire disk sat in woodstove-ready pieces.

Without hesitation, Latin leapt up, vaulted himself over several disks and landed with another mighty smash, breaking a second disk in half. After he had split the second disk the same way, he stopped to check the blade on the maul.

Mark was down on one knee, laughing.

"What in the world was that?" Danny asked, shouting.

Latin looked around. "What? Isn't this the wood you wanted split?"

"That's how you split wood?"

"Umm. Why? How do you guys split wood?"

"Not like that. We, um…we don't do it like that," Danny said.

"Oh, okay. I'm sorry. I'm doing it wrong? How do you do it?"

Mark started chuckling and laughter spread to the others. After a while, even Latin laughed a bit, although he did not know why.

When they stopped, Latin said, "What? What's funny?"

"See that pile over there over there?" Mark said, pointing to a modest pile of split wood.

"Yeah."

"Okay, that was one disk. We split that this morning."

Latin said, "Okay, good. What?"

Mark said, "No, Latin, you're not getting it. All three of us, and it took us all morning."

"To do that little bit?" Latin asked. "Really?"

Mark sat down. He said, "Well, first, we use a big cant hook to get one disk flat on the ground, then we use that as a chopping block, which means we have to lever one of the other disks up onto it. That usually takes, I don't know, fifteen minutes, at least.

"And that's how I got my ankle banged up," Mark added.

"Then we get out the wedges and tap one in with a hammer. Then we drive it in with the sledge. Then we drive a second wedge. Usually a third wedge cracks the disk. We can't just pop them with the maul until they're already in quarters," Mark explained.

"You did the whole afternoon's work for the entire crew in what, seven or eight minutes?"

The four young men stood in silence until finally, Latin said, "Sooooo…I guess that means we get to take the rest of the afternoon off?"

After a hearty laugh and a very long rest break, Tom, Mark and Danny loaded the split wood onto the cart while Latin put an edge on the second splitting maul and freshened up the first one.

Mark and Tom left for town with the wagonload of firewood and all the tools, while Latin packed his gear.

"You mentioned Paul before. Who is Paul?" Latin asked on the walk back.

Danny said, "He's the clerk of the Wood Gild."

"Oh, right. Arthur mentioned him. I still get the names mixed up. Are all three of you in the Wood Gild?"

"Yes. I'm a member. Tom and Mark are apprentices."

"What's the difference, again? Arthur explained the Gilds last night, but I'm not sure I understood the difference between Gild members and apprentices."

Danny stopped suddenly and sat on a fallen log beside the path. He held his head with both hands.

"Are you okay?"

"Uh, lightheaded. Happens sometimes. Dizzy. I sit for a minute. It gets better."

Latin sat next to him and put a hand on Danny's back. After Danny sat, he took a few deep breaths. Feeling recovered, he nodded and stood up slowly.

"Maybe you should have the doctor look at you?"

Danny shook his head gently and said, "No, there's nothing wrong with me. It's like this with everyone. It's from the food, the lack of variety."

"Simple hunger, probably."

"I guess. Not much to be done about it, I suppose. Let's keep going. What were we talking about?"

"Gilds."

Danny nodded. "That's complicated," he said. "And it's changing, with the Gilds. It's a lot different than it used to be. When there were more

Friends, being in a Gild meant more than it does now. It's still important, but with things as they are, everybody's hungry, we all work too hard, and there's not enough of anything to go around. Being a Gild member really doesn't make much difference. Back when we had more, Gild members tended to get more benefit from it."

"I'm not sure I get your meaning."

"Okay, I'll give you an example…tea. We used to have all kinds of tea. We drank tea all the time. Gild members could get their favorite kinds and have it at home whenever they wanted. Everybody else drank what was served in the Gild hall. It wasn't bad, mind you, but the choice went to the Gild members."

"Oh, I see. Now that there's no tea at all, everybody's out of tea, even the Gild members."

"Exactly. It's the same with everything…soap, candles, honey, whatever."

"Why is everything so bad?"

Danny thought before answering. "There isn't just one reason," he said after a while. "It's a lot of things. Everything relies on trade. We're strong in some things, like cloth. We make the best cloth around. We make our own clothes, and for years we traded with the other houses to send clothes to them in exchange for what we needed. We still do, but there are fewer people here making clothes, so we have less to trade. Also, I think we get less in return than we used to, but I don't know, maybe that's not so. It sure seems that way."

"You don't think the Trader is stealing from the town, do you?"

"Oh no, nothing like that. He's a good guy, the best. It's just…if the other houses have less to give and they don't need what we have as much as we need what they have, it puts us in a weak position."

"I see."

"But, that's not the big problem."

"What's the big problem?"

Danny stopped and sat on one of the rocks in the creek. Latin sat down next to him.

Quietly, Danny said, "We're dying out."

Latin closed his eyes and sighed, then looked out across the creek, shady in the dusk. "I thought that might be happening," he said. "Was there a sickness?"

"There's always a sickness. We're all starving. Anyone who gets a cough or a cut that turns hot, for the most part, they go in a hurry. Kids, old people…there's far too much to do, and any little mistake can mean the end."

"The doctor does what he can, I guess?"

"He tries. He helps when he can, but it's up to nature, you know? If she's going to take you, there's nothing Doctor Dash can do."

Latin nodded.

"What's worse," Danny said, "and don't tell anybody I told you this, but there was a time this winter when people would leave in the middle of the night and set out for one of the other houses. Winterthur, mostly, but some went to Longwood, I'm sure."

"Winterthur?"

"Yeah, Winterthur is a full day's hike for a healthy person, with lots of dangerous road along the way. It's different there. They're not free like we are. There are books of rules and harsh punishments for breaking them or disobeying orders. There are all kinds of gossip about how crazy and strange they are, but there is food, apparently, and a little easier living. I've never been there, so I can't say for sure. I know a few Arden House people who vanished, and I expect that's where they went."

"Longwood is another house?"

"I've never seen it. I'm not even sure it's real. They're supposed to have fresh fruit all the time, clean clothes every day, wine at every meal. Longwood's just a myth."

"Friends stopped leaving?" Latin asked.

"Yeah. It's been a couple of months. I guess anybody who hasn't left already is going to stay."

After a pause, Latin said, "I guess that explains a little why everyone was so excited to see us."

Danny snickered, "Yeah, well…Autumn, anyway."

Latin didn't understand at first. "Oh," he said when he figured it out.

Danny said, "Are you two married? Are you a couple, or only traveling together?"

Latin looked at Danny. "We're a couple. We're together. We're not married, yet, but…"

"Okay, I understand. Of course. I was simply asking—no offense."

"I guess I didn't realize how things are."

"We need babies."

"Right," Latin said, standing. "I get it now. We better get back before we lose the last bit of light."

"Okay. You're not upset that I asked, are you? You understand."

"I'm not upset, Danny. I'm not upset at all. Thank you. Thank you for explaining how things are. I'm only trying to figure out how I can help."

"Sure."

CHAPTER 12

"Doctor Dash, we met at dinner. I'm Autumn," she said, shaking hands with the man leaning against a gatepost, smoking a pipe and watching over a field of animals.

"Oh, hello, Autumn. I was hoping you'd come to chat at some point."

"What are those?"

"These are alpacas. They don't have alpacas where you come from?"

"No. I've never seen one before. We have sheep; I guess they would be distant relatives."

"Well, alpacas have great wool. We use it for our winter coats, and the wool is also worth quite a bit in trade. They're not much to eat, but if we get hungry enough, and it comes to that, they can be okay. What's your training? Do you have much experience with animals?"

"My mother is an herbalist. She trained me in chemistry, extracting oils from plants, and using catalysts to make reactions. She taught me the basics of biology, as well, so I know some about the organs, the systems, and how to recognize the common ways they can go wrong. I know about infections, cleaning, and distilling, that sort of thing. I've delivered two babies, and I've seen my mother deliver many more. I've seen about a thousand teeth pulled, and I've pulled some myself. I've watched appendixes come out, but not done any myself. I've worked on animals: goats, sheep and horses. Delivering their young, mostly, but also treating some injuries. I've had to put down a few that got mauled by foxes or coyotes. I have done quite a few autopsies, where Ma would find things, such as squirrels, rabbits, and cats that had died, and we took them apart to look at all the organs and see how they fit together."

The doctor's face was pale with a mix of disbelief and astonishment.

"What?" Autumn asked.

"I'd keep most of that to myself if I were you," he said.

"Why?" she asked.

"Don't get me wrong. I think it's fantastic, but some of those practices are not held with high regard around here, especially by some of our more weighty Friends."

"Weighty?"

"Older Friends of influence."

"But who could have anything against science and the study of nature?"

"Oh, I'm not saying they have anything against those studies. It's complicated. We can talk about that later. Here, have a look at these alpaca and tell me what you see."

"There's obviously something wrong with that brown one, poor darling. How long has she been sick?"

"I don't know, two or three days maybe," Doctor Dash said, taking a long series of puffs from his pipe. "The man who came over to feed them last night said this one was staggering around, not eating. When I came over to look at her this morning, she was down on her side like this, and she's been whimpering and snorting."

"Have you examined her?"

"No, I was waiting to see if any of the others got sick before I got close. Caution, you will find…"

"They look fine," Autumn said, jumping over the fence and crouching down to look at the sickly alpaca.

"Oh, I wouldn't do that if I were you. She's sick. It might be catching. You don't know how she's going to react," the doctor said, aghast.

Autumn hummed softly and asked, "Ohhh, poor little creature, you don't feel well at all, do you?" She petted the alpaca and rubbed its nose, then brushed her hand gently against the side of the alpaca's long, wooly neck. "There, there little one," she said, petting the sad alpaca's head.

"It's a bad tooth," Autumn said.

"Really, how can you tell?"

"This side of her face is hot and swollen."

"Are you sure it's not contagious?"

"Contagious? It's an infected tooth. She's in pain, and she can't eat. I can knock her out, pull it, and pack it with gauze and clove oil, and she'll be right as rain in two days."

"Knock her out?"

"I'll need my backpack. You don't carry chloroform do you?"

"Carry what?"

"Do you have any rope? I'll tie her feet together to be safe. Never know with something this big."

"What?"

Autumn stood, leaving the alpaca lying quietly in the grass.

"Is there someone else we should ask before we work on her? I mean, whose alpaca is she?"

"What do you mean?"

"I mean, who owns her?"

"Slow down, Autumn. This is all a bit quick, don't you think?"

"Quicker the better. I don't know how alpacas carry pain, but they seem gentle and it's not healthy for any creature to be like that any longer than can be helped. Plus, she's already weak from not eating."

Doctor Dash knocked the burnt ashes out of his pipe with the force of his rising frustration.

"This is not the way we do things around…"

He stopped midsentence at the sound of a galloping horse approaching. They both looked up the path to see a frantic young man on a gray mule headed directly for them.

"Accident, Doc. Broken arm. Little William Morrison. Looks bad. Come, hurry."

The doctor jumped up on the back of the mule, and they rode off before Autumn could say a word.

She looked back at the sick alpaca. "I'm sorry, girl. I've got to go."

Autumn began at a jog, gradually stretching out her legs and covering ground more quickly. She flew out from the little path, past the Craft Shop and all the way down the length of the long green, at top speed. Instead of going to the Doctor's office in the basement of Arden House, she ran straight to the little house in the rocks by the creek. Mara was tidying up in the kitchen, moving out the last of their things, when Autumn crashed through the front door, panting.

"Can't talk, need bag," Autumn blurted. She grabbed her pack from the floor under the kitchen table and then sprinted back up the rocky path to Arden House.

As she approached the basement door, the doctor walked out with a resigned frown.

"What? What is it?" Autumn huffed. "Internal bleeding?"

The doctor leaned back against the door and started filling his pipe, but his hands were shaking so severely that he dropped more tobacco on the ground than went in the pipe.

"Doctor, what are you doing? Is he in there? Is he alive? What is his condition?"

The doctor said, "There's nothing we can do. Yes, it's a broken arm, at least. Probably more. He's cold and pale, as they get with this sort of injury. It'll be a long night for him, I'm afraid, and I doubt he'll make it. Sometimes they do survive with breaks if the damage is contained, but..."

"But what?"

"Well, you know, maybe it's best for him if he doesn't have to deal with all that."

"What in the world are you talking about?"

"His arm is crushed. It will never be normal again, even if he does live. The pain can be never-ending, you know, from all the damage. It's a shame."

Autumn stepped close to the doctor, leaned forward, and said with quiet intensity, "Doctor, what are you doing out here? Get in there and set the bone, treat the shock, help the patient. You treat the patient."

The Doctor stared at Autumn with a frozen mix of panic and indignant offense.

"Oh," Autumn said, recoiling slightly. "Okay, um...I see, right. Well, if you're not going to do anything for him and you say he's a lost cause, hopefully dying, then why don't you let me work on him? I'll see what I can do. I can't make it much worse than it is already, right?"

The doctor said, "No, I can't let you do that…"

"Why?" Autumn demanded.

"You could make it worse. We must do no h-harm," Dash stammered.

"Harm? You're the one that's doing him harm by leaving him in there, doing nothing. That's harm! Just because you don't know what you're doing isn't going to stop me from trying. From what I've seen, this place can't afford to lose anyone that can be saved. Not one person. I'm going in there. I'm treating this patient. If you want to stop me call the Constable? Fine! Do whatever you think you need to do. You go right ahead. They'll have to drag me out of here kicking and screaming."

Autumn pushed Dash slightly to one side as she charged through the door.

CHAPTER 13

The infirmary was cold, dark, and empty. The only furniture was a rickety wooden workbench against the far wall. A crumpled boy, sobbing weakly and shivering, lay curled toward one end of the workbench.

Doctor Dash followed Autumn closely across the room.

"Do you have any camphorated alcohol?" Autumn asked.

"Any what?"

Autumn looked at Dash in disgust. "Do you know who his parents are?"

"Of course I know, but his father is dead."

"Go get his mother," Autumn snarled.

"What?"

"You heard me. I need his mother. Get his mother, please."

"Why?"

"Why? Because he's a hurt little kid. He needs his mother."

"But he lives at the school now."

"I don't care if he mends his own clothes and cuts his own hair! He's hurt; get his mother. What kind of place is this? The first thing you do with a hurt kid is to get their mother. I am going to see what I can do here with him. You, please, find his mother and get her here."

Doctor Dash left in a huff.

Autumn slipped off her backpack, untied the leather strap that held it closed, and pulled out her sleeping bag, her old clothes, and her medical kits.

"Okay, William, can you hear me?"

"Y-y-y-yeah," he stammered, teeth chattering, choking on sobs.

"Oh, you're wet. How did you hurt your arm?"

"I fell, rock hopping…creek."

"It's your right arm, this arm?" She touched the arm in question.

"Yes." William winced.

"Okay. You're going to be fine. Here's what we're going to do. We're going to get you out of those clothes and warmed up, then we're going to set that arm, put a little splint on it, maybe a plaster if I can get something together, and we'll see what else we need to do as we go along. Okay?"

"I'm going to die," William wept.

"Die? You're not going to die, William. Absolutely not."

"You're only saying that to calm me. I can feel it already setting in, the death," William said, choking, gasping for breath.

"Nonsense, you're in shock. Maybe with Doctor Dash you might have died, but I'm here now and I know what I'm doing. You wait and see, okay?" Autumn pulled a pair of scissors from her kit and cut off his wet clothes, being careful with his arm although working quickly. "That's quite a watch you have there. My friend Latin has one very much like it. It's quite special to him."

"It's his. He gave it to me."

"He did? You leave that on, then. That watch has seen people through much worse troubles than a broken arm."

Autumn put her old pants on William's legs and wrapped all of her old shirts around his stomach and his good arm. She rolled up William's clothes, jammed them into her backpack, and stuffed the whole pile under his knees, propping up his feet. She unrolled her sleeping bag, shook it out, and covered William with it.

Moving close and holding the side of his neck, Autumn said calmly, "Okay, William, you're going to warm up and feel better in a few minutes, but I'm going to need a little help from you with this part. Okay?"

William shuddered and panted. "I'm dizzy," he said.

"I'm going to give you some medicine in your leg. It's going to make you feel much better all at once, okay? Don't be afraid; if you think something feels strange, it's the medicine, got it? I'm going to need you to stay awake, if you can, to answer questions for me. Can you do that?"

Little William shook violently from the cold and shock. "I will," he said.

Autumn opened her medicine kit and slid out a glass vial half-full of amber syrup. With one hand, she opened the wooden box that contained her glass and steel hypodermic needle and ground glass plunger. She screwed the needle tip onto the glass stock, put the tip into the vial, and drew the plunger out, pulling the amber liquid up into the syringe. She put the box down, tapped the side of the syringe to knock any air bubbles to the top, and pushed a few drops out of the needle. All of this took less than ten seconds, and Autumn's movements were smooth and calm. She pulled the blankets aside and slipped the needle quickly and gently into William's thigh. He didn't flinch. Autumn was pushing the plunger down when the doctor came through the door.

"My God!" he said. "What are you doing?"

"I'm treating his pain and shock. I need heat and light, immediately. Lanterns, candles, anything. A pot of boiling water would be helpful, anything with heat. Do you have any camphor? Does that chimney work? Can it be made to work?"

Doctor Dash was overwhelmed and could not respond.

"Forget everything else, please get candles and lanterns immediately." Dash left, shaking his head.

"Are you with me? Are you in there, William?"

"Yes, I'm here. What's happening? What did you give me?"

"Morphium. Do you know what that is?"

"No."

"Well, you will. You'll like it. Here's what's next: I'm going to fix your arm. It's not going to hurt, I promise. In fact, chances are that it'll feel a good deal better as soon as I'm done."

"I'm scared."

"I know you're scared. Here, we need a cocoon."

"A what?"

"Here, I'll show you." Autumn stood close beside William on the bench and put her left palm flat against the skin of his chest. She put her right hand on the top of his head and said, "Open your eyes."

He did, and Autumn lowered her face to his. She looked directly into his eyes from six inches away.

"I am with you," she said.

He nodded.

"I am wrapping you in light. I am holding you here in safety, healing, and heat. You are going to hum. Can you hum for me?"

William hummed, weak and unsteady.

Autumn hummed along with him, varying her pitch, still looking into his eyes. "Follow me," she said.

Gradually, William found a pitch that harmonized with Autumn's. She nodded encouragement, and he continued as she kept humming, kept her eyes with his, and drew her hands down to his hurt arm.

Autumn heard the doctor come through the door. She raised her hand, emphatically motioning for him to stop, then quickly put that hand back on William's arm and continued her work. She ran her fingers gently over the lump in his forearm. She put extremely light pressure on his wrist with one hand while she felt the lump in his arm respond with the other. She did similar tests around his elbow with movements so subtle and quick that Doctor Dash could not see them.

William was humming steadily, his thoughts occupied with Autumn's eyes and the sound of his voice harmonizing with hers. His brain was soaked with morphine sulfate. When William stopped humming to breathe, Autumn breathed. When he started humming again, she followed along.

With no warning, Autumn held the elbow of William's broken arm firmly against the bench with one hand. With her other hand, she pulled the wrist of that arm away from the pinned elbow nearly an inch and a half, separating the bone at the break. Then, she turned his wrist slightly clockwise while holding his elbow still. When she felt the bone stop moving, she eased his wrist back down so that the muscles and ligaments of his arm could contract to their natural lengths, settling back into position.

William was still humming.

By the time William's mother arrived, Autumn was wrapping his arm in a splint.

CHAPTER 14

Latin and Danny walked into the wood lot as Tom and Mark finished unloading and stacking the cartload of split wood.

A scowling old man limped up to Latin and stood in his way. He breathed with forced huffs that shook the wispy, pale-blond hair on the edges of his round face. The top of his head was bald. "Latin?" he demanded.

Mark stepped in, saying, "Yes, Paul, this is Latin. Latin, this is Paul, the clerk of the Wood Gild."

Latin extended his hand to shake Paul's and said, "Pleased to meet you, Paul. I'm Latin Tillich."

Paul made no motion, so Latin withdrew his hand meekly.

"I know your type," Paul said. "You think you know better than everyone else."

"I don't," Latin said plainly.

"You think you're some kind of expert, some kind of woodsman, huh?"

"I don't know about that. I've split some wood. I've spent a lot of time in the woods. I hope there's some way I can be helpful."

"The boys tell me you can split a cartload of wood in fifteen minutes. Is that right?"

Latin said, "I don't know how much wood a cartload is, exactly. I've always carried my own split wood in a wheelbarrow or by hand, but I guess fifteen minutes is about right, depending on the type of wood, of course, and the weather."

Paul got angrier. He said, "Don't get smart with me, boy. Since you're not a Quaker, you probably don't know about the honesty testimony."

"That's so," Latin admitted. "I don't know as much about those things as I would like. I hope to learn."

"It means if you say you can do something, you better be able to deliver on what you say. It's a matter of honor."

Latin nodded. "I don't know what to say. I can split firewood. That's not an uncommon skill to have. I have it. I'm not..."

Paul cut him off by saying sharply, "So you wouldn't mind if I have one of my teams bring in a solid disk tomorrow morning? You say you can split a solid disk without wedges, and I'd like you to come show me that you're honest, that you can do what you say."

Latin hesitated, then said, "That would be fine, sure. Certainly. I'll do my best. Can I ask, though, if there are any other tools around? Maybe something with more of an edge on it, or something lighter? Are there any sharpening files, stones, or other mauls I could take a look at and maybe work on a bit before I use them?"

Paul's head flushed crimson with rage. "You don't think we know what we're doing around here, I suppose? You must think you've landed in some backward, no-good..."

Latin interrupted by holding out his hands, palms down, saying, "I'm sorry, I'm sorry...I meant no insult. I thought that if you wanted to see what I could do, I could do much more with a sharper maul. In fact, I've made my own splitting maul design back home. It was quite popular and in considerable demand."

"Oh, was it? I see. We don't even know the right tools to use for the job. Well then, it sounds like you must want to try out for one of the Wood Gild apprenticeships?"

Latin withdrew, saying, "I don't know. That seems sudden. This is only my first day. I thought I might look around a bit at the other Gilds and try to get a feel for things before I started to..."

"Nonsense! You know so much...I am giving you a gift. A dozen young men in town have asked for a chance to apprentice with us. If you're as good as you're making yourself out to be, then you should have a chance to prove yourself."

"I'm not making myself out to be anything except..."

"No, no. I heard you. Changing your story now won't help your cause. You might learn to think before you speak, young man."

"Fine, agreed. What do I have to do to try out for an apprenticeship? How does that work?"

"It's simple. I pick one of the current apprentices to compete against you in a Gild challenge. The Wood Gild Apprentice test, by tradition, is to drop, limb, saw, split, and stack a thirty-foot poplar trunk. We'll find a pair of trees about the same size. You get one, and the other apprentice will get one, side by side. You both get a saw, an axe, a cant hook, a splitting maul, and three wedges. Your split firewood must be eighteen inches long, with no piece weighing more than twenty pounds, and it must be stacked six feet high. First man finished with his tree wins. If you win, you get the apprenticeship and the other apprentice is out of the Gild. If you lose, you can't challenge again for three months and you have to do whatever work the Wood Gild gives you for three weeks."

Latin shrugged and said, "Okay, when?"

Latin's flip acceptance infuriated Paul far more than anything else Latin had said before. "Tomorrow morning, right after breakfast, and I'm choosing Mark as your apprentice to challenge."

Latin recoiled, "Not Mark, he's hurt. That wouldn't be fair. No, not Mark."

Paul shook with fury, "Fair? You don't seem to understand the way things work around here, do you boy? Clerks run the Gilds. This is my Gild. You got here yesterday, and you're telling me how things should be done? We have a word for that..."

Latin interrupted Paul to apologize, saying, "Look, I don't want any trouble. I'm not trying to tell anyone anything...I want to chop wood. I want to help."

Paul spoke through gritted teeth, "You show up tomorrow morning and we'll see..."

"Latin, Latin! Thank goodness I found you. We've been looking every-where." Cousin David interrupted, running into the wood lot out of breath.

"Cousin David, what? Is something wrong?" Latin asked, backing away from Paul.

David said, "You should probably come with me. Autumn's in a bit of...well, you should probably come with me."

"Is she hurt?"

"No, not hurt, I'll explain on the way. Excuse us, Paul."

Paul said, "Latin, if you don't show up tomorrow morning, I'll make it known that you're a big talker. You won't be welcomed in the Wood Gild, and probably no other Gild will have you either. Understood?"

Latin said, "Paul, I'm sorry you feel that way. I intend to be here in the morning, and I'll do my best to be helpful. That's about all I can say right now. I'm sorry, I need to go."

As they walked briskly toward Arden House, David said, "I'm sorry about all of this. I should have warned you about Paul. Not everyone here is understanding and helpful like Arthur, right? What did you do to upset him?"

"Honestly, I have no idea. I'll think about it later."

"You've got to take that challenge tomorrow morning. I'm telling you, if you don't, nobody will ever trust you around here. If you take it and lose, it's no big deal; it's only a few weeks of lousy work. Everybody knows what Paul is like to deal with, so nobody's going to think less of you because he got cross."

"Thank you, but I'm more worried about Autumn than myself right now. She's got herself into trouble as well?"

"I don't know. I was told to find you and get you to Arden House. I heard a rumor that there was an accident and Autumn and Doctor Dash disagreed on what should be done."

"Oh dear," Latin said, shaking his head with worry.

CHAPTER 15

"There she is," David said, showing Latin through the door into the infirmary.

Autumn had nearly finished splinting William's arm with wide swaths of heavy fabric. Cousin Susan was standing near, holding the little boy's other hand.

Latin approached silently and did not speak.

Autumn turned her head quickly and pointed to the door to let Latin know that they would talk outside.

"What happened?" Latin whispered as Autumn came out of the infirmary a few minutes later and closed the door.

"Broken arm. I feel I may have put us in a spot of trouble."

"That's curious. I seem to have gotten myself into trouble as well. Mine is with the clerk of the Wood Gild. What did you do?"

"Me? I fixed this kid's arm. Their doctor isn't much of a doctor. Susan works as his nurse, and she's very skilled and does quite a bit of good, but, apparently, the doctor just stands around, smokes his pipe and lets nature take its course."

"Is the boy going to be okay?"

"I think so. It's too early to tell. It was a bad break and he was left cold and wet far longer than he should have been, but I believe I've got him going the right direction."

"So what's the trouble?"

"I'm not sure, exactly, except that the doctor didn't seem too happy about me working on the kid. I'm afraid he's worked the town into a bit of a righteous frenzy. I wouldn't be surprised if he's put some religious voodoo in place to hide the fact that he doesn't know what he's doing."

Susan came out of the infirmary and closed the door. "He's asleep and breathing normally. I'll go back in and keep an eye on him, but I wanted to come out to ask if there's anything specific I should look for?"

Autumn patted her on the shoulder. "Thank you. He'll probably get sick when he wakes up. I left a bucket next to the bed. He's more scared than anything, I think. His mother has gone to get him clothes. Poor child was convinced he was going to die."

Susan said, "Well, I couldn't say for sure, but he had every right to be afraid. I've seen kids die here from similar injuries, and sometimes it takes so, so long. It's been horrible. I understand why William was afraid."

"William?" Latin asked.

"Yeah, little William Morrison," Susan said.

Autumn said, "You gave that boy your father's watch?"

"I did. He broke his arm on the way back from leading me to the Wood Gild crew?"

"Yes, rock hopping."

Latin went pale.

Arthur walked briskly around the corner of Arden House and joined Autumn, Latin, and Susan in front of the door of the infirmary. "How is our young patient doing?" Arthur asked.

"I've set the bone and treated his shock and chill. There is a light splint on his arm right now, which will keep the bone in place while the swelling goes down. In a few days, he'll need a cast."

"I'll go keep an eye on him. His mother and I will stay with him to-night and come find you if anything changes?" Susan asked.

Autumn made a prayerful bow toward Susan and said, "That is most helpful, thank you. When he wakes up, he'll need the bucket and his arm will hurt, of course, but the splint will keep things in place. He can move around as best he's able."

Arthur fixed his flustered hair and stroked his chin for a few moments, thinking, then said, "Good. Thank you. That's splendid news about William. Excellent." Then Arthur sank back into thought, staring into the ground. Quietly, he muttered, "I must say, I didn't expect the two of you to cause this much trouble so quickly."

"I'm afraid I also got into a bit of a disagreement with Paul in the Wood Gild."

"Yes, I heard. That is of lesser concern, so long as you attend the challenge in the morning."

"I intend to."

"No, Autumn is the one who's gotten into a bind, although… I have some ideas on how we may proceed. Autumn, I think it would be best if you stayed out of view here in the infirmary until after dinner."

Autumn nodded that she would.

"Send Susan over to the Gild Hall to get you some dinner, but you stay here in the infirmary and tend to young William until I come to get you later. Latin, you should probably steer clear of Paul if possible. Eat as good a dinner as you can and get a good nights sleep and rest up for tomorrow. I'm going to see if I can manage a difficult conversation with our good doctor."

CHAPTER 16

Cousin David took pity on Latin and bumped his way toward him at the end of the dinner line. "Latin, care to join us for dinner?"

"Sure, yes."

"We'll be upstairs. We'll save you a seat."

Latin nodded.

Latin found Cousin David and sat in the empty seat he offered.

"Latin, these are all the guys from the Craft Gild: Jim, John, James, and Harold. Don't expect you'll remember all the names."

Latin shook hands all around. A short, curvy girl with enormous green eyes wedged herself between Latin and David. "Could I join you? Is there room?"

Jim, John, James, and Harold shifted down both sides of the table with an urgency that took Latin by surprise. After three seconds of clamorous adjusting, they had squeezed together enough to create a space that would have been ample for a family of four. John, next to Cousin David, reached back to brush a speck of dirt from the bench with a welcoming flourish. "Sit here, Belle," he said.

"Introduce me!" Belle urged, jabbing an elbow hard into David's ribs.

"Ow! Latin, this is Belle, she's…um…I don't know, Belle, what are you doing these days?"

Belle rolled her eyes and held her hand out to shake hands with Latin. "I have been helping the Garden Gild and, you know, around. I'm pleased to meet you Latin."

Shaking her hand, Latin said, "Pleased to meet you as well."

Belle sat directly in front of Latin, then everyone else adjusted back into the extra open space.

James asked, "So…Latin, David tells me you made friends with Paul today?"

"That guy is impossible. I honestly don't know what happened."

Cousin David said, "Don't worry about it. Everybody knows he's difficult, and this apprentice test he's set up for you tomorrow morning is his way of making sure you know he's the boss in the wood lot."

Belle leaned in with a smile and said, "I know you're going to win and make gimpy old Paul look like a fool."

"Thank you, but I don't want to make anyone look like a fool. I only want to help out and chop some firewood. I don't know how it came to be such a big deal."

"You shave?" Belle asked, reaching across the table, touching Latin's jaw.

Latin fought the impulse to flinch. He stayed still and let her keep her hand on his face as long as she wanted. She left it to linger there a little longer than anyone at the table was comfortable with. They squirmed.

"I do shave," Latin said, finally.

Latin and Belle stared at each other calmly long enough to force Cousin David to speak just to break the silence. "Belle, you leave Latin alone," he said, "He's only been here one day, and he's already gotten into six month's worth of trouble. Let him be."

Belle looked away, pretending to look for empty seats at other tables.

"So, you all heard there's a Called Meeting tonight?" James asked.

"No!" Belle gasped. "We're still having the dance, right?"

James shrugged and said, "I guess. Brock is going to make an announcement."

"Oh, we better have the dance," Belle said with a suggestive wink.

"What's the Called Meeting for?" Cousin David asked.

James said, "I heard it was about Autumn."

Everyone at the table looked to Latin. "What's a Called Meeting? It sounds bad."

David said, "Yes, it's usually not good. They're for a specific purpose, usually to deal with a crisis."

Latin nodded. "The dance? Would that be here in the Gild Hall?"

Belle said, "Oh yes! We move all the tables and benches out of the way, our little band plays, and we have popcorn and mead."

"Honey beer?" Latin asked.

David shrugged and said, "Yeah, well, not really. It was honey beer, but we ran out months ago, and they've been adding water to it to stretch it. It's pretty much only water now, but, if you use your imagination, it can be okay."

Latin nodded and said, "I expect I'll go to the Called Meeting, though, if it's to do with Autumn."

Cousin David said, "Of course."

Belle rolled her eyes and got up to leave.

Before she had taken a full step away from the table, Arthur took her seat on the bench across from Latin and said, "Evening, fellas."

Everyone at table said, "Evening, Arthur."

Arthur motioned for Latin to lean in toward him.

Latin leaned in, but not enough.

Arthur got up and walked around the table, covered his mouth against Latin's ear and whispered. "Go to the dance or go home and sleep. Do not go to the Called Meeting. It's going to be okay, I promise. Autumn will be fine. Can you do that for me?"

Latin nodded, "Of course. Okay."

Arthur nodded in understanding and said, "Good. I must go. There's much to be done."

"Good Evening! Good Evening! Good Evening!" Brock yelled from the stage. The conversations in the Gild Hall gradually died away. Brock announced that the Called Meeting and the Dance would both start after dinner. The Dance would be in the Gild Hall, and the Called Meeting in Arden House.

As the Craft Gild table moved to break up after announcements, a bright young man with glasses approached Latin and said, "Friend Latin, it's a pleasure to meet you. My name is Joe Clark. I work in the Trade Gild, mostly. This is my sister, Annette."

"Hello, Joe, pleased to meet you. Annette, we met earlier, right? At lunch?"

"We did yes, briefly."

Latin looked around at all of the tables and benches being moved. He said, "Thank you for welcoming me. So much is happening. Is this normal?"

Annette said, "Yes, it takes about twenty minutes to put everything away, hang the drapes, light the big candle lanterns, and set the tables and chairs for the dance. The music makes a big difference, too, as well as the fire in the fireplace."

"The fire makes a huge difference," Joe said.

"Why don't they light it for dinner?" Latin asked.

"Not enough wood, and everyone being in the same room naturally heats it up," Joe said.

Latin asked, "Will you two be going to the dance or the Called Meeting?"

Annette said, "Called Meeting. This is important business, I believe. I'm eager to hear the facts. I fear that some Friends have already drawn conclusions without the benefit of knowing what took place. Of course, you'll be going to the Called Meeting?"

Latin shook his head.

"No? But Autumn…"

"I know, and it's important, for certain, but Autumn is perfectly capable of handling herself, whatever happens. I know she'll be fine."

Annette raised an eyebrow in shock. "I'm sure," she said. "Not that you would be there to intervene, but to hear her side…"

Joe stopped her, saying "Annette, easy now. Let our new Friends find their way."

Joe smiled at Latin and said, "I suspect there are forces at work here that are not ours to understand."

Latin nodded and said, "As always."

Annette's face lightened. "Right, well…yes. You wouldn't want to miss your first Arden House Dance. They really can be quite fun."

Joe wandered off and left Latin alone with Annette.

After an awkward pause, Latin said, "Yours is such important work, teaching children. It means so much to them, I'm sure, but it takes a lot of patience. Do you enjoy it? You like that kind of work?"

"I do. I love it. I've wanted to be a teacher in the Arden School since, well, forever. It's always what I wanted to be."

"You like to teach?"

"I like to learn. I love to learn, and that's really all it is, learning and showing them that they can learn. I get to watch them struggle with difficult things and succeed. It's amazing to be a part of that," Annette said, smiling and blushing.

Suddenly, Belle spun out of the flow of people moving tables and benches and stopped herself directly between Latin and Annette.

"Hey! I saw him first," Belle teased, interrupting.

"What?" Annette fumed.

"Joking, joking. Come on, lighten up. Relax a little. Get your nose out of a book for a minute and learn to have fun," Belle said, grabbing Latin's hand.

"Oh, hi, Belle," Annette said with a forced smile.

"Don't you love the way his face is clean and smooth?" Belle said, fawning.

"I do, and do you know why I like a man with a smooth face?"

"For kissing, like a regular girl would?"

"No, because it's evidence of capability. It proves that he knows how to properly sharpen and maintain a razor-sharp edge on a piece of metal. That's attractive. It means he's attentive to details and that he learns. I like that. That attracts me. It makes me think he's the kind of man I'd like to spend more time with."

Belle shot back, "Well, whatever. All that's probably true. Who knows? I know I'd like to kiss that smooth face properly, is all."

Annette blushed.

Latin also blushed and said, "Yes, okay, well…that's nice. What kind of band do you have? It's been a long time since I've heard music."

Annette said, "Friend Latin, I'm sure Belle will be glad to explain the dance scene to you. It has been a pleasure to see you again. Good luck with your Wood Gild challenge tomorrow, and, if you're ever interested in seeing how the Arden School operates, please feel free to stop by and visit any time. I'll be glad to show you around and introduce you to the children. I imagine you must have some interesting stories to tell."

"I will , Annette. I'm looking forward to it," Latin said, bowing subtly as she left.

Belle took Latin's hand, pulled him slightly toward her, leaned in, and whispered into Latin's ear, "Annette's a nice girl and a good teacher, but I'm more of a traditional, old-fashioned girl. I think it's best when a man is in charge and he tells a girl how things are. That's how I think things should be."

Cousin David stepped in to rescue Latin, saying, "Give him some air, Belle. Leave him alone. You like him. We get it. You've made yourself clear, okay? Good heavens."

Belle looked Latin straight in the eyes and said, "Well, Latin, have I? Have I made myself clear?"

Latin nodded, confused.

"I live across the garden from the Craft Shop," Belle said, lingering a moment longer than necessary, then sauntered away.

"That girl is trouble," Cousin David said.

"You know what?" Latin said, "It's been a long day. There's been so much new, my head is spinning a little. I think turning in early and getting a solid, long night of sleep would do me a world of good. I'd like to be at my best for the Wood Gild challenge tomorrow, and I'm not really familiar with our new place down by the creek."

Cousin David nodded, "I understand. That's an amazing place, by the way. I'm more than a little jealous that you're down there."

"It is a magical little house, isn't it?" Latin said.

"Oh, indeed."

"So, I'm going to go and settle in, unpack, you know. I don't feel up to dancing tonight."

"Sure. Of course. Would you like company?"

"No, no thank you. I'm fine. I'm tired. I'll probably be asleep before the dance even starts."

Cousin David shook Latin's hand. "Sure, you got it. Have a good night and I'll see you at breakfast."

"Thank you."

CHAPTER 17

Together, Autumn and Arthur walked into the Peace Room. The room was dimly lit and packed tightly with unsettled people. The only two empty chairs were together near the fireplace, so Arthur and Autumn sat in them. Without a word from anyone, the room fell silent. Even those standing against the walls were still.

As the minutes passed, the room gradually calmed until finally, Arthur spoke, "I thank you, Friends for taking the time to be here to discuss the events of the day. I would like to begin by inviting Autumn to explain her view so that we might all better understand what's taken place."

After a long pause, Autumn stood and recounted the day's events. She spoke of her visit with the sick alpaca, the specifics of the conversation she had with the Doctor, the run back to the house for her medicine bag, the exact medicines she gave William, why she gave them, what effect they had, how she settled him with her mother's humming method, and how she set the bone.

There were gasps and a few moans at the bone-setting section of the story, but Autumn continued.

She explained the splint and the swelling, and she described how she would make a cast, if gypsum could be found to make plaster, and how she would use starch if no gypsum was available.

When she was finished, she sat, leaning forward, prepared for a rush of attacks, questions, and protests, but there was only silence.

Arthur finally spoke, "Doctor Dash, that was a lot of information. Does Autumn's account of the day fit with your experience?"

After a painfully long pause, the doctor said, "No."

A ripple went through the crowd.

The doctor rose to speak, took his pipe out of his mouth and said, "Autumn isn't being fair to herself when it comes to the matter of relieving his pain, calming him, and warming him. Her work was masterful and completely beyond my understanding. Autumn has a powerful combination of a healing gift and a great deal of precious scientific education that is essential to put a gift like that to work. What she did today saved a life. I'm certain of it. Furthermore, if young William's arm heals the way I expect it will, he will be completely restored to health, as if the bone had never been broken. I hold that any credit for this young man's work from now on will be shared between him and Autumn, due to this young girls work today. She has made a massive contribution to Arden House in her short time here. I will not speak of what is to be done by this Meeting in response to what she's done, but, for myself, I do celebrate it with joy and unquestioning thankfulness."

There was another long silence.

The shaking voice of an old lady rose into the room. She said, "Clerk, I speak to some questions I have, which I know are shared by many Members of this Meeting. I would like to be able to direct my questions directly to this young lady."

"I understand, Friend Sarah. Thank you for giving voice to the questions in a spirit of kindness."

"Young lady, are we to understand that you gave the child an injection of some kind?"

"I did, yes."

"The use of injections of any kind has long been strictly forbidden in Arden House. Did you feel that, because you are not a Member here, you did not need to follow the leadings of the long history of Friends?"

Autumn stood to respond, saying clearly, "I know that I have much to learn from the long history of Friends. I am eager to do so. At the same time, there are some facts, some realities, about science and medicine that I have come to know through experience and my own direct observation, and I know these could be of great value to the Friends of Arden House. I know that injections can be extremely harmful, even deadly, if administered incorrectly. I know that sterilizing all equipment used during the preparation and administration of an injection is of the absolute, utmost importance to guard against any negative effects from contamination or infection."

There was a tremor of unease in the room, but Autumn continued, "Furthermore, I know exactly how to sterilize equipment to prevent infection. I've done the sterilization dozens of times and administered dozens of injections. To be plain, they don't always help, and sometimes they do harm, but we're compelled to act, to try to heal what can be healed, and give comfort when that's all there is to give."

Autumn continued, "It comes down to this…I am new to the testimonies of Quakers, but I'll put this as simply as I can…When someone is hurt or sick, there is risk in acting. There is also risk in not acting. In these cases, a choice without risk is not available to us. If we act, we either help or we learn how not to help next time. If we do nothing, we do not help and we do not learn."

Autumn sat and braced for heated debate, but none came—only silence greeted her.

After a long period of quiet, Arthur said, "I believe I have a clear sense of where this Meeting is going, and I'd like to test that now. Is it the sense of this meeting that Autumn should be Apprenticed to the Doctor and, also, be taken to Lady Ledger with a word of introduction from this Meeting first thing tomorrow morning?"

Autumn looked at Arthur for explanation, but all he did was nod in agreement along with nearly everyone else in the room. Two people in the back of the room shook hands, and then everyone started shaking hands, saying their goodbyes, and leaving. Many Friends shook Autumn's hand with a smile and winked at the doctor before leaving.

"Lady Ledger?" Autumn asked Arthur as they walked out into the cold night.

"All is well. It's late, and you've had a long day. Check on your patient, then sleep. I'll do my best to explain everything at breakfast."

CHAPTER 18

On their way to the Gild Hall for breakfast, Autumn and Latin stopped at the infirmary. There was a note on the workbench from Susan.

"Young William awoke in the middle of the night, feeling much better. He wanted to sleep at his mother's house. He could walk and hold the lantern in his good arm, so I let him go. His color was good, and he and his mother both said, 'Thank Autumn for us,' several dozen times," Autumn read.

Latin smiled. He said, "It must give you an amazing feeling to be able to do that, to be able to help someone like that. You probably saved his life. What does that feel like?"

Autumn shrugged. "I don't know. It doesn't feel like anything. In the moment, when it's happening, I'm too focused on what I am doing to step back and feel much. Now, after it's over, I don't know. It's just…over, like it's not my business anymore. I'm hungry, I need breakfast. Let's eat."

In the quiet Gild Hall, Autumn and Latin sat at a bench with Arthur, Ruth, and Doctor Dash, who had already started eating.

Autumn was excited at the sight of breakfast, "Hey, steak and eggs, this is my kind of breakfast, nice. I guess it's not all thin soup around here after all?"

An uncomfortable look went around the table.

"What?" Autumn asked.

Doctor Dash said, "It's alpaca steak."

Autumn winced. "Oh no. The one from yesterday? The one with the bad tooth?"

Arthur nodded.

Autumn sighed, "Well, that's a shame. I'm truly sorry about that. Wish I could have helped them both."

Doctor Dash said, "I stopped at the infirmary this morning and saw the note that William felt well enough to go home last night. Congratulations, that's exceptional work."

"Thank you, and thanks again for your help. I could not have done that alone. Also, thank you for your help at last night's Meeting. Your words were much appreciated."

"It was nothing. You are the one who should be thanked."

Autumn said. "Okay, so when is someone going to explain to me who Lady Ledger is and where I'm going this morning?"

A rapid series of coy glances circled the table, with Autumn finally looking to Ruth for an answer. Ruth only smiled and said, "It's a clear, pleasant morning for a walk. What about you, Latin? Are you ready for your challenge this morning?"

"I believe so, thank you," Latin said.

"I'm sure you'll do fine," Ruth said with a reassuring pat on Latin's shoulder as she left to carry her dishes down to the kitchen.

When she returned, Ruth said, "Autumn, let's get going. I've got four lunch sacks here. Do you have room in your backpack for these?"

Autumn asked, "Yes, but why four?"

There was no answer forthcoming. Autumn quickly finished her meal and wedged the four lunch bags into her pack, slung it over her shoulder, and hurried to catch up with Ruth. Latin reached out to wish Autumn safe travels, but his hands were too late for her to see.

She was gone and out the door.

Latin tried to smoothly extend the motion of his outstretched hands to pick up Autumn's bowl.

Arthur, his voice full of empathy, said, "Don't worry, Latin. Her mind is on other things today."

Once they'd settled into a steady walking pace on the lane beside the vegetable gardens, Autumn asked again about Lady Ledger.

Finally, Ruth explained, "She was a member of Arden House, long ago, a lifetime ago. I was born at Bellevue House and moved to Arden House with my family when I was young, so Lady and I didn't do many things together, directly. While I did not know her well, I certainly knew of her. She was raised in curious circumstances, I'm told. Nobody will say what happened, exactly. At least they've never told me. She was involved with Arthur for a time, romantically, I believe, but that was long before Arthur and I had noticed each other."

Autumn struggled to picture what Ruth described.

They turned off into the woods and meandered along a narrow path. They walked for most of the morning, at times seeming quite lost, until eventually Ruth said, "Oh, there it is," as they emerged into a clearing with a towering heap of bamboo reeds and dry brush in its center. At the far edge of the clearing, sunk partially into the ground, was a rough mud-brick roof attached to the front of an old barn.

"She lives in there?"

"She did. Let's see."

"Hello! Lady!…Lady Ledger!" Ruth called.

There was no answer.

"How long has it been since anyone has seen her?"

"Seen her?" Ruth asked, walking across the clearing.

A shotgun boomed. Autumn dove to the ground. Ruth crouched down.

"Go away! Get away! Right Away!" came the shouts of a frail voice from deep inside the barn.

"Lady! Lady, it's me, Ruth. Ruth from Arden House! Arthur sent us. Arthur! Arthur sent us with someone to meet you."

There was a long, uncertain pause, then the rasping voice called out, "Don't bring your sickness around here! Get lost! I won't fire another warning shot. Next one is coming chest high."

Autumn stepped in front of Ruth and spoke loudly, "Please? My name is Autumn. I'm not sick. I'd like to talk to you, please? I am not from Arden House. I've only just arrived here. I honestly don't know why these people want me to meet you, but they won't stop telling me I've got to talk to you. Can we please talk for a moment so they'll leave me alone?"

"No! Get lost! Go away!" came softer calls, followed by an extended fit of coughing.

"Can I just come inside long enough to make everyone think we talked? Maybe then they'll let me get back to work at the infirmary."

There were sounds of shuffling and movement from inside. The little voice said, "Anybody who walks through this doorway here, right here, if I don't like the look of them…I'll shoot 'em! I'll shoot 'em dead!" There was another loud fit of coughing.

Ruth whispered to Autumn, "Go! That means she wants you to come in through the porch door."

Autumn shook her head, standing her ground. "What? No. I don't think that's what she meant at all. I think she meant that she would shoot anyone who came through that door. I'm pretty sure that's what she means."

"Yeah, it's fine. Trust me. Go on in," Ruth urged.

Autumn stood firm. "No. No, I'm pretty sure that's not what she meant. If you're so sure, why don't you go through there?"

Ruth said, "Trust me. That's how she is. She's invited you to come through the porch door. That's her way. She wants to talk to you."

Autumn rolled her eyes, sighed, then started forward, humming a lilting tune out loud as she approached the doorway.

"I am here. I am coming in," Autumn announced. "Please, no more shooting, okay?" Autumn passed through a low opening into a porch with hundreds of sealed jars, assorted bricks, piles of sticks and clumps of roots, blown-glass pieces, and various pipes tied in bundles.

Lady said, "Don't touch anything or I'll put a hex on you so strong, you'll grow warts on your face for the rest of your life."

Autumn followed the voice into a little room where she saw a tiny, shriveled old woman sitting sideways in an Adirondack chair. She held a shotgun pointed at the square opening where a window had been, long ago. The room was piled high with boxes full of books. Every box had eight or ten jars on top, many labeled with ink on yellowed paper scraps held on with pieces of grapevine tied in identical square knots.

Autumn was frozen in place, astonished at the overwhelming clutter and disarray. There was no safe place to put her feet. She waved from across the room and said, "Hi. My name is Autumn. In Arden House, they call you Lady, is that what you like to be called?"

"Lady is fine. What do you want? Why are you here? You're not sick. You're not in the motherly way. You didn't come to sell or trade. Why are you bothering me? And tell me the truth, or I'll know and I'll put a hex on you that makes your eyelids fall off."

Autumn smiled.

"Don't smile at me, child. I am an angry old witch. I have powerful magic and I'm about to die, so I don't care about anything, you hear? Don't test me. I'll make your eyeballs dry up and fall right out of your head."

Autumn laughed. Lady moved the shotgun a bit.

"You're not a witch. You're a healer, or you were. It looks as if you may have retired. In any case, you know there are no hexes or curses, except in the minds of people who make up stories to explain what they don't understand; they're only myths and empty secrets to fill the void."

Lady coughed for a while, then asked, "Secrets? What secrets do you know?"

"I expect that you know most of the same secrets I do, and more, although I probably know some that even you don't know."

"I doubt that very much," Lady said.

Autumn shrugged, then said, "Well, maybe not. Not many, maybe a few. We know the same kinds of secrets because we follow the same path. It's plain from these things, the things you have all around you."

"What are you talking about, child? That's nonsense, I know the old secrets, the ones that nobody else knows, and, when I die, they'll all die with me."

"Really? I don't think that's what's going to happen."

"Oh, pretty young one, time comes for us all. I'm quite old. Child, you get on out of here now. You're tiring me out and getting on my last nerve."

Autumn smiled and took a half step back, then said, "Okay, Lady, I'll go. Before I go, however, let me say, first, that I'm not going to get warts from any hex from you because warts are caused by viruses in the skin that are present absolutely everywhere. Furthermore, if I were to get warts, I would know that warts are caused by aerobic viruses, which means they need air. Since they need air, they can be killed by preventing air from getting to them, usually a few days, sometimes a week. That's simple and can be done with any kind of poultice that dries on the outside and stays wet on the inside. I usually use a mustard poultice for warts because mustard grows everywhere, as you know. Also, the mix is easy to make, it has an odor that helps people believe it's medicinal, and mustard plaster is not much good for anything else, which I'm sure you also know."

Lady's mouth fell open. She sat forward in her big chair.

Autumn shifted her weight on her hips. "Want me to go on? This process here, with these six stacked glass cylinders where the bottom three all have cracked sides…I did this exact same thing myself, back home"

Working her way slowly through the clutter, Autumn held her nose over the broken cylinders and sniffed slightly. "Yep, that's the same smell. I was trying to set up a chain distillation process to extract pure alcohol from sour mash using only one fire. I could never get it to work, though. From all the broken glass, I'd say you didn't either."

Lady relaxed, lowered the shotgun to the ground and leaned back, smiling. "Keep talking, child."

"My mother taught me. I've moved into Arden House. They're eager to have someone around who can heal their illnesses, and I'd like to help them. However, I don't have any supplies, and I don't know where any of the herbs grow in this area. It seems like you're retired, and you've got this whole witch persona…I know that can take a lot of work to establish. You like to be left alone and I won't spoil that for you, I promise. I hope there's some way that we can talk, because I'd like to learn from you and I hope that somehow I can be helpful to you."

Lady gave a quick sob of joy, then bit the back of her finger. "Come here, child," she said, opening her arms. Autumn walked gingerly through the piles and kneeled by the chair, holding Lady's ancient, frail shoulders as she wept in joy.

"I thought I was going to die and all of this was going to rot away. You'll use it? I can pass it all on to you?"

"Yes. Oh, yes. Yes," Autumn said, her eyes also damp.

"This is wondrous news. Oh, I'm so thankful! I'll show you the greenhouse. We'll need a map. I can show you where the wild herbs grow, even if I can't get there with you. We'll need paper. You'll have to write these things down. Put on water for tea. I could eat, maybe a little. Did you bring food?"

CHAPTER 19

Latin left breakfast and walked across the lane to the wood lot. Mark, Tom, Danny, and most of the rest of the Wood Gild men were talking in a cluster around the door of the wood shed.

Latin walked up quietly and nodded silent greetings.

A young man who had been sitting on a stool inside the wood shed stood and ducked under the doorframe to avoid knocking it with his forehead. He was a foot taller than everyone else in the Gild, and so much taller than Latin that he had to stoop slightly to shake hands with him.

"I'm Tall Carl," the man said.

"Good heavens," Latin exclaimed.

"Paul picked me to be your opponent for the Challenge."

Latin winced in pain as Tall Carl's grip nearly crushed the bones in Latin's fingers as they shook hands.

"Pleased to meet you," Latin said, forcing a smile.

"Nothing personal, Latin, I'm sure you're a nice guy and all. I hope after this, we can be friends, but there's no way you're going to knock me out of the Gild. I won't have it. I'm the senior apprentice. I'm in line for the next Gild Member position. Good luck, though. I expect I'll beat you by about two hours."

"Oh, okay, well, that's, you know…interesting," Latin said, looking down.

Paul limped out of the back of the woodshed and sat on the stool where Tall Carl had been. He said, "Okay men, here is the plan. The wagons are all hitched up and loaded with gear. We're going to head up to the worksite on the other side of the creek up the hill behind the cotton field. There are two poplars over there that Tall Carl and Latin will use for their test. I'll keep an eye on them while the rest of us will work across the clearing."

"Where are we going to work?" Latin asked.

Paul said, "Behind the cotton field, but you don't need to worry about how to get there; we'll all go together in the wagons."

"I can't…I'm sorry, I can't ride in the wagon, sir."

"What?"

Latin blushed and looked into the faces around him for help.

Mark stepped forward and said, "It's the horses, Paul. Latin can't be around horses."

Paul smiled and pretended that he hadn't heard of Latin's fear. "Is that true?"

Latin nodded that it was.

"You want to join the Wood Gild, but you can't stand to be around horses?"

Latin kicked at the wood chips they were standing on.

"That sounds like quite a handicap."

"If you'll tell me how to get there. I'll walk."

Mark said, "I'll walk with him."

Paul shrugged. "Whatever. Let's go. I'm not going to make Carl wait for you, though."

"Thanks," Latin muttered to Mark as they started walking. "When did Paul decide to test me against Tall Carl? I thought it was going to be you. How's the ankle? Are you sure you can walk with me?"

"No problem. The ankle's fine. In fact, we should probably jog a little if we can. It's about two miles, I guess, and Tall Carl is probably the best we have at straight-out splitting like this. If you give Carl too much of a head start, well, he'll be that much harder to catch."

"Okay, let's go. I'll follow," Latin said, breaking into a trot to keep up with Mark.

Carl's tree was dropping to the ground when Latin and Mark hustled into the clearing. Paul said, "Latin, your axe, saw, maul, and hook are all over there by your tree. You better get to it. Haven't started yet and you're already behind."

Latin squinted up into the canopy and wandered around his tree twice, learning how the branches were set. His arms made soft gestures in the air as he thought of how he might safely fell the tree so it was easy to work once it was down. As Latin thought and planned, Carl was madly cutting limbs from his tree and throwing them in a pile at a vicious pace.

Latin eventually decided how he wanted the tree to fall and started his first light, tentative cuts into the trunk with the saw. After scratching the bark, he stepped back and looked at the lines, the canopy, and the ground where he intended the tree to land. He approached the tree again and started his first felling cuts. He stopped after thirty seconds and frowned curiously at the saw blade, which was badly rusted and completely dull. Latin stopped and looked around the forest. The morning was cool and dry. Latin was sweaty and tired from the run, so he wanted to settle into a comfortable pace for a while as he worked on his felling cuts with the dull saw, but the blade was in such poor condition that Latin could make no progress at all without forcing the blade into the tree with all his strength on every cut. He was quickly out of breath.

Latin walked over to watch Tall Carl slashing branches from his tree, punching at them with the saw. "Is your saw sharp?" Latin asked.

"I guess, sharp enough," Carl said with a shrug.

Latin walked over to Paul and asked, "Is there a saw file in the wagon?"

"A saw file? I don't think so. Go look if you want. Can't you cut with yours the way it is? Carl is doing fine. I think they're about the same."

Latin looked quickly in the back of the wagon. There was no file.

"Paul?"

"What?"

"I am going to run back to the wood lot and get a file to sharpen my saw. That doesn't break the rules or anything, does it?"

"You're going to do what?"

"My saw is dull. It won't cut. I am going to run back, get a file, and sharpen my saw. I'm asking if that breaks the rules of the challenge, or if that's allowed."

"It's allowed, sure, but…"

Latin nodded and started jogging back to town.

"Where are you going?" Mark shouted across the clearing where the rest of the Gild was working.

Latin waved, but did not answer.

The path back was easy, downhill running. Latin slowed some to catch his breath as he approached the wood lot, then walked as he went into the barn to the dusty room that held their tools. He picked a saw file out of a bucket and a flat sharpening stone from the workbench, then started jogging back toward the work site.

As soon as he left the wood lot, he saw Belle.

"I'm surprised to see you here, Latin. I thought you were challenging for the Wood Gild apprenticeship this morning."

"Oh, hey Belle. Yes, I am. It's actually happening right now. I got a dull saw and came back for a file. I've got to run, though, Tall Carl is already way ahead of me."

"Tall Carl? Okay, good luck. Do you have lunch packed?"

Latin had started running, but stopped. "No. No, I should have, but I guess I forgot."

Belle interrupted, saying, "Don't worry about it. Go. Go chop. I'll bring lunch to you."

"Really? You'd do that?"

"Of course. I'd be glad to. Sure. You go, run. I'll be over there later."

"We're working behind the cotton field."

"I know where you are. Go."

Back at the worksite, Paul rolled his eyes as Latin stopped to catch his breath. Finally, Latin knelt and tucked the saw, blade-up, between his knees.

As Paul mumbled loudly about wasted time and pointlessness, Latin focused. He drew the file across the cutting edge of each tooth with light pressure and a steady angle. He worked each tooth until it hissed against the file. Latin skipped a few teeth near the handle to save time. During his run and sharpening, Tall Carl had removed all of the limbs from his tree and cut six disks from the trunk. He was well into cutting his seventh when

Latin continued the cuts that would drop his tree.

The sharpened saw was easy to pull through the soft wood and threw generous handfuls of sawdust in thick plumes on every stroke. Wood dust flew. Latin moved quickly and carefully. The angled cuts in the tree trunk converged quickly. Latin knocked the loose wedge of wood out onto the ground with a tap from the handle of the saw, then he moved around to the back of the tree and started a straight cut toward the missing wedge on the other side.

After a few minutes, there was a deep, wet pop from the core of the tree. It started to move. The trunk lurched over the missing wedge and fell simply and quickly, landing with a gentle thud. Latin set to work removing the limbs with rhythmic bursts from the saw. As he worked, Latin scanned the trunk for knots, scars, and disturbances in the grain that would make sawing and splitting difficult.

Once all of the limbs were off, Latin started slicing the trunk into eighteen-inch-thick disks. Even with a sharpened saw, a disk took a long time and energy to cut. Latin would count to twenty sawing with one hand, then switch to the other hand for a count of twenty. Soon after Latin's first disk fell to the ground with a thud, Tall Carl dropped his tenth and stopped for a break. Latin kept sawing.

"Hey Latin?" Tall Carl called out.

"Yeah?" Latin answered without stopping.

"You went back for a saw file?"

"I did, yes."

"It looks like that saw is cutting much better now. You're making good progress. I think you're catching up."

"Slightly, maybe, well…that's the plan, anyway."

"Can I borrow the file to sharpen my saw?"

Latin stopped sawing and turned to look at Carl. "Really?" Latin asked.

"Please?"

"I guess, sure. Go ahead," Latin said with a nod to the file sitting on his backpack.

"Thank you," Carl said, picking up the file and looking at it curiously.

Latin went back to sawing and continued until he had finished his second disk, then looked around, realizing that Carl had not yet started sawing again after his break.

Carl was holding his saw flat against the stump of his tree, raking the file back and forth across the blade tips, quickly ruining his saw. Paul had gone across the clearing to check on the others.

Latin considered stopping Tall Carl and explaining how to sharpen a saw, but decided against it.

When Paul realized that Latin and Carl had both stopped sawing, he limped back across to have check on them.

When he saw what Carl was doing, he shouted out, "Carl? Stop! What in the world are you doing?"

Carl stopped and looked up at Paul approaching. He said, "What? I'm trying to sharpen this saw. Am I doing it wrong?"

"Doing it wrong? You're ruining it, not sharpening it. Here, let me show you. How have you worked in the Wood Gild this long without anyone ever showing you how to sharpen a saw?"

Latin cleared his throat loudly as Paul was taking Tall Carl's saw.

Paul stared over at Latin. Latin did not look away. He stared back.

Paul pursed his lips. With a disgusted sneer, he handed the saw back.

Tall Carl said, "I guess it would be a bit unfair for you to help me out like this during a Gild challenge."

"I suppose," Paul spat.

"Could you talk me through it if I did the sharpening myself?" Carl asked.

Paul nodded yes, handed the saw back to Carl and explained the sharpening process with a great deal of pointing and correction.

Latin cut disks three, four, five, and six while Paul and Tall Carl struggled with the ruined saw.

Over the course of the morning, Latin got closer and closer to Carl.

When Carl finished cutting his twentieth and final disk, he stopped for lunch.

A few minutes later, as Latin was in the middle of sawing his final disk,

Belle sauntered across the clearing and started setting out a picnic blanket next to Latin's backpack.

"How's it going?" she asked, handing Latin a large Mason jar full of water. She gave a slight nod to Tall Carl resting on his side of the worksite.

Latin sat, winced while stretching his back and said, "Well, I haven't injured myself. That's good. I'm catching up, but still behind him by a few minutes, maybe twenty."

"I brought you a little something to eat."

"That's so kind of you. I sure could use it. What did you bring?"

"I thought you would be hungry, so I brought extra, and a little something special. Here you go; I hope you like it."

Belle pulled Latin's backpack around so that it blocked Carl from seeing, then reached into her cloth bag and set out a large sack of the regular mix with a colorful blend of dried fruit added in, as well as three big pieces of corn bread, a wedge of cheese, and a handful of peanuts.

Latin laughed. "Wherever did you get all of this?"

"Keep this to yourself. I'm not supposed to have these things. Maybe if you eat some, get your energy up, and take a little break, maybe you can catch him this afternoon?"

"Sure, thank you. Energy has to come from somewhere." Latin sat down and started eating, chewing carefully, savoring the unusual tastes.

Belle got up and knelt behind Latin, rubbing his shoulders. Latin looked around to see if anyone was watching, but then relaxed, letting Belle work his tired muscles.

"It feels like your right side is doing all the work."

"I don't saw as well with my left. I try to count to keep the work even, but my right side is stronger. My only hope is to catch up on the chopping, and I can do that pretty well left-handed, so…yeah, I don't know, I can't saw as well left-handed, I guess."

Belle went to work digging into Latin's muscles with her thumbs and strong, open palms.

"Ow!"

"Is that too much?"

"I don't know."

"Does it hurt?"

"I can't tell."

"You said 'Ow.'"

"That probably wasn't the right thing to say; please keep going. I think you're helping, thank you."

Belle kept working his shoulders while Latin ate.

Tall Carl started using his long cant hook to twist his disks around, then shoved one up on top of another and rocked it back and forth to get it level and solid for splitting. After winding up his great long arms and legs into wild, violent spasms, he mashed the maul into the top disk, sending wood chips flying off in all directions. Latin chuckled.

"What are you laughing at?" Belle asked.

"He chops like an animal. This is going to be fun."

"There's more than one way to chop wood?"

"Sure. Look at him. Look at all that wasted effort. Everything he did with the cant hook was wasted energy. Coming to a complete stop between each movement? That's the worst technique I've ever seen. He could split wood three times as fast as he does, using half the energy."

"Really?"

"Sure. I'll finish sawing off my last disk in a few minutes, then I'll catch him in no time at all. Thank you for everything. That lunch and massage were both big helps," Latin said, standing stiffly.

"You're welcome. I hope it does help. Go get him. I'll check in on you later."

As soon as his last disk cracked and fell, Latin picked up his maul and sharpened it lazily for several minutes.

Without moving a single disk, Latin climbed to the top of one that had fallen sideways across another. He swung the maul around his head a few times to loosen up and get the feel of things, then he leaped down onto a disk that was leaning against two others. His feet caught the edge of it and his first hit split the disk cleanly in half with one exploding crack.

Carl stopped and looked up.

Paul stood up and leaned on his cane to get a closer view.

Latin spun, leaping and landing in looping circles, slinging his maul up and down in long, graceful arcs with smooth and even speed. His feet danced quickly, shifting his weight in seamless transitions between strokes, letting the momentum of the spinning maul carry him from one disk to another, catching his toes on the edges of the disks. He did not stop moving until six of his disks were split in half.

"What in the hell is that?!" Carl asked when Latin stopped.

"What? Splitting wood. That's not how you guys split wood?" Latin said with a grin.

Latin stretched, shrugged his shoulders and went to work. He settled into a groove, crushing every single hit, cracking the pieces along the grain, and flicking the split pieces out of his way with his feet between planting them for splitting strikes.

In minutes, Latin had passed Carl and was leaving him comfortably behind.

Much later, when he stopped to catch his breath and get a drink of water, Latin was surprised to find that a curious audience had gathered at the edge of clearing, watching him. Seeing his surprise, they started scattered clapping and whistling, including Belle who was standing with little William, his arm in a sling and his prized watch displayed proudly on his good arm.

William waved. Latin decided to take a break and nodded for Belle and William to come over to his backpack.

"Did you bring any more food? Can you rub my shoulders again?" Latin asked.

Belle slipped a bag of mix with dried fruit and nuts into Latin's hand and started rubbing his shoulders. Using William as a shield to keep everyone from seeing what he was eating, Latin snuck several fistfuls of mix into his mouth and washed them down with water from the Mason jar.

William said, "Can you teach me to split like that, when my arm is better?"

"Absolutely. You'll be great at it," Latin said with a confident nod.

Later in the afternoon, when Latin split his last piece of firewood, he did not stop, but walked directly to the far end of Tall Carl's disks and started working on splitting them.

Paul looked away.

After Latin had finished three of Tall Carl's disks, they started to get too close to each other to swing safely.

Latin stopped chopping and walked over, extending his hand to Tall Carl.

"It's all got to be stacked," Tall Carl said.

"I know," Latin said, out of breath. "Let's stack it together."

They shook hands.

Latin handed a water bottle up to Tall Carl.

"Welcome to the Wood Gild," Tall Carl said.

"Thank you, but I don't want to take anyone's spot. I've only been here two days. It wouldn't be right."

"Are you kidding? You've got amazing skills. Wasn't even close."

"I suppose, but…"

"Honestly, Latin, I don't mind. You beat me by a mile, fair and square. Seriously, you belong here. I hope you can teach me how to split like that."

"Well, yeah, okay, thank you. I appreciate it. I'll do my best. You'll pick it up in no time. With those great long arms of yours, you're a natural."

"Where did you learn to do that?" Carl asked.

"My Grandfather," Latin said. "First, you've got to give yourself more time to get the maul head up to speed. If you start here, you have, what, three feet? Start down here. Start each stroke with the weight hanging down, relaxed, in front of you. Draw it back and up behind you, like this…"

CHAPTER 20

Autumn walked across the clearing toward Ruth. She said, "I understand now. Thank you for bringing me to her."

"What happened?"

"That's difficult to explain. Lady and I have many things to discuss. I trust you to understand."

"I expect so. She'll come back to Arden House with us?"

"What do you mean?"

"She's agreed to come with us?"

"Oh no, I'm staying. I'll be staying here for a while."

"You? Here?"

"Lady has things to teach me. Things I can't really explain right now. Could you please have someone bring us a few things?"

"I suppose, but…"

"We'll need clothes for Lady."

"What? Are you sure?"

"Yes, and food."

In Lady's barn, Autumn lit the rusty woodstove, stoked it for several minutes and put the cast iron kettle on for tea.

"When I die, I want you to take me out to the pyre there," Lady said, pointing out to the tower of brush held together with bamboo poles in the clearing. "Put me in the center of that and light me up. Wait for night, but nobody else, okay? Just you."

"I will."

"I don't have long, Autumn. I can feel it. It's close. I know; I've seen enough things die."

"It's okay, I'll be here," Autumn said, continuing to make tea.

"You aren't scared to be around dying?"

"I guess not. I've seen enough things die."

"There is so much to tell. I don't know where to start."

"Tea. Let's start with some tea," Autumn said, pouring boiling water into the empty teapot and fumbling in her backpack for her pouch of tea leaves.

Lady chuckled, "Oh, you do know what you're doing."

"Well, I know how to make tea."

"That's a good sign, but do you know why it's done that way?"

"Heating the pot?" Autumn asked, emptying the teapot into a bucket by the stove.

"Tell me."

"You get the teapot as hot as possible before putting the tea in so that when you pour the boiling water on the tea leaves, all of the heat in the water is used to draw the tannins out of the leaves and none of it is wasted on warming up the ceramic of the teapot, which otherwise would be room temperature."

"This is going to be fun," Lady said with a grin. "It's been so long since I could speak plainly with anyone."

"There's not much firewood here. Is there somewhere I can fetch more?"

"Back in the woods behind the barn. Go through there and out the back. There's a path back to the other clearing where the greenhouse is, and, along the way, on the right side, there's a little stack of wood under a canvas tarp—but it's quite old."

"I'll see what I can find. You don't keep the fire going, usually?"

"No, I bundle up nights. I can't get around so well, especially not carrying anything."

"Okay, well, the tea is steeping. I'll be right back." Autumn took the wood-carrying strap, found the covered pile along the path behind the barn, gathered a load of wood, and was heading back toward the house when she heard a shotgun blast from the barn.

Autumn screamed and ran toward the barn, dropping the firewood behind her. "Lady!" she screamed.

"Don't come any closer! Don't come in the house, or I'll blow you full of holes, you scurvy bastards!" Lady shouted from inside.

Autumn called into the barn, "Whoa, whoa…hold it there. Easy now, Lady, it's me. It's me."

"Who in the hell are you?!"

"I'm Autumn, remember?"

Silence.

"Lady, do you see the steaming teapot on the table beside your chair? I made that. I warmed the pot first because I know about heat transfer and the release of tannic acids."

No response.

"Lady, you're going to teach me about your experiments. You have a greenhouse, some herbs, and things growing. You're going to give me your equipment. We're going to make medicines together."

"We are? I told you all that?" Lady asked.

"Yes, and when you die, I'm going to put you on the pyre out in the yard and cremate you, but for now, I've made tea. I went for firewood, but I dropped it when I heard the shotgun. Can I come in now? The tea is ready."

"I suppose so."

Autumn stuck her head around the corner into the cluttered room, eyes wide. She waved at Lady. "Don't shoot?"

Lady lowered the shotgun. Autumn tiptoed in.

"Here, let me hold that for you," Autumn said, lifting the warm shotgun off the arm of the chair.

"Where are you taking my shotgun?"

"I'm putting it across the room, here."

"But I like having it close."

"I think it's better over here for now."

"Why?"

"Lady, do you know how many times you've shot that thing today?"

"No. More than once?"

"Yes. More than once. It'll be right over here if we need it," Autumn said, leaning the shotgun behind a bookshelf full of chains, ropes, cables, pulleys, and differential gear rigs.

CHAPTER 21

Paul sat on a log and let Latin come to him to shake hands.

"Congratulations," he said.

"Thank you. We'll stack the rest later."

"I suppose."

"Would you prefer that we did it now, before dinner?"

"I don't care."

"Okay, so now that I'm apprenticed to the Wood Gild, I wonder if I could start working on building a forge?"

"For what?"

"To melt down scrap and make new tools like lighter splitting mauls and better axe heads. We could make chain and brackets, hinges, and parts for carts and wheel bearings. We could make nails and all kinds of things; then we wouldn't have to trade for them."

"No."

"No? That's it? Just no?"

"No, we don't need it. We've never had one. We don't need one. You wouldn't know how to build a working forge anyway. It would be a huge waste of time. Time that we don't have to waste."

"Never?"

"Never."

"What if we put up enough wood to get us through next winter? Could we work on it then?"

"Do you have any idea how much wood we burn in a winter?"

"No, I'm asking. If we had that much set aside, could we work on a forge then?"

"Maybe."

"Okay, how much did we burn last winter?"

"One hundred twenty-five cords, but the winters are getting worse and longer, so make it one hundred fifty."

"One hundred fifty cords?"

"Yeah. If you and the boys can fell, split, haul, and stack one hundred fifty cords in the wood lot, you can work on a forge during the day."

"During the day?"

"You can do what you like at night, as long as you're fit to work, rested, and awake during the day."

"I can work on a forge at night?"

"Do what you like. I can't stop you from wasting your time at night, as long as you're ready to chop wood during the day."

Mark, Danny, and Tom walked across town with Latin.

Arthur met them on the path near the Gild Hall and said, "I hear congratulations are in order."

Arthur and Latin shook hands. "Thank you," Latin said.

"Friends, could I talk to Latin for a moment?"

"Sure, we'll save you a seat at dinner?"

"Yes, please. I'll see you there."

"What is it, Arthur? Is everything okay?"

"Everything is fine," Arthur said. "Latin, we need to ask you a favor. I know there's not much light left in the day, but could you go with Constable Pete to take some clothes and things to Autumn?"

CHAPTER 22

"My long-term memory is fine. I remember everything. I know where all the books are…well…most of the books. It's new things; I don't seem to have any way to hold them."

Autumn said, "That's fine. I'll take care of everything. I can write notes for you. I'll take care of it."

Lady coughed for a spell, then said, "I know where some of the books are."

"Don't worry about it."

"I'm going to die, Autumn. I can feel it."

"Right, so, yes. That is a concern."

"Where do we start?"

"I would like to start by making some kind of way that you can remember that you know me and that you trust me. That way we won't have any more close calls with the shotgun."

"How would that work?" Lady wondered, sipping her tea.

"I don't know. Why don't you tell me one special secret, something nobody else would ever know? Then, if you don't remember me, I'll tell you the secret back. Maybe a closely held secret will connect with your long-term memory enough for you to conclude that I must be someone you know and trust. Maybe that will work?"

After thinking for a while, Lady said, "Okay, but what secret?"

"Well, Lady, I don't know. That's kind of the point of a secret."

"Don't get snippy with me, young lady. Just because my memory is going…"

"Okay. You're right. I'm sorry."

After another long spell of deep thought, Lady said, "I could tell you my name, my real name. That would do it for sure, if anything would."

"Nobody knows your real name?"

"Nobody alive."

"Okay, what is it?"

"What is what?"

"What is your real name?"

"I'm not telling you that."

"Lady, we're going to use it as a way to try to remind you that, since I know your secret, you must know me, right?"

"How is my own name going to remind me that…Oh, because if you know my real name, then I must have told you…Oh, that's clever…Did you think of that?"

"No, it was your idea," Autumn said, laughing.

"Was it really?"

"Sure. As far as you know, it was."

Lady looked off into the distance, thinking, then said, "Still, I'm not telling you my real name. Nobody knows my name."

Autumn started clearing space in the room for a second chair. "More tea?" she offered.

Lady asked, "What is your name again?"

"I'm Autumn. What's your name?"

"Nice try, but my memory isn't that bad."

"Just checking."

Autumn said, "Okay, here's an idea. What if you write your real name on a card and give it to me. I will promise not to read it. However, if you forget who I am again, I'll show you the card. You'll see that it's your name. You'll know that you must have given me the card, which might jog your memory, but I still won't know your name."

Lady considered it. "Hmmmm. That's brilliant. How do I know you won't read it?"

"You trust me; that's the whole point. When you see the card, you'll know that you trusted me not to read it. Otherwise, you would have simply told me your name."

Lady nodded in agreement. "Yes…yes, I see," she said, "I've got a whole lifetime's worth of work in this house. I thought it was going to all rot. Now, though, I can pass it all on to you."

"Yes, won't that be fantastic? Please write your name with this pencil on this card."

"My real name?"

"Yes."

"Are you sure about this?"

"I am, and so are you."

"Okay, here," Lady said, writing on the card with a shaky hand. She handed the card to Autumn, who immediately folded it in half and stuck it in her pocket.

"Okay then. Let's get to work. Is there something we should discuss first, or should we pick a box and get started?" Autumn asked.

Lady looked around the room and said, "You should keep the shotgun, too."

"Yes, I'll keep the shotgun over there, out of reach," Autumn confirmed.

"But what if someone comes and wants to take things or cause trouble?"

"Oh, I'll shoot them, for sure," Autumn said confidently.

Lady nodded, "Okay, good. Let's start with the brown notebook over there, under the glass dome."

"This one?"

"No, the thicker one."

"Okay, what's this?"

"These are maps I've made over the years of where all the wild herbs grow in the area."

Autumn and Lady spent the rest of the afternoon looking at maps and discussing all the different herbs that grew wild in the area, what could be done with them, and how. Autumn took meticulous notes in her notebook from home.

When they finished with the maps, Lady said, "Okay, now those black ones down there," pointing to a set of fifteen identical black notebooks in a wooden crate.

"What are those?"

"That's everything having to do with limiting the spread of infectious disease. I've made that a particular area of focus for quite some time."

Autumn nodded and said, "That's exciting, but it's quite cold and will be getting dark before too long…How about if I go get another load of wood? Then I could get us a steady fire going and perhaps make some dinner? I've brought some food."

"Before you go, could I ask a favor?"

"For certain."

"I hate to ask it."

"No, anything, really, please let me know how I can help."

"I've gotten so I can hardly walk. I need help."

"Sure, Lady, I'm glad to help. Anything, you name it."

"I need a bath. I would so adore a hot bath. I know it's a lot to ask. I'll understand if you can't bring yourself…"

"Nonsense! This is my specialty. You rest. I will take care of everything. I understand. I'll get the stove going for water. Would you like some miso soup?"

"You have miso?"

"I do. My mother and I made it ourselves. I carry a little for emergencies."

"Are you an angel?"

"I am not."

Autumn brought in several loads of wood, breaking what she could with her hands and ripping the rest with a dull, rusty saw she found in the back of the barn. She washed out a rusty old cast iron pot, set it on the stove and filled it with water for the bath. She cleaned out the bathtub and drew several buckets of well water. She filled the cistern in the kitchen, checking in with Lady every few minutes to remind her of who she was and what was happening.

While the water was heating up, Autumn wandered through the little side rooms and nooks around the barn. She compiled an inventory of the herbal samples, glassware, scalpels, and other scientific equipment that were stuck among the piles of rags, sawdust, and dead leaves on the floor.

From back in the sitting room, there was a gunshot and Lady's excited shouting. "I hear you in there, you dirty rats, taking my things! Come in here where I can see you and I'll shoot you full of holes."

"Oh, my God! Lady, it's me, it's me, Autumn. Where did you get a pistol? I'm getting your bath ready. Here, don't shoot, look at this card," she said, frantically pulling the folded card out of her pocket.

Agitated, Lady shouted, "Card? Look at what card? I can't read that card! Get out of here! Who in the hell are you?"

"Lady, you know me. I'm Autumn. I'm fixing you a bath. That's why all the water is heating on the woodstove. I brought in all that wood stacked there. You couldn't have done that yourself, right? I'm going to burn you on the pyre when you die. Remember? Put the gun down, please?"

Curious, Lady asked, "What's on the card?"

"Your real name."

"Nonsense."

"It is. You wrote it on here so that I could…wait a minute, where did you get the pistol?"

"I keep it under the cushions. Read me the card."

"No, I'm not supposed…you…oh, forget it. I will read you the card, but can I have the pistol please?"

"Why should I?"

"Because I don't want you to shoot me while I'm fumbling around trying to read your shaky handwriting."

"I'm not handing it over, but I'll put it down," Lady said, resting the pistol on the arm of her chair.

Autumn rolled her eyes and unfolded the card. "Fran? Your real name is Fran?"

"Autumn? You said your name is Autumn?"

"Yes?"

"Hey, that works. My idea about telling you my name…it works precisely the way I imagined it would. When is dinner going to be ready? That miso smells fantastic. I haven't eaten in…I don't…"

"You don't remember the last time you ate?"

"Well, no, but with my memory, that's not saying much."

"It'll take the bath water a while to heat up. Here, try some soup."

Autumn cleared the few remaining sticks and leaves out of the old claw-foot tub and pressed the crumbling cork stopper into the drain to keep the water from running out on to the dirt floor of the barn. She brought the three large buckets of water from the top of the woodstove and dumped them one at a time into the tub.

"Ready to wash up?"

"Yes, although I think I may need some help getting there."

"That's fine. Here, take my arm."

Lady tried to pull herself up on Autumn's arm. "I'm so weak. I'm stuck. I'm sorry, let's forget about the bath."

"Not a chance," Autumn said, gently lifting up from under both of Lady's arms.

It took a few seconds for Autumn to register the unspeakable mess Lady left behind when she stood up.

"I'm so sorry about this," Lady said, sick with embarrassment.

"Think nothing of it. It's easily dealt with. Can you stand?"

"No. I really don't think I can."

"Okay, right. Here, hold on to this," Autumn said, improvising a walker by emptying and stacking three wooden crates. "Can you hold yourself up on this?"

"Yes, yes, that's fine," Lady said, her arms shaking.

"You hold yourself here for one minute. I'm going to get you out of these clothes?"

"Okay, but how are you…"

Without explaining, Autumn drew her pocket knife, flipped it open, and cut off Lady's pants with two quick slices from ankle to hip. Continuing the motion, she cut Lady's shirt off with two long cuts up the sleeves and down the back. Autumn let the whole mess drop into the chair. She pulled a tan wool blanket from the couch and wrapped it around Lady.

"Can you move your feet?"

"Maybe," Lady said, shaking.

"How about if I carry you?"

"Are you sure you can?"

"Let's see," Autumn said, gently leaning Lady back into a cradle she made by locking her hands in front of herself. She picked Lady up in the blanket without straining.

"You okay?"

"I'm fine. Can you really carry me?"

"No problem. You don't weigh much at all. Let's get you washed up."

Lady sat in the warm washtub with a bar of lye soap and a rough cloth. She scrubbed as Autumn drew more water and set it to heat on the wood-stove. As the water was heating, Autumn dragged Lady's chair out into the yard, across the clearing, and tucked it into the tower of dried bamboo stalks and fallen branches of Lady's pyre.

"Autumn, I'm okay. I'm okay, Autumn. Don't mind me, just washing up. I know you're there, Autumn," Lady repeated to herself as Autumn worked.

Autumn replaced Lady's sitting chair with a sturdy Adirondack model she found in the barn. She lined it with spare blankets and padding. Next to the chair, she fashioned a commode from an upside-down crate.

After draining the tub and refilling it three times, Autumn finally said, "Lady, I think you're about done. Do you want to do another tub-full?"

"No, it's been fantastic, thank you. I'm ready now."

Autumn lifted her carefully and dried her as she stood in the tub. "Let's go, sweetheart," Autumn said as she lifted Lady up out of the tub, wrapped her in a quilt, and carried her back into the sitting room.

"My chair?"

"It's been dealt with. We'll make this comfortable for you. It might take some time, but we'll get it right."

It was while she was arranging the pads and quilts in the new chair that Autumn noticed the lumps. They were various sizes and deep under Lady's skin, all over her torso.

"My tumors," Lady said.

"I'm so sorry."

"Oh, don't be. I've had some of them for quite a while. There are more and more all the time. They don't hurt."

"Hmmmm," Autumn pondered. "What's to be done about that?"

"There's nothing to do. They're everywhere. They've had ages to settle in. They have deep roots. There's no stopping them."

"I suppose you're right," Autumn said, wondering.

There was a knock at the door.

"Lady, don't be afraid. I know what this is. I sent for some things from Arden House."

Autumn was surprised and visibly cross to see Latin at the door.

"What are you doing here?" she snapped.

"What do you mean? Ruth said you asked for things. I brought them and came with Constable Pete to see if you're okay and if you need any help."

"I thought they'd send one of the boys."

"Well, I'm sorry, it's me. Why don't you…are you okay?"

"I'm fine. Thank you for the things. I need to get back…"

"Can't we talk for a minute outside? Please? Is that too much to ask?"

"Actually, it would be more of a problem than you expect. It's late and dark, you should head back now."

Latin huffed, "I walked all the way over here, carried all these things miles for you. Can we talk for five minutes to reconnect?"

Autumn rolled her eyes and called back into the house, "I'm going outside to see our visitor off. I won't be long."

"Latin, I understand why you're asking, but I can't explain right now. I have to be here. This is my place right now. This is where I belong."

"You're staying here long-term? You're moving out of Arden House? We promised to take care of the little house in the woods."

"You know what, I can't do this with you now. I can't have this conversation right here. I am staying. You are not. You go back to Arden House, now, please?"

Latin said, "But there's news to do with the Wood Gild."

"What? Make it quick."

Latin recoiled as if smacked. "You know what, never mind. I'll tell you later…maybe," he said as he turned away into the darkness.

CHAPTER 23

Latin arrived back at the Gild Hall too late for dinner. He begged a bowl of thin, lukewarm soup from the cook and sat by himself on a bench down in the basement while the others cleaned up.

Annette took pity on him and sat down to talk.

"Congratulations. You know, some people are born here, live their whole lives here, work hard for years, and never hold Gild positions. You and Autumn have been in town less than three days, and you're both apprentices."

Latin frowned with confusion and fatigue, "Well, yes, thank you. I'm thankful."

Annette nodded, "I heard Autumn's studying with Lady for a while."

"Yes, it seems that's her intention."

"I also heard you had an idea to set up a forge and start trying to craft some new tools, some better splitting mauls for the Wood Gild?"

"Word travels fast around here."

"You have no idea."

"Yes, well, I thought about a forge, but there are complications."

"Paul?"

"Yes. He is one. I can't tell if he's being spiteful or if he really has a point that getting wood split is more urgent."

"I suppose in an important way, it doesn't matter what his motivation is, only what his decision is, since he's the clerk of the Wood Gild."

Latin nodded, "That's a good point, and well said."

"Latin, I think you have a good idea for a forge, and we need more of that kind of thinking around here. I went through the town library and found two books that you might find helpful. One is about the basics of metallurgy. I'm not sure how helpful it will be, but the other has all kinds of diagrams and measurements in it that look like they might be specific to forges—except it's in German."

"Why would the Arden House library have a German book about forge design?"

"I have no idea; I thought it might be helpful."

"It's fascinating. Thank you. I'm eager to see them."

"How about now? I have them at my house. Would you like to come over? We could visit. I'd like to talk, if we could. I have a little tea and a few other little goodies hidden away."

"Oh certainly, wonderful. I'd like that, yes."

Annette stood, beaming.

Latin walked beside Annette on the path across the center of the long, open garden green.

"Where do you live?"

"Right there behind the little theatre. I share the house with a few other girls."

"That's a nice place."

"Not as nice as your stone house in the woods."

"You heard?"

"Of course, there are no secrets here. We're all jealous, but it's good that you're there. I'd like to come visit sometime."

When the girls talking around the woodstove saw Latin come through the door behind Annette, they rose up in a flurry of hair fixing, face clearing, and clothes adjusting that went on awkwardly as Annette introduced them.

"It's a pleasure to meet you all," Latin said, flush with fatigue and embarrassment.

Immediately, Annette said, "We have some books to discuss. We're going to be talking in my room. Is there water for tea?"

One of the girls said, "No, but I'll put some on and bring it in when it's done."

"I'll come out and get it, thank you," Annette said.

CHAPTER 24

Autumn got Lady dressed in Arden House clothes and settled her into the new, clean chair.

"Not bad for a day's work," Lady boasted. "I'm exhausted, but you did everything."

"Would you like more miso? Or some dried oats? We have plenty of dried oats."

"No, dear. I'm fine, but you go ahead. I know you must be hungry after doing so much."

Autumn fixed herself a little dinner and said, "I think from the notebooks and the maps that we went over earlier, I can do a good enough job of finding and using what grows naturally around here. Plus, I'm familiar with some of them from back home. What about the greenhouse? You said you had one? Where is it? What do you have in there that I'm not likely to figure out on my own?"

"I have to tell you something."

"What?"

"When I was a young woman, the first time I came to this house…this is difficult for me to talk about."

"Should it be avoided?"

"You're all business, aren't you? I'm trying to tell you my secrets, and I don't think I've met a girl yet who didn't want to know another's secrets—until now. No, Autumn, it's important that you know this."

Autumn nodded respectfully and stirred her miso.

Lady said, "I had a brother, Henry, who was two years older than me. We lived in the Arden School. Back in those days, most children lived with their parents, but we lived at the school. Mother and Father were not warm and caring people. Henry and I chose to live at the school. Our parents were children during the Reduction. They saw it. They lived through it. All those years later, it wasn't something they ever healed from, if you know what I mean. They had scars. Not on their skin, although they had those scars as well. There were scars inside them, in their hearts, in their souls, you know? So much loss, so much violence, and so much pain."

"I can only imagine what that must have been like for them."

"They did their best for us, but the most they could manage was to be distant. I say that with respect. Everyone wants to be close to their children, but, for them, the damage was toxic and they kept their distance to save us from it. Henry and I knew how it was. We never resented them for it. We both respected what they'd been through and what it had taken out of them. We never felt like it was our fault or that they didn't love us, but they were wounded, crippled souls."

After a long pause, Autumn asked, "Did they ever talk about it? About what happened? I've always wondered what really happened."

"Oh no, never. Well, the truth is…they never stopped talking about it. They never talked about anything else. They could say, 'Please pass the carrots,' in a voice so full of pain and grief and loss that you would know from their voice that they'd seen horrors beyond our worst nightmares. The loss left them hollowed. Their voices echoed from all that vast emptiness left inside them. They were survivors. That's all they ever did, was survive."

"I wonder if it was helpful and healing for them to see you and Henry grow up, living your lives?"

"No. I understand why you'd say so, but I know they didn't see it that way. They were always afraid for us. Afraid something would happen to us like what happened to them, or worse, whatever that could be. When they tried to do anything with us, it hurt them too much. It was as if being with us brought them closer to all that grief, so we kept our distance too, to honor their struggle. The town looked after us. We learned the arts and crafts. We studied the Gilds and practiced the Quaker way. We were Arden children, and I have to say that despite the way our parents suffered, we were quite happy. I have such pleasant memories of that time. Even with the lean times, growing up in Arden seems like such a dream to me now.

And then everything changed."

"What happened?"

Lady thought, staring off through the walls for long minutes, "I can't talk about this directly, except to say that Henry…"

Lady fell into a fit of sobbing, coughing and weeping. Autumn held her and wrapped her in another layer of quilts. It was a long cry, deep and dark. Autumn let it run, then, finally, when Lady was able to speak, she said, "A crazy, foaming-mouthed dog bit Henry, here, on this fleshy bit on the hand." She pointed to the section of her right hand between the thumb and fore finger, "We knew it was serious, and the doctor back then did everything he could. What everyone feared would happen, did. Henry got the sickness. The doctor, my parents, they couldn't be with him, carry him those last steps."

Lady sank back into another spasm of coughing and sobbing. Autumn held her through. Finally, Autumn said, "You don't have to say it. I'm not going to say it either. It doesn't need to be said."

"Okay," Lady whispered.

Autumn said, "And afterward, the people in town didn't understand how you could have?"

"No, it's not that. Most of them understood. A few of them even thanked me and told me that what I'd done was strong and right, but still, it stuck to me. It was like I carried the shame and grief around with me everywhere. No one in town wanted anything to do with me."

"Oh, yes. I've seen that happen."

"It wasn't that I'd done anything wrong, so much as that I was stained by it. I wasn't shunned or driven out or anything, but there was a coldness, you know? A separation where there hadn't been one before. A few times, my people tried to talk to me, but it felt like charity. Like they it took an act of bravery just to talk to me.

"I tried to stay, but after a few months, I could tell it was no good, so I packed up some things and I left. I went to Bellevue House for a while. They were kind and took me in. I might have made a life there, but I met the man who lived in this house, back when it was a house. Everyone called him Doctor Miller. He was a magnificent man. In the beginning, I would visit. He was a man of science, always doing experiments, taking notes, measuring and weighing things, trying to put together different compounds, making medicines, treating the sick. I started helping, then I took on other chores. Eventually, I started sleeping on his porch from time to time instead of walking home.

This place was once a center of activity, if you can believe that. The doctors from all five houses would come talk to Dr. Miller and ask about their toughest cases. Dr. Miller was convinced that he could treat most anything, and he was absolutely obsessed with finding a way to produce penicillin."

Lady coughed for several minutes. Autumn gave her a cup of water to drink.

"Day and night, petri dishes, dozens of rabbits and goats numbered in cages with thermometers, hundreds of tedious measurements, dozens of different bread molds, countless titrations, all different catalysts, herbs and mixing methods.

"Whenever there was a patient that any of the doctors thought would be a good test case for him, they sent a messenger to fetch him, and Doctor Miller would leave at a moments notice, day or night, and go administer his latest compound."

"He sounds like quite a man."

"Oh, and handsome—my goodness, me. He was older, of course, too old for there to ever be anything between us. And he loved medicine so much. Nothing ever came to pass between us, although, I'm not ashamed to say I would not have been sorry if it had."

"Did he ever create a successful antibiotic?"

"Yes. The year before he died, he did. That spring and summer, he had a string of eleven cases that all responded. It was a thrilling time. All eleven patients had blood infections; high fevers and were on death's door. Every one of them broke their fevers in a matter of hours and recovered entirely inside a week. He was sure it wasn't exactly penicillin because the process was different from the one described in the books, but it was something similar, and it worked. It worked on old people, young people, some with a rash, some not. It was magical. I'd never seen the Doctor so happy, so excited."

"What happened?"

"All the medicine that worked came from one batch. Everything he did to try to make the same medicine again always failed. He couldn't figure out why. He followed his notes perfectly. He was a meticulous note taker. He ran the same experiment over and over and over. He quit sleeping, quit eating. In the end, it killed him. Having made it once, but not being able to reproduce it and not know why, it was too much. At least five times, he scrapped everything and started over from scratch, but nothing."

"A working antibiotic would be…it would change everything."

"I know, wouldn't it be grand? We lose so many people to plain sepsis from cuts and scrapes. I mean, even a simple topical antibiotic would save countless lives. I worked on it after Doctor Miller died. I read his notes and went over all his experiments. I didn't understand all of it, but I tried what I could. Eventually I gave up and focused on the herbal compounds I could grow and work with."

"Are all of Doctor Miller's notes still here?"

"Oh, sure, they're all in the wooden crate behind the couch. I pull them out and look at them every once in a while, when I was feeling sad and missing him, or lonely."

"Would you mind if I take them with me, back to Arden House?"

"Oh, Autumn, you have to. Yes. Take them and do what you can. I hope you can get it done. Maybe someday?"

"Maybe, we'll see."

"I know I've let this place run down. I'm sorry about that. I wish it was better shape to hand down to you, but this is how it is. The stomach tumors got big enough I could feel them a year ago, and, since then, I've been hanging on, sure that all of this would die with me. I've done a poor job of keeping records in the greenhouse the last few years as well. I've moved things around; we'll have to go out there tomorrow and see how much I remember, do some proper labeling."

"That sounds perfect. I look forward to it. I know you're tired, but can I ask one more question before we turn in?"

"Okay."

"Why the gun? Why the angry witch act?"

"Oh, that's my own foolishness. People got so they were too much for me to deal with. They'd come and demand creams and salves, and they'd bring their sick children sneezing all over me and their pregnant daughters and chicken pox. They'd say, 'Fix them. Make them better. Cure it.' They never asked about what I needed. They never asked what they could bring, how they could help, or how many hours it took to make their medicines. They would bring ten eggs to pay for something that took me three weeks to cook down from stinking root paste and two years before that to figure out and test. Not that I needed payment, mind you, but it came to be too much, their indifference. So one day I basically quit. I got fed up and started running them all off. Eventually, they stopped coming."

CHAPTER 25

With the door closed tightly and latched with a hook, Annette handed the two books to Latin. She sat at the foot of her bed, leaving the chair for Latin. She lit a lantern and hung it from a long, curved hook on the far wall.

"These look perfect," Latin smiled. "Thank you."

"Of course. Yes. They're for you. Keep them as long as you like."

"I don't know how much help they'll be, though."

"Because of Paul? What's his problem?"

"He says we need to put up firewood, a lot of firewood, before we work on anything 'extra' like a forge."

"You can do it. How much is it?"

"One hundred fifty cords."

"Oh."

"I have some ideas about how the work crews could get more done, but even working perfectly, that's a great deal of wood."

"Would that even fit in the wood lot?"

"Yes, but it wouldn't leave much space."

"It's never been that full before."

"That doesn't surprise me. I think he's making a point."

"Seems like it's really gotten you down."

"Oh, not really, it's not that."

"What's bothering you?"

"Oh, it's Autumn, and I'm so tired, and missing home. It's been long week."

Annette settled in and gave Latin the warmest, most inviting smile he had ever seen. She said, "Go on."

"Oh, Annette, I don't know. Maybe it's just that I need some time to adjust. There has been so much change, so quickly, all at once. I'm waiting for things to calm down for a few days."

"Of course."

"I don't know where I'm going to fit here. I don't know how to get along with this many people. I feel…"

"I imagine you feel like a stranger here."

"Yes, that's it exactly."

"You'll get used to it. You're already highly regarded because of your uncle and your abilities. I bet you'll get comfortable here in a few days and it'll be as if you've lived here your whole life."

"That's a pretty thought."

"I'll do my best to help you along. How about if I get us some tea? We'll break out my hidden stash of molasses cookies and we'll talk about books or whatever else comes to mind?"

Later, Latin was giggling on the floor of Annette's bedroom while she lay on the bed, propped up on an elbow, telling the story of the time her brother set off a keg of fireworks during Meeting. Latin tried to hold back a yawn as he said, "I wish I could have seen the look on Arthur's face."

"Ruth's was better."

There was a long pause. Annette smiled down at Latin, curious of what he would do.

"I'm about to fall asleep," Latin said. "I have my first real day of work tomorrow."

Annette raised her eyebrows with invitation.

Latin stirred to his feet.

"You don't have to go," she said.

Latin froze, then he settled back to the floor. "Oh?"

"No. You don't have to go anywhere. You can sleep right here."

Latin rubbed his eyes and looked around the room. "Oh."

They stared at each other intensely. Annette was nodding her head slowly and slightly.

"Oh my goodness," Latin said, finally standing and looking about for his pack. "I want to stay, but I'm going to go home. I'm not sure why. Okay?"

"Sure, take the lantern, and don't forget the books," Annette said softly.

"Thank you, please don't take it the wrong way, my going, I only…"

"Latin."

"Yeah?"

"It's fine, really. I enjoyed visiting with you. You're welcome back any time. Go rest."

CHAPTER 26

Lady's rusty woodstove clicked while it cooled to a low simmer in the frozen spring dawn. Lady reclined in her chair, eyes closed, breathing deeply with her head wobbling against a pillow wedged beside her head and the side of the chair.

Autumn slept facedown on the moldy couch, wrapped tightly in a cocoon of blankets.

There was a timid knocking at the door.

Lady awoke with a jolt and started screaming, "Aaah! Look out! I'm armed. I have a shotgun! I'm going to shoot the next thing that moves! Get out, get out!"

Autumn fell while trying to stand up. Tangled and wrestling with her blankets, she shouted up from the floor, "Fran! It's me, I'm on the couch, sleeping. It's Autumn. Your name is Fran."

"No, I know that. I know you. I know who I am. I know who you are. There's actually someone here. There's someone knocking on the door. Where is my shotgun? Why did you take my shotgun? Where is the pistol? Where is my chair? Why is all of this happening at once?"

Autumn fought her way out of the blankets and stood. "Why? You're really asking me why I took your shotgun?" Autumn rubbed her eyes and checked the door. There was a cowering little boy in Arden House clothes on the doorstep.

"Come in, please."

The boy stood still, holding a note, shaking it at Autumn. Autumn took it, unfolded it, and read out loud, "Come immediately. Ten-year-old girl fell down brick steps, landed awkwardly. Several obvious broken bones, hit her head, unconscious. Breathing with difficulty. I doubt she has long.

Most urgent."

"I'm sorry, I know it's cold, but could you please wait outside for a moment?" Autumn asked the little boy.

Happy to be able to move away from the house, the boy left without hesitation and stood in the yard.

Autumn closed the door, added fresh logs to the stove, and put water on for tea.

She read the letter again to Lady.

Lady said, "Well, you'd better go. Is there anything you need from Dr. Miller's surgical kit, the big one? It's over there. Take the whole thing if you need it."

Autumn sat down.

"Autumn?" Lady asked.

Autumn didn't answer, but stared at the letter.

"Autumn? You've got to go in a hurry. This is serious. This girl doesn't have much time, from the sound of it. She's probably broken some ribs. There's bleeding and her lungs are filling up. You have to do a cavity puncture to drain it, see if it's bloody or clear."

"I'm not going," Autumn said, checking the kettle.

"What? Not going? You have to go. You must go. You can't choose to help some people and not others. You must go. You know that."

"I must? I honestly don't know what that means. Listen, I'm looking at you, your face, your sunken eyes. I'm not going to nurse you back to health. You know that, right? You're dying. How long do you think you have? It could be today, couldn't it?"

Lady sighed, then said, "Autumn, you can't do anything for me. Nature's going to its course. She'll see me through. I don't mind going this last mile alone."

"Oh, I don't doubt that for a minute. That's not what's keeping me here, not today."

"What then?"

"It's the greenhouse and your plants, the medicines growing there. You and I have to go through there so that you can explain what you have, what it is, what it's for, and how to use it. I have to label those plants."

"Autumn, don't be absurd. This girl is dying. We can label plants any time."

"No."

"No?"

"I have a sense, Lady. Maybe it's a premonition, I don't know. I feel like, if I don't take this chance to be with you right now, I might never get it. I've learned from painful mistakes not to go against these kinds of feelings when I have them.

Lady shook her head. "I don't know. I know what you mean, but with a girl's life at stake, I don't know if I believe it's right to follow feelings like that.

"Believe it or not, I'm writing Dash to let him know he's on his own."

"You're not playing around, are you?"

"No, I am not," Autumn confirmed while writing on the note. She read her response aloud, "Do your best. I am not available."

CHAPTER 27

Latin awoke alone, freezing and stiff, in the little house built into the rocks. The sound of the creek tinkled with thin sheets of ice that had formed on the rocks, then slid off, washed downstream by the swirling water around them.

After a dozen pathetic jumping jacks to warm up after dressing, Latin stretched under his backpack while he walked up the rocky path. Since he was early for breakfast, he turned into the wood lot and wandered into the barn and looked through the old axe handles, spare saw blades, coils of dirty rope, scrap metal, and broken nails. He walked back out into the yard and looked around, surveying. Suddenly, he dropped his pack and pulled out his notebook and pencil. He wrote figures quickly, checked his work, and then picked up a coil of rope and started counting out even measures using the length of his arm as a guide. He tied a knot in the rope and went about the wood lot measuring, dropping pieces of wood as markers, and driving sticks into the ground.

Latin was standing back, checking the angles of his markers, when Paul limped into the wood lot.

"What in the world are you doing?"

"I'm laying out the yard so that we'll know when we've put up the full one hundred fifty cords and we can start using daylight work hours on the forge."

"Are you kidding me?"

"Not at all. One hundred fifty cords, each cord is one hundred twenty-eight cubic feet, so we need nineteen thousand two hundred cubic feet of wood. I rounded up to nineteen thousand five hundred to keep it simple."

"Simple?"

"Yes, because we cut eighteen-inch logs and stack five feet high, every foot of stacked wood is seven and a half cubic feet, so we need exactly two thousand six hundred feet of stacked wood or about eight hundred sixty-six yards. This part of the wood lot is seventy-five yards wide exactly, so we need to stack each row from one end to the other for eleven and a half rows. We might manage a row a week, so in twelve weeks, we'll be done, minus what the town burns while we're chopping of course, so maybe fourteen weeks."

"You don't get it, do you?"

"Get what?"

"Latin, there is a history here. You would do well to think more about what has taken place in the past and what led to things being so lean, so painful, and such a struggle now. We don't have any reserves, we're losing people, and we're losing livestock. Latin, Arden House can't even manage proper shoes for everyone. We couldn't stack one hundred fifty cords of wood if we put everyone in town on the project and did nothing else all summer."

"I don't think that's so."

"That kind of naive blindness isn't going to help. Our backs are against the wall, here, Latin. This could very well be our last summer, the last season of Arden House. We've lost seven people since last fall. Seven! We don't call them deserters, but they are. Nobody blames them; this is not living. And even with the deaths and deserters, we still ran out of food over the winter. We didn't grow enough, didn't trade enough to keep us going. Everyone here is run down because all we have left are seeds and grain. There's no protein. There comes a point when a place gets run down so much it can't recover. Many think Arden House has already past that point. I believe it has. We're desperately holding on for now, trying to last as long as we can. You come along with your crazy plans for one hundred fifty cords of wood and stakes in the ground, when all we have are twelve broken-down slackers who only work when they feel like it and four sick and hungry horses? You'll hurt everybody with this nonsense, and there's no use in it. I won't allow it."

"But…"

"No! How dare you talk back to me, boy? Do you know what I've given for this town? What I've done? I'm the clerk of the Wood Gild for a reason, you know. I've earned this. Did it occur to you that someone else might know better than you what's right for a town you've been in for less than a week? If you start pushing these boys, they don't know any better, and they'll work harder than they're able. They'll break. They can't eat well, and they won't recover. Someone's going to get hurt or killed, and it's going to be your fault for selfishly demanding that your projects take time away from real work."

"I didn't…"

"Keep your mind on your work and do what you're supposed to do. It's good to have new people, new thinking. I'm not against it, but you've got to at least try to fit in, to follow the ways of the place where you are, and to change it gradually."

"Then let me make the forge, let me start, at least. Splitting will be easier once we've got some better maul heads, and what we learn making the maul heads, we can use to make other things. It could be a source of trade for us. We could make horseshoes and wagon parts and chain. It could really make a difference. It could make things better."

"Forget it. No. We can't get distracted from our real work until we've set aside enough wood for next winter. It's been too dry this season for the seeds to start. It looks like we'll have nothing to trade again this fall. What we have to do is focus on our job: wood. That's it. This conversation is over. I'm going to breakfast."

As Paul hobbled away, Latin said, "I understand, Paul. During work hours, I will focus on chopping wood with the tools we have until we've set aside our eleven and a half rows. At night, though, and Saturdays and Sundays, I'm going to work on a forge."

Paul limped off with a shrug.

CHAPTER 28

Autumn wrapped Lady in a heavy blanket and carried her past the bamboo tower to the greenhouse on the other side of the clearing. Lady coughed most of the way. When they arrived, Autumn sat her on a wooden bench outside the greenhouse, where Lady coughed without stopping for many long minutes.

"Do you want to go back to the house?" Autumn asked.

Lady shook her head and waved her hands, continuing to cough louder and louder. Eventually, she spit out a wet, bloody knot the size of a grape and stopped coughing.

"Water?"

"Sure, here," Autumn said, handing her a bottle.

Lady took a drink, then deep breath and said, "Well…that's new."

"We should get to work?"

"Yes, no time to waste. You have your notebook?"

"I do."

"Okay, well, what about labels?"

"I'm going to number all the pots with a piece of coal and make notes in my book here about what the numbers mean."

"Okay, well, you can see the basic layout, the pots all sit on this wire mesh, so when I would water with the can, the extra drains out between the blocks in the floor. I have been too sick to tend anything for most of the winter, but it's stayed warm enough in here that I expect everything to bounce back once spring comes."

"Okay, well, we can start with these, I know what these are."

"You do?"

"Those are morphine poppies. I know all about scarring the bulbs and extracting with methanol, let's move on to these."

"Those are Echinacea. They'll come up late. You know about making the tea?"

"Roots only. Do you roast them or dry them?

"I've always dried them and that's worked fine."

"Just roots?"

"No, the leaves are active as well, only less so. You can mix them in equal parts for general use, but I like to keep a bit of the pure root extract around for emergencies and extreme cases."

"Are these potted samples of the ones that grow wild?"

"Oh no, the wild ones aren't good for much, I find. These have darker flowers and the roots are much more acidic. I've planted them a few places around, and I think they'll take, but I keep the potted samples just in case."

Autumn filled her notebook and worked on loose pieces of scrap paper, making label cards and tying them on with string during Lady's long coughing fits, which were ominously close together.

"Should we stop? Let's go back to the house and warm up, get some tea and dinner?" Autumn suggested at one point.

"It sounds nice, but I don't think we should. Let's keep on until we get all the way down to the end. These pots here are Floss Flower. They need heat. If they come up in the spring, you can crush the little white flowers into a paste with a bit of wax. It's good for skin infections, blisters, and rashes. Although, it depends on the cause, of course. Don't use them to treat an allergic reaction, but, if there's some kind of infection, sometimes it can be helpful."

Autumn wrote legibly, but kept pace with Lady.

CHAPTER 29

Latin huffed, "Mix? That's it?" as he sat down roughly at the Wood Gild table in the Gild Hall.

"There's been some bad news," said Mark.

"Oh, I'm sorry, I'm in a foul mood. Had an argument with Paul this morning. What's the news?"

"Alice Weaver, one of the young girls who helps with the kitchen, she fell down the back steps behind the Gild Hall this morning."

"She fell?"

"It was dark, and she was carrying a heavy bucket. It was a bad fall."

"She's hurt?"

"Badly hurt. Bleeding inside, I heard. They sent for Autumn."

Latin ate his mix.

"What were you and Paul talking about?"

"That man is impossible. I asked if I could have time during the day to build a forge to make us some better, lighter, sharper splitting mauls, but he wouldn't listen. He said no, not until we set aside one hundred fifty cords of split firewood."

Everyone at the table scoffed.

"I know it sounds like a lot."

"It sounds impossible."

"Well, I do have some ideas that I think could improve our efficiency quite a bit."

"Efficiency, Latin? Do you have any idea how long it takes us to set aside a single cord of wood, with cutting down the tree, taking off the limbs, sawing the disks, splitting, hauling, and stacking? Efficiency isn't going to get us to one hundred fifty cords. Not ever. We can hardly keep up as it is, and we all work hard."

Latin said, "Maybe. Maybe you're right, I don't know. If we really put our minds to it, how long do you think it would take to set aside an extra cord of wood?"

"On top of what the town burns every day?"

"Yes, in addition to that, to put aside a cord of wood above what was burned while we were working."

After some shrugs and stammering, Mark said, "A week?"

Most of the others nodded in agreement.

"About a week," Mark confirmed.

"I bet we could put aside a cord today, in one day, if we wanted to."

"One day?"

"Yes. Let's try it?"

"I don't know. What are we going to do differently?"

"First of all, we've got to sharpen everything. I mean, every saw, every blade, every axe, and every maul. We've got to sharpen at every break, at lunch, all the time. That's an easy thing to fix and will make a huge difference."

Mark shrugged. "I guess," he said.

"You'll see. Also, we shouldn't work in crews spread out all over the place."

"How do you think we should work?"

"As one crew. Pick one spot to work each day and do all of our work together in that one spot to save on time coming, going, and moving between spots."

"Okay."

"And we should not split out in the field."

"What do you mean?"

"We should drop a tree, remove the limbs and cut the trunk parts only as much as we have to make them lie in the bottom of the wagon. We should haul them whole. They'll slide around less, we'll get more wood in each load, and we'll keep the horses moving all day long, instead of sitting around waiting for us to split wood before hauling it."

"Okay, we can try that."

"Mark, can you pick a work site that's not too far way from town and take the whole Gild, all three carts, and half of the saws? Then, try to get back here with a cart full of unsplit wood as soon as you can without hurrying?"

"What are you going to do?"

"First, I'm going to go get a helper, then I'm going to get to work sharpening. I'll send sharpened saws back with the first cartload that drops off wood for me to split."

Latin leaned his head to the left to avoid striking it on the low doorjamb of the side entrance to the Arden House Lower School.

"Annette, I apologize for the interruption. Could I have a word with you?"

"Of course, we were just sitting down to Gathering."

"Can we step outside for a moment?"

"Of course, this isn't bad news about Alice, is it?"

"No. I only know they sent for Autumn."

"That's good. I hope she can help."

"I came to ask how William is doing. Did he come to school today? Is his arm hurting him?"

"Oh, he's fine. He's there in the circle. He hasn't complained once. It was generous of you to give him your watch. I don't think I've ever seen any boy as proud of anything in my whole life."

"Good. I'm glad. I wonder if I could borrow him for a few days for light work with the Wood Gild."

"Light work with the Wood Gild?"

"Yes. I don't want to pull him away from his studies, but I'm going to be sharpening blades over then next couple of days. I thought it might be helpful for him to come learn how that's done. I think he may have some talent for that type of work, don't you agree?"

"Oh, certainly, his gentle touch and attention to detail would be well suited to that. His splint won't be a problem?"

"I expect he'll be fine."

"You can have him for a week on two conditions."

"What are they?"

"First, he has to agree to it."

"I don't think that will be a problem."

"Right, neither do I."

"And the second condition?"

"After the week, you and William come back to the school and give the rest of the class a presentation of what he's learned, and, Let anyone else who wants learn sharpening, you will teach them."

"Agreed, gladly. Thank you."

Latin centered the ancient, rusted saw blade in the vise and turned the handle.

"Are you sure this is worth working on?" William asked. "It looks like junk."

"It is in poor condition, but after a bit of care, this saw will be easier to cut with than a better looking blade with dull teeth. Here is your file."

"But it's all rusty."

"The rust will work out of it as you go. Here, hold the end like this with your splinted hand."

"Okay."

"Take the other end with your good hand."

"Like this?"

"Exactly, yes. Then put the file in one of these channels at an angle like this."

Latin demonstrated with his file, then William put his file against the blade.

"Then drag the file gently toward you, kind of like you're trying to wipe a little bit of oil off the outside of an egg, only lightly."

"Okay, like this?"

"That's perfect."

"Don't you have to do it harder to get it sharp?"

"Oh no, lighter makes it sharper."

"How many times?"

"Start with ten on each tooth, and of course you have to alternate the angle, see? So tend to every other one, then take the whole blade out of the vice, turn it around, and do the ones you skipped. While you're working on that one, I'll work on this one. We'll send one sharp saw back to the work crew once the first load gets here. We'll keep one for ourselves to saw what they drop off."

The first wagon arrived as Latin and William were fastening their finished saw blades back into their handles.

"You were right, Latin. Hauling the wood in solid blocks makes it much easier to control the wagons, and I think we get about twice as much wood per load this way."

"The horses didn't struggle with it?" Latin asked from a distance.

"Not at all. They were much more sure-footed because the weight was lower and they didn't have to worry about it sliding around like it does in split pieces."

Latin watched from the barn as they levered the pieces off.

"Here is a sharp saw to take back to the crew. This should help fell trees faster. If you think of it, have Mark send a dull saw back with the next load, and we'll work on that this afternoon. Come to think of it, could one of you stay here and help me saw these into disks?"

"I'll stay," Danny volunteered.

Belle came into the wood lot and waved.

Latin and Danny stopped sawing and went over to say hello.

"Heard what you boys are trying to do. I brought snacks and water." Belle slipped a wadded handkerchief out of her pocket and handed it to Latin.

"Dried apples?" Latin asked. "Where do you get these little treasures all the time?"

"Just a few things I squirreled away. I'm out, or I would have brought more."

Latin shared the leathery pieces with Danny and William.

"This is fine, thank you. Every little bit helps."

"Did you hear about Autumn?"

"No, was she able to help Alice?"

"She didn't come."

"What?"

"She didn't come back from Lady's house. Autumn sent a note back to the doctor that he should do whatever he could to help her, but that she was too busy to come back."

Belle, Danny, and William all stared at Latin, who frowned. "That doesn't sound like something Autumn would ever do. That can't be right. There must be something else going on. There's more to this."

Belle said, "I know. You look tense, Latin. Are your shoulders sore?"

"What? I don't know. Yes?"

"Here, let me rub them for you."

William and Danny wandered off politely.

CHAPTER 30

Later, when Lady fell into another strong coughing fit, Autumn ran back to the house to get the lantern so they could continue after the sun went down. Lady was gasping for breath when Autumn got back.

"That's enough, I'm carrying you back to the house."

"No," Lady whispered. "These last plants here in the end room, these are all spices and cooking herbs, and some are uncommon. Let's do the special ones. You can figure out the rest of them without me. In the corner, there in the glazed blue pot, that is a special type of chive that can be used to make a strong diuretic tea with dandelion…"

"Well, that's it."

"We can figure the rest of it out later; thank you, Lady."

"I hope we did right."

"We did. Let me carry you back to the house. Can you carry the lantern?"

"Let me see. No."

"That's fine. We'll blow it out and leave it here."

"Wait, put me down," Lady said, falling into a deep coughing fit that shook her viciously.

Autumn looked away to hide tears as the coughing rocked Lady in her arms. When Lady finished and spit the blood onto the floor of the greenhouse, Autumn gave her the water bottle and said, "There's no point in you suffering this much , Lady. I can make this much easier for you if you like. I can speed things along and lessen the pain, if you like."

Lady reached up with her cold, shaking hand and grasped Autumn's ear. She whispered, "Come here, listen. I'm not ready. Not tonight. I want one more sunrise. Tomorrow, I'll be ready. Not now, do you understand?

There's so much more to tell you, tomorrow."

Autumn shook with a short sob, then said, "I'll carry you back to the house now, okay?"

"Yes, please."

As they crossed the yard together, Lady gasped, "Oh, stars! Stop. Let me see. Stop! Put me down."

"Lady, I don't think we should. I need to get you inside and warmed up. The ground is cold."

"I don't want to go inside. Put me down. Put me down."

Autumn sat down on the ground with Lady cradled in her lap, still wrapped in the blanket. "Can you see the stars?" Autumn asked.

Lady cried, choking, coughing, and weeping.

Autumn held her close, letting her own hot tears fall onto Lady's.

Lady whispered, "Autumn, let the secrets go. Let everything go. Don't be afraid to let go. Love with your whole self, seek the truth, follow science…Study with that fierce drive you have, but don't let the secrets that you can't solve haunt you. Let the mysteries be."

"Okay, I understand. I'll do my best."

"I'm not ready…" Lady choked, gasped, and shook.

Autumn held her, weeping wildly.

Suddenly, the shaking stopped, and Autumn was alone in the dark.

CHAPTER 31

"I need help tonight, Belle"

"With what?"

"I need bricks, cinder blocks, supplies, and a place to build a forge."

"Sounds like the Craft Shop. I'll get word to David. I'm sure he'll give you a tour. What about the dance? Are you coming to the concert?"

"I don't know. I'm quite tired already. I have a long afternoon of chopping ahead of me, then the forge, and tomorrow is Saturday, so if I could get it built tonight, perhaps I could do the first test-firing tomorrow."

"Test-firing?"

"A forge like this is a complicated. It's got to get extremely hot to melt the scrap. The ventilation and insulation have to be perfect and we have to pour off the waste in a specific way to avoid foaming. I probably won't get it all right the first time, but it'll be a start. I don't think I'm going to have time to have fun for a while."

"Okay. Do you have much more to chop today?"

"Yes, many hours of splitting. I'll work until dark, if I can manage that long."

Belle thought as she rubbed his shoulders. She whispered into his ear, "Be careful. I will leave you to work, but I will come back at dusk. Would you like to eat dinner with me tonight?"

"Sure, I'll meet you in the Gild Hall."

"No, I mean alone."

She continued to work his shoulders while he thought. "Alone?" he said.

"Together, somewhere away from the Gild Hall. I'll bring dinner."

"Okay, where?"

"No need to decide now. I'll bring a picnic and we can go wherever."

CHAPTER 32

"Did we make it?"

"We did, with three feet to spare. Our stack is twenty feet long and five feet high. Well over a full cord and we did it in one day."

"I can't move my arms," Latin groaned, sitting on the splitting stump.

"Let's go eat," Danny said.

As the rest of the Wood Gild went to eat together, Latin peeled off and walked across the wood lot toward Belle, who grinned.

Stopping and shaking hands with William on the way, Latin said, "We could not have done it without your help today. Do you think you'd like to come help us again tomorrow?"

"I would, yeah, sure. As soon as my arm is healed up, I'd like to try splitting with you. Do you think I could?"

"Of course, you'll be great."

"Are you coming to dinner?"

"No, I've got a…I'm going to…No, but I'll see you in the morning."

"Okay."

"Hey, William?"

"Yeah?"

"What time is it?"

"Let's see…it's…oh, five fifteen, by my watch." William said as he walked away grinning ear to ear.

"Can I carry your pack for you?"

"Oh, no thanks. Actually, getting it on was a little difficult, but, now that it's there, I don't notice it."

"Did you get your splitting done?"

"We did. We stacked a whole cord. That's a cord, there."

"In one day?"

"We can do better, much better—we're just getting started."

"How are you feeling, you look pretty tired."

"I'll be okay. I need some rest."

"Are you still going to the Craft Shop to work on the forge with David?"

"Yes, he's meeting me there after dinner."

"Okay, then let's eat."

"Sounds good to me, where would you like to go?"

"Well, I hope you don't mind, but I started the woodstove at your place and put the kettle on. I brought you an extra pair of underclothes from the supply room. I thought you might want to wash up and get out of those sweaty clothes."

Latin put a hand on Belle's shoulder to steady himself. "Really, you did all of that?"

"I did. I hope that's okay. I know that was Autumn's place, but since she's not here...I hope it's not a problem."

"Honestly, I don't know for sure if she'd be upset about that or not. Frankly, right now I'm so tired, sore, sweaty, and cold that I really don't care. I think it's fantastic, and I can't thank you enough."

"Well...let's go then."

"And you made dinner, too?"

"I did. It's here in the bag. It's nothing special."

"Somehow I doubt that," Latin said, bumping shoulders with Belle as they walked together into the dim forest.

"This is amazing! Where in the world did you get honey and all this wonderful cheese?"

"Oh, I've been saving it for a special occasion. This seemed like a good time. After this, though, it's nothing but mix and eggs, sorry to say."

"That's fine; this is delicious! And this bread?"

"I got that from the Gild Hall. They're actually serving this with regular dinner tonight, so I can't take credit for the bread."

"Well, thank you, anyway. This is nice with the candles and the clean, dry clothes. A fellow could get used to this kind of treatment." Latin sipped his tea.

"Have you had enough to eat?"

"Yes, I've had plenty. Thank you again."

Belle went about clearing the dinner things and stowing the leftovers back in her bag. "How are your arms?"

"Dinner helped, but they're sore— my shoulders and back. You know, it's to be expected. I'll be fine. In a week or two, I'll have my chopping muscles back, and I'll be fine."

"Would it help if I rubbed them?"

"Oh no, I'm fine. They're fine. Thank you."

"It's so wonderful here. The attention to detail that Mara put into this kitchen is impressive."

"It is."

"And this spot, so close to the creek that you can hear it gurgling, it's like heaven."

"You know, on second thought, I would really like it if you could work on my muscles a little," Latin said, blushing and looking down.

"Of course," said Belle in a low tone. She moved toward the back of the house and motioned with her head for Latin to follow her.

"Back there?"

Belle didn't reply. She just walked into the back.

"Take you shirt off. Lie on your stomach."

He did.

She started with his shoulders, working lightly. Her hands were warm and soft and strong. Latin exhaled and began to relax, letting her work.

After a time on his shoulders, she moved to his back, loosening and opening several knotted muscles there. Then, she focused on the middle of his back, between his shoulder blades. Carefully, she worked up toward his head and back down.

After slowly building from light kneading to harder digging and rubbing all along his back, Belle finally put one hand on the back of Latin's neck and the other at the base of his spine. She leaned over him, pressing down, stretching him.

Latin produced a deep guttural moan as the ache of long-carried burdens was lifted up and out of him.

"Breathe in," Belle reminded him after he had stopped for some time.

Latin drew in a huge, open breath. He let it out. Gradually, his breathing returned to normal.

"You're well? That was okay."

"I'm fine. I'm drooling."

"Good. That's good. You drool. Get some rest. I'll wake you up in a while; we'll go up to the Craft Shop."

"Where did you learn to do that?" Latin asked as they walked slowly along the big garden toward the Craft Shop.

"My sister."

"I didn't know you had a sister. What's her name?"

"We called each other sister."

"Oh, I'm sorry."

"No, she's fine. She's alive. She went to Longwood House a long time ago."

"She moved there?"

"We're not supposed to talk about it."

"You learned body work from her?"

"We learned from each other."

CHAPTER 33

Latin and Belle walked slowly to the Craft Shop, enjoying the stars over the long garden.

Cousin David greeted them. "Belle, good to see you. I'm surprised you're not at the concert."

"I had dinner with Latin. I'll wander over and see the concert later, I suppose. I wanted to see if there was anything I could do to help build a forge."

David said, "Right, well, Latin, you've done this before, right? We haven't had anything more than a pottery kiln here for a long time. I certainly don't know how to make a working forge."

Latin said, "Well, there's not that much to it, really. Only to get the metal hot enough to melt and separate out."

"So what kinds of things are we going to need?"

"I'm not sure, exactly. There are lots of ways to do things, as you know, depending on what you have on hand. Why don't you show me around the Craft Shop, and I'll think as we go?"

"Sure, well, this the first floor. You can see the workstations for various specialists. There is a drafting table, some design tools, and a drawing desk. Following around this hall, there are workshops for leatherwork, carving, and furniture repair. This little closet is for the tinkers who fix the weaving looms and various little machines around town."

"Got it. This is quite helpful. What's upstairs?"

"Let's go up the back steps. Belle, you want to lead the way?"

"Up here are, well, basically piles of related sorts of things. As you can see, here we have a pile of lanterns, in various states of repair. This is our candle-making setup, except we don't have any good wicks right now.

These are a bunch of pottery wheels that don't work anymore. Here is our basket-weaving pile. Many of those could be fixed, I believe. I guess that's why we keep them instead of throwing them out—I'm not sure, really. And this is a drawer full of dull sheep shears. That's from back when we had more sheep. As you can see, it's not our most prosperous endeavor."

"No, it's great. There's a lot here to work with. Thank you for showing me. What's that?"

"Oh, that's an old sheet."

"No, under the sheet."

"Oh, that's…I'm not sure. Let's look. Oh, right, this is an old machine we used to use to spin the honey out of honeycombs. It had a handle off that way and some gears in this part, and something or other broke with it, so here it sits."

"All good to know. Can we go and see if there are enough bricks and cinder blocks to start building something?"

"Sure, let's take a look."

Holding up his lantern to light the yard, David said, "There is this open spot where the pottery kiln gets set up."

"Yes, this concrete pad will be perfect. How long has this been here?"

"It's always been here."

"It won't be needed for pottery firing soon?"

David said, "No, I checked earlier. They don't have plans to do anything for several weeks."

"And this pile of bricks and cinder blocks?"

"That's all scrap. You can use whatever you need."

Latin took the lantern and walked around the pile. "This is perfect. Can we use one of these big pieces of slate?"

"Sure, yeah. It's all junk."

Latin handed the lantern to Belle and stood looking back and forth between the pile and the concrete pad, planning.

Finally, Belle said, "So…how is this going work?"

Latin stroked his chin. "What you build and how you build it depends on what you're trying to melt down and what you want to do with it. We need to build a firebox that draws air in from the bottom and blows it up and out through the top. Inside that firebox, we need an insulated crucible that holds the metal. We'll make castings, then what we'll do is make a mold in a box with wet sand in the shape we're trying to make. Later, we can make a real impression cast, but for now, we can use a sand cast. They're easy to make and work well enough to make something that's useful and proves that we can do this."

"How hot does it have to get to melt scrap metal?"

"I don't know. Very, very hot. It depends on what kind of scrap we're trying to melt. If we get soft alloys, they'll be easier to melt, but then whatever we make from them will be soft—which is okay for some things, but not others. At any rate, we really should have charcoal for this, but making charcoal is a project in itself. I think we'll be okay with hardwood. If the fire doesn't get hot enough, though, we won't be able to melt our scraps down and they won't pour. We'll also need some way to pick up the crucible full of hot metal. Usually, they use long tongs because it's too hot to get within arm's reach."

David said, "It's getting cold. Let's go inside and sit by the woodstove."

Inside the Craft Shop, they gathered in the sitting room, David said, "How are we going to get the crucible out of the firebox? Is there a door, or do we have to dismantle the fire box while it's hot?"

"Back home, we had a little door in the side that opened out and we could reach in with the long tongs and pull the crucible out. But, a hinge and door assembly that can take that much heat would take a lot of effort to build. We could do it, but it would take a long time."

David said, "If we had tongs long enough, we could use them to remove enough bricks to get to the crucible."

"Maybe."

Belle said, "Why don't you build the top of the forge out of something light, that's a single piece? You could make cap shaped like a cone out of those flat slate pieces and the long metal bars behind the wood shed."

Latin looked at David. "Rebar?"

David nodded.

Latin said, "Keep going, Belle."

"If you build the cap to fit the forge and set it on top of the firebox like a hat, you could get ladders on either side, pass a long pole through the top, climb the ladders each holding one end of the long pole, and lift the cap straight up off the top. You could carry it off and set it down, then lift the crucible out. Know what I mean? Is that a bad idea?"

David and Latin both nodded. Latin said, "No. No, it's not a bad idea at all. I'm thinking. We'll need a crucible. Something that won't melt."

"Porcelain?" David asked.

"That would be perfect. Do you have something in mind?"

"I do," David said, getting up, taking the lantern, and walking off toward the Craft Shop basement.

"You like my idea?" Belle said, blinking slowly at Latin.

"I do. It's a fine idea. I'm working out how we might build it, how we might join the slate pieces to the rebar."

"Can you bend rebar?"

"Yes, but not easily. It has to be heated. We could use a tray forge for that, though. I bet we could work it like a flexible tent; when it's sitting on something, it's held up like a pyramid by its own weight, but, when you pick it up, it folds in on itself."

David set a large porcelain vase on the floor in front of the fireplace.

Latin looked inside. "It doesn't have a hole in the bottom?"

"No."

"They usually have holes."

"Those are planters. This is a vase."

"Nice. It's a good size and certainly heavy enough. It should be easy to grip around the neck. How about tongs? Have anything down there for tongs?"

David said, "We have fireplace tongs."

"If we wear heavy gloves, they might be okay. I was telling Belle, I have an idea for the top; I'll need to work with the rebar and slate a little bit. I think I can put something together. Do you have any cabling? Old wire?"

"Sure."

"I can work that out."

David said, "Do you want to start tonight? You look beat. You must be exhausted."

"I'm okay. Belle did something to my back earlier. I feel like a new man. Is it okay if I look around the scrap heap a little bit?"

"Sure. I'll start stacking blocks for the firebox. You don't need mortar or anything, right?"

"No, just dry. We'll take it all apart after we use it."

Working by lantern light on the flagstone flat behind the Craft Shop, Latin showed David the basics of how to build the firebox, and David figured out the rest on his own. Belle helped Latin build the removable pyramid top with eight pieces of rebar and four triangular pieces of slate. They practiced picking it up by standing on opposite sides, pinching the top between two long poles, and lifting it.

"Seems to work pretty well," Belle said.

"It's perfect."

"My goodness, what are you all working on so late at night?" Susan asked as she admired David's work.

"Hey, sweetheart," David said. "This is going to be our forge."

"Hi, Latin. Hi, Belle."

"Hello."

"Hi, Susan. Are you coming home from the infirmary?"

"Yes, no sign of Autumn."

"How is Alice?"

Susan frowned. "Doctor Dash is with her now. I don't want to say it, but I doubt she'll make it through the night. There's nothing we can do."

"Do you think Autumn could have helped her, if she had come?" Latin asked.

"Who knows? She could have operated, but Doctor Dash says he doesn't think it would have made any difference. The way she landed, there was too much damage, he thinks."

"Did you stop at the concert at all?" David asked.

"No, I heard as I passed by, but I'm tired and wasn't in the mood. I went home. When you weren't there, I came looking for you."

"I think we're about done?" David asked, looking to Latin.

"We're done. We've made a lot of progress. Thank you so much. Go sleep. Thank you. Do you need the lantern?"

Susan said, "Oh no, we're only around the corner. You keep it."

CHAPTER 34

The fire had burned out in the woodstove by the time Latin got back to his little house. He was too tired to relight it before going to bed, so he shivered under the covers, moving his legs in big circles to generate heat. He lit the candle lantern to read Annette's metalworking books. He read one page, blew out the lantern, and fell asleep.

When the town bell rang frantically in the predawn freeze, Latin wove the far-off sound into his aching, dreaming confusion, then awoke with a jolt.

He ran outside and held his breath, listening to the strange sound of many people moving at night.

"Fire! Fire! Fire!" was shouted from the lookout platform at the top of Arden House so loudly that it reached him clearly in the woods.

Latin threw off his bedclothes, put on his work clothes, grabbed his pack, and rushed out. He scurried up the stony path to town in the dark. When he got to the corner by the garden, he saw a commotion of lanterns and people running toward Arden House, but no fire.

"Where's the fire?" he asked of the first man he saw.

"Outside town. We're hitching up wagons."

"To horses?" Latin asked in a whisper.

Latin ran along, following the flow of the others. Cousin David appeared from a side path with a lantern.

"Bad news. It looks to be Lady's house."

"Where Autumn is?"

"Yeah, from what they could tell from the lookout, that's got to be it. It might have already jumped to the trees and could spread rapidly if we can't get there and put it out quickly."

"I've been there. Can I borrow your lantern? I'll run."

"Are you sure?"

"Yeah, I'll get there."

Latin took David's lantern and dashed off through the woods in the dark, crashing and sprinting by himself. Soon, lost and freezing, he stopped to catch his breath. He heard the far-off commotion of carriages and horses. Unable to find the path, he pressed along, keeping his course parallel to the sound of the men on the road.

Eventually, the dim first light of the day helped him find his way. As he got close, he could smell the fire, then see the glow against the lightening sky, then feel the heat.

When he finally burst into the clearing, he discovered that it wasn't Lady's house that was burning, but the massive column of bamboo, brush, and trash in the yard. Autumn was unhurt, and she was talking with Doctor Dash and Constable Pete.

"You're okay?" Latin asked, running up to them.

"Lady died," Autumn said coldly.

"You're okay?

"I'm fine, Latin. Lady died."

"Yeah, but…" Latin collapsed, retching and catching his breath. "The whole town is on the way."

"I know," Autumn said, "Many of them are already here. Soon, it will be light enough."

"Light enough for what?" Latin asked, but Autumn had turned away and was talking to the Constable Pete again.

"I'm sorry, Constable Pete. I know it's caused a lot of commotion, but she made me promise that I would burn her on the pyre."

"You could have waited for daytime. You could have warned us. A wildfire, even at this time of year, could be disastrous. It's likely that the men from Bellevue have seen this and are on their way as well. We'll have to explain this to them, I suppose?"

"I take full responsibility. I'll explain, and, if there's trouble, I will find a way to set things right. I promised Lady I would honor her wishes.

There's no harm done. I don't mind taking the blame for any inconvenience that might have been caused by everyone thinking something was wrong."

Constable Pete and Doctor Dash stared, dumbstruck.

"But can I ask a favor?" Autumn continued.

"I wouldn't, if I were you. We're having the funeral, later today, for the little girl who was injured."

"Oh no. I'm so sorry to hear that. That's terrible."

"Go ahead and ask your favor, if you must," said the doctor.

"Since you're all here, all the men and carriages and carts and horses and everything, could I ask that we load what we can from the house? Maybe the people who won't have room to ride the carts back could take an armful of the lighter things? It's going to be a big job to move all of the gear, books, and plants back to Arden House, but many hands will make light work of it."

"What?"

"Well, since you've got all these carts and people here, and we're all going back to Arden House anyway, could we start taking things now? I've already packed the fragile things into boxes. Those can be carried by hand—whatever is easier for everyone."

Constable Pete said, "We can't just take a whole house's worth of things back with us."

"No? Why not? One armload at a time."

"It's not ours."

"Everything is ours. Lady gave everything in the house to me before she died. She gave me the house—and the barn too, but that's for later. The books and tools and plants are priceless. Let's go, let's start loading up these carts. It's plenty light now, but those clouds look threatening. We don't want things to get wet, do we? Let's pull that first cart right up to the door there. Careful not to rub the markings off the sides of those pots."

Although there were grumbles and objections, Autumn kept making direct appeals for specific tasks to be done by individuals until a pattern emerged: people entered through one door, picked up a box, and either carried it to the wagons which had started lining up in the front yard or simply started back toward Arden House with it.

"Where does all of this go?" someone asked.

"Please take it all to the infirmary and the storage rooms in the basement, thank you."

A long, slow procession of wood-hauling carts and weary Ardenites loaded down with books, notebooks, equipment boxes, needles, glassware, slides, plants, samples, notebooks, tinctures, cases, ash, pill presses, glassware, and flowerpots wound its way back to Arden House.

Latin walked home along the woods path, empty-handed, kicking rocks along the way.

CHAPTER 35

Latin staggered into the Gild Hall as breakfast was being cleaned up and put away. There were sacks of mix set out on a table for people returning late from the fire. Latin took two and headed for the wood lot. From the shed, he took a wheelbarrow nearly full of wood and an armful of rusty scrap that looked promising to melt down, as well as a hatchet for splitting kindling.

Walking along the garden green, he saw young William sitting on a tree stump, reading a book.

"No work today?"

"I got put on light duty until my arm heals up. It doesn't hurt, but they told me take it easy for two more weeks anyway."

"That's probably wise. You didn't go to the fire this morning?"

"No, they never let us do anything fun. What are you doing? Where are you going with all that stuff?"

"I'm working on a forge to melt down metal scraps and make new axes, splitting mauls, and stuff like that. Want to come along?"

"Sure. Feels like rain to me."

"Definitely going to rain."

William and Latin walked into the back yard of the Craft Shop together to find Cousin David assembling the forge. William helped to finish stacking the bricks around porcelain crucible, which was already half-full with scrap metal. Latin adjusted a few bricks, changed the angle of the air intake slightly, and made sure the chimney was clear. He let William start the fire and tend it as it grew. The rain started. Large drops popped into steam as they landed on hot brick.

They spent the afternoon building up the fire, making it as hot as possible. Every few minutes, Latin would climb up on a ladder to look down into the crucible.

"It's glowing. It's bright red, but it's not melting at all. We should have charcoal."

Cousin David said, "Would it help to have more insulation around the firebox?"

Latin nodded. "Yes. That would help."

When Annette stopped by, all three of them were soaked and discouraged. "How's it going?"

"It's not melting. Not hot enough."

"Because of the rain?"

"No, I don't think the rain has much to do with it. It's not hot enough. We need charcoal and a different design."

"Is there anything I can do to help?"

"No, I don't think so. Let's shut it down, guys."

William and David poured buckets of water into the firebox, sending a gout of steam into the air and a gush of sooty water running off the sides of the concrete pad and into the grass.

Annette said, "Well, don't get too discouraged. You can try again, do something different next time."

Latin said, "We will. We need to try charcoal, which will get it much hotter, and we should probably be more selective about what scrap we start with. It's not a wasted day; we learned some things."

"Did you go to the funeral?"

"For the little girl? No. I couldn't. Did you go?"

"I did. It was…" Annette stopped to wipe her eyes and blow her nose. "It was so sad. We've lost so many people. It never gets easier."

"I'm so sorry," Latin said, hugging Annette. "Sorry there's so much pain."

"She was such a dear little girl."

"I'm so sorry. It makes it even worse, I imagine, to think that Autumn might have been able to help if she had come?"

Annette shook her head, "No, I don't think anyone's blaming her—at least not yet. Right now, there's nothing…just hurt."

"I understand. Did they cancel the dance tonight?"

"No, they decided to go ahead with it. I guess it's for the best. I don't know. Music does seem to be one of the few things that can help, if only a little. Will you go?"

"No, I'm going home. I'm beat. I need rest."

CHAPTER 36

Latin slept through the rainy afternoon and night. The next morning, he was walking slowly up the cold, stony path from the house by the creek to Arden House when he saw Arthur headed down the path toward him.

"Good morning, Arthur, is everything okay? Were you coming down to see me?"

"Good morning, Latin. Yes, all is well. I'll walk with you. I wonder if I might ask about Autumn?"

"Sure, I mean, what's the question?"

"She spent the night in the infirmary. Susan tells us that Autumn has asked not to speak to anyone."

"And you want me to go talk to her? Is she in trouble?"

Arthur rubbed his chin. "Well, not trouble, exactly, but I do have some questions I'd like to ask her."

"Yes, so do I," Latin added.

"I wonder if you might go talk to her after breakfast?"

"Talk to her?"

"Perhaps? To see if you can find out what her intentions are? If she needs anything?"

Latin said, "Well, I don't know how much she'll tell me, but I can go ask."

"I would appreciate that, thank you. Please come find me after Meeting for Worship and let me know how it goes?"

"Meeting for Worship is after breakfast?"

"Yes, upstairs in the Gild Hall."

"Of course, Arthur. I will."

Once they reached the corner of the big garden, Arthur said, "If you'll excuse me, Latin, I need to talk to some people down in the laundry," and Arthur turned down a different path.

Latin sat with Cousin David and Susan at breakfast.

"Sorry about the forge," Susan said.

"Thank you. Didn't really expect the first one to work perfectly," Latin said with a shrug.

David said, "We're going to start designing and building the next one this afternoon."

Latin nodded, "Yes, after Meeting. Arthur's asked me to go to the infirmary and talk to Autumn."

Susan looked surprised. "Really? I don't think she's ready for visitors yet. She's asked not to be interrupted."

"I understand, but Arthur asked me to try to talk to her and I agreed to try."

Susan nodded, "I should at least go in first and tell her you're coming."

"Okay, thank you. Afterward, can I sit with you at Meeting? I've never been to one before."

"Sure, we'll be there. We'll save you a spot."

Susan came out of the infirmary and shrugged. She said, "I think this is a bad time to talk to her, but go ahead."

"Thank you," Latin said, going in. "Hi?" he called into the boxes and clutter.

"Not now, Latin. Please?" Autumn answered, hidden in the piles of Lady's things in the infirmary.

"Autumn? What's going on? Arthur asked me to come find out how you are."

"Outside," she said, getting up off the floor.

Latin followed Autumn outside. They sat on a tree stump carved into a bench overlooking the garden.

Latin said, "You look like you've been crying. Are you okay? Can I help at all?"

"No, I don't think so. Only time."

"Can we connect? Can we talk? It feels like things have changed."

"Changed? Yes, it's changed. Everything has changed around us. And we've changed with it."

Latin looked like he had been smacked in the face. "I hadn't thought of it that way. That makes sense now that you say it."

"Latin, look, don't act surprised. You know how life is. You know better than anyone; things change in an instant, and they're never the same again."

Latin was bewildered. "Never the same again? How do you mean?"

"When we came here, when we walked into Arden House together, everything changed for us. Our worlds changed. You realize that, right?"

"I guess."

"It's not just the two of us in the woods any more, Latin, and we're not going back."

Latin frowned. He knew what she was saying. His eyes grew watery. He looked away.

Autumn said, "Awww, you liked it when it was just the two of us?"

"Yes, I did. Didn't you?"

"I did. I liked it. It was a sweet time."

"It snowed, we..."

"Stop. Latin, we've got to adapt. You know how it is. We have to be resilient. Things are different now. We're part of something larger than ourselves."

"But, what about us? Didn't we have something?"

"We did. Latin, I'm sorry. I know this is going to hurt you. There's just no way around it. I'm afraid that things aren't going to work out the way you had hoped they would."

"What?"

"Arden House changed things. Lady changed things. She changed me. I have a part to play here. This little girl that died, maybe I could have helped her if I had come back, but I didn't. Those were my choices. You see how things are. Latin, I have a lifetime's worth of work to do here. You see how it is. This place needs all the help it can get, and I think I can help, you know, with the medicine. You can help, too. You'll find a way."

"But what about our house by the creek? You could come there when you want. I'm not asking for anything. I want you to know that we can rest together whenever you're not working, whenever you want to do something else."

"I'm not going to do anything else, Latin. This is my work, here in the infirmary, and I'm going to put everything I have into it. Late nights, days on end—there's not going to be room for anything else. Nothing's going to happen between us, at least not now. Later…I doubt it, but who knows? But not now, not soon."

"But, but…why? Why does it have to be like that? Why can't there be something, if only something different."

Autumn looked at him coldly.

Latin asked, "You're not coming back to the house?"

"I think it's best if I don't. I want to be clear, at least, so there's no confusion. At least I can do that."

Latin shuddered and looked away so that she wouldn't see his eyes.

"Latin, I'm sorry. Obviously, this is going to be hard for you, but I'm not going to be able to help you through this. I have to get back to work."

"But, but…I left my…"

"I know. I'm sorry about that," Autumn said, standing, taking a step back, then turning and walking back into the infirmary.

Latin was sniffling and wiping his nose when Belle came out of the garden and said, "Latin, what's wrong? What happened? Are you okay?"

Latin shook his head and said, "No."

Belle sat down next to him, put an arm around him, and held him while he composed himself. She said, "Want to go to my place? I'll make you some tea."

"I can't. I have to go to Meeting and tell Arthur about my conversation with Autumn, that we're parting ways." Latin frowned damply.

"Oh, that's terrible." Belle let a smile slip. "Come with me. Let's find

Arthur and talk to him before Meeting so you don't have to sit through the whole hour."

"Arthur?"

"Belle, I'm headed in to Meeting. Join us?"

"Arthur, could you please talk to Latin for a quick minute before Meeting? He talked to Autumn. He's a bit upset."

"Of course, Latin. I'm sorry, are you okay? What's the matter?"

"Arthur, I'm fine, except that Autumn has decided to move into the infirmary to focus entirely on her work there. She's taken her things out of our little house by the creek, and she doesn't plan to come back."

Arthur held Latin's shoulders and said, "Oh my goodness, Latin. I understand why you'd be upset, of course."

Belle stepped up and said, "If it's okay, we're going to go have a cup of tea and talk things through."

Arthur nodded. "That's fine, of course, although Meeting for Worship can also be quite helpful in times like this."

"I'm a bit raw just now," Latin said. "If it's okay, I'd like to take some time alone?"

Arthur nodded and shook Latin's hand. "Let me know if there's anything I can do to help."

As they walked away, Belle said, "Tea at my house?"

"Won't your housemates be there?"

"They'll all be at Meeting."

"Yes. That sounds nice. Thank you so much."

Belle smiled and held Latin's hand as she walked him away from the Gild Hall.

CHAPTER 37

Latin enjoyed having tea with Belle, but he soon recovered from the shock of Autumn's news and was restless to get to work on the next version of the forge. He left Belle early in the afternoon and went to the drafting room in the Craft Shop for the rest of the day. On the massive, tilted table, he drew plans for a much larger forge that would burn charcoal. It would be fully enclosed and insulated, with a hinged door for removing the crucible.

Every night that week, after long days chopping wood, he would eat a quick dinner and go to the Craft Shop to tinker and plan. With Cousin David's help, he started by working on converting one of the old steel drums into an oven for making charcoal. After dark, he would light the lantern and draw up plans for making a more precise mold for a maul head, using as much geometry as he could remember from his work with his grandfather.

Autumn stayed in the infirmary. Susan was her only visitor. People reported seeing her lantern lit through the night. Susan said she took short naps on the examination table and spent the rest of the time reading Lady's notebooks, going through supplies, labeling and relabeling boxes, and writing pages and pages of notes. It was rumored that guilt had driven her insane.

After weeks of splitting wood every day, Latin pulled a muscle deep in his right shoulder. He spent three days on light duty, sharpening blades and saws and cleaning up around the wood lot. The others picked up the slack. They were quick studies and learned Latin's splitting technique effectively.

Late into the evenings, Latin and David worked in the Craft Shop, building the charcoal oven and piecing together a larger, hotter forge. Their first batch of charcoal took all night, but was a complete success. They made several batches of light, dry charcoal. Latin estimated that it would take five loads of charcoal to fuel a full run of the forge. Latin walked around town scouring the various scrap heaps and rusted piles of old metal. He ground off the rust to see the quality of the metal underneath and gathered only the highest quality scrap to melt in the big forge.

No rain came during April, raising concerns about the health of the early crops. The spring wheat looked pitiful. However, the Garden Gild persevered, hauling massive loads of wild ramps out of the forest. The cook made a soup from a mixture of fresh ramps, onions, and the first young radishes and every one ate greedily.

Some nights, Latin slept in the Craft Shop while a batch of charcoal cooked in the drum. Some nights, he slept in the spare bed in Susan and David's house. Some nights, he slept on the floor in Annette's room. Other nights, he and Belle slept in the little house by the creek in the woods.

Wild rumors continued to fly around town about what Autumn was doing in the infirmary.

CHAPTER 38

Days later, Susan passed a note to Arthur after Meeting.

Arthur, Please come visit the infirmary when you're free.
Thank you, Autumn.

"Autumn?" Arthur called into the chaotic array of boxes.

"Yes, Arthur. Thank you for coming. Please come in, let me fix you some tea."

"I've brought Ruth along."

"Splendid. Tea for both of you, then?"

"Tea?"

"Chamomile or Lemon Ginger?"

"Are you kidding?"

"No, Lady had a nice stash of tea."

"Lemon Ginger, please," Ruth said.

"For us both," said Arthur.

Autumn put the kettle on the woodstove that she and Susan had installed in the infirmary. "I suppose I owe a bit of an explanation for all this."

"I don't know that you owe us anything, but we would enjoy one—if you have one to give."

"Yes, well…as you can see, Arden House has inherited a treasure trove of medicinal information, tools, and raw materials from Lady Ledger."

Looking around at the junk, Arthur said, "If you say so."

"Oh, I do. Arthur, I do. We have the beginnings of a real, working infirmary where we could actually practice some medicine and seriously help people."

"Really?"

"Oh yes."

Ruth said, "Okay, that could eventually be good. I mean, over a long time, that could, I guess, contribute."

"No, listen! The things we can do with these supplies, the medicines we can make, the compounds we can extract from our plants—these are items of intense value, immediately."

"What?"

"We can trade them."

Arthur huffed, dismissing her.

"Arthur, this isn't the kind of medicine you're used to. This isn't like putting honey in your tea if you have a cough. We can sterilize instruments and perform safe procedures. We can extract teeth with real painkillers. We could perform basic surgeries with anesthesia. We can properly set broken bones and cauterize open wounds. We can really make a difference now."

Ruth said, "Okay, I understand, but how often do those kinds of things come up here? I know we've had a few accidents recently, but there just aren't that many of us here."

Autumn said, "Not only us, all five houses. Imagine! Once I establish a reputation for being able to cure things—not old hocus-pocus and hoping things go well, but actually practicing medicine that is safe and effective. Imagine what that could mean for us."

"You mean people would come here for treatment?" Ruth said, looking around at the dirt and clutter, wrinkling her nose.

"We'll clean this all up. It will be safe, clean, and orderly in no time at all. Susan is a capable assistant, and I can teach other nurses. Elsie and Esther have already said they're interested. We can do this."

"You really think people will come here for this?"

"Not at first, no. It's going to take some travel and some good luck, and, although the medicine is real science, I must be honest that adding in a little hocus-pocus can go a long way getting people to trust us."

"Oh?"

"Yes. That's where I'm going to need a little help if you don't mind."

"Help?"

"Yes, I need you to start some rumors."

"I think I know someone who might be helpful with that," Ruth smiled, looking at Arthur.

"There need to be stories about how I'm a mystic healer. Strange medicines with amazing results, and so forth."

"Well, you did set young William's broken arm successfully."

"Agreed, true stories are even better."

"I see."

"Word has to spread beyond Arden House. Maybe Trader Jack can help spread the word that Arden House has a practicing healer?"

"Do we? Do we have a practicing healer?" Ruth asked.

"Yes, yes we do," Autumn answered.

"Don't you think that's a bit pretentious? I mean, shouldn't we say that you're studying to be a healer, that you're an apprentice, or that someday you'd like to be a healer?"

"No, no Arthur, that's the last thing we want. We want people to have confidence, to be sure that I know what I'm doing."

"But what if someone has an injury or illness you can't cure. Surely there are things you won't be able to fix."

"Of course, and we'll be honest right up front that there's not much we can do. We won't ever ask for payment in those cases."

"Payment?"

"Oh, yes. Payment. Trade."

Arthur thought, looking around at the boxes with new optimism, seeing them in a new light.

"How much?"

"It depends on what the problem is and how much I can do to help. Dentistry is a very good area to focus on. The pain is so bad and the cure is often quick and effective, depending on what's wrong. Imagine if you have a toothache, or your child has a toothache, and there's someone with medicine that will make it stop hurting immediately. How much would you be willing to trade? A lot, right?"

"One must be careful not to take advantage."

"What do you mean, Ruth?"

"It wouldn't be right, if there were a sick child or injured person, to barter for a higher price."

"No? Why not? If there is a demand for meat, meat prices go up, right? If someone wants an infected molar pulled and they're willing to trade a whole flock of chickens to have the pain go away and the problem fixed in a matter minutes, well, how is that different?"

Arthur thought. "It is, but I'm not sure exactly how. You make an interesting point, though."

"And nobody would have to pay if the treatment didn't work. I won't get paid for trying, only for results."

Ruth asked, "Would you negotiate terms up front, before you do anything?"

"Of course. I will examine for free, make a diagnosis, and propose a treatment—if I have one, along with an offer of what we'll take in return. I'd expect some haggling, of course, but before I did any healing, payment would need to be agreed upon."

Arthur stroked his chin. "Can you cure warts?"

"Warts, sure that's a simple skin virus that we treat with mustard poultice. It's easy to make, the ingredients are easy to find and it works every time."

Arthur sat down. "You've worked as a healer before?"

"Arthur, this is what I was raised to do. My mother trained me my whole life for this."

"How much would you charge to clear up warts?"

Autumn laughed.

"Nothing, Arthur. I'm not going to charge Friends; we only charge outsiders."

"Oh, I know, but let's say someone comes in from Longwood House and they have warts they want removed. How much?"

"What are they trading, and how badly do we need what they're trading?"

"I see," Arthur said, staring off into the distance. "Yes, rumors, yes. I believe I can help with that."

CHAPTER 39

Nightmares came to visit Latin. He would awaken with a spasm of terror in the middle of the night. It did not matter where he was sleeping or how long and hard he worked during the day, the dreams found him. They were cryptic and horrifying, full of panic and punctuated by long sequences of being chased through the woods, driven forward by the hot breath of a faceless terror.

All he could do was light a lantern and start his day. He would go to the Wood Shed and sharpen all the axes and mauls. Once he finished the indoor work, he would string a rope between two trees in the wood lot, hang a lantern from it, and split wood through the night.

When the sun went down, he went to the Craft Shop to either make more charcoal or work on the big forge.

The rest of the crew worked all day just to provide Latin with enough wood to split. They cut and hauled and sawed disks, then Latin chopped. The rest of the gild picked up the pieces, stacked them and went for more. The stacks grew out toward the marker strings and end posts, filling up the yard until it became difficult to turn the wagons around. They started driving the wagons in, throwing the uncut logs off one side, and pulling straight out of the other side.

At one point, he nearly had to stop because of blisters on his hands, but then Annette talked someone in the Craft Gild into making Latin a pair of work gloves from scraps of leather. With the gloves and a rising supply of protein coming in from early beans, Latin hoped to be able to finish the one hundred fifty cords before he wore himself out, assuming he could avoid injury.

CHAPTER 40

Autumn was startled awake from a midmorning nap on the exam table by frantic knocking on the infirmary door. Trader Jack stepped in and said, "Autumn, there are men from Winterthur House. It's an emergency. They've sent for you. They've sent for you specifically. I have my horse here. I'm to bring you to Winterthur House immediately. Their men are waiting up the street to accompany us, serve as lookouts, and get us safely there."

Autumn leaped off the bench. "I'm ready. Let me grab my things and we can go."

Autumn climbed up behind Trader Jack on his horse. He clicked twice, and the horse sped down the narrow streets of Arden House at a fast trot. Once they met the other men by the barn, they headed off together, building speed until they were rushing down an open path at a staggering gallop that Autumn did not believe the horses could sustain for long. They raced in formation for miles. They went through a long series of ruins and dead places, then into a section of woods and open fields. They darted across a ramshackle bridge that spanned a large creek. They ran through twists and turns of faint trails in the woods, until finally they raced through an open iron gate in a massive stone wall. Autumn looked back to see four men in ornate green armor closing the gate behind them.

Inside the gate, the road was smooth and the fields were all meticulously plowed and planted. The horses slowed to a gentle trot. In the distance, placed along the tree line at the far edges of the fields, Autumn saw several tall wooden platforms with roofs. On the closest watch tower, Autumn counted six men in brilliant green uniforms holding binoculars, long telescopes, and enormous guns.

They rode along a gracefully curving road between two lush wheat fields. A massive herd of immaculate black and white cows stood grazing in a rich pasture beside a barn. At a place where the road divided, the company turned right and crossed a finely built bridge over a little creek. They ducked through a tangle of wooded paths to emerge from the woods at the front door of the largest, most ornate building Autumn had ever seen.

The square building was seven stories tall, freshly painted light brown, and perfectly pristine. There were magnificent rows of potted flowers along stone paths leading down to a concrete pool. Other paths curved away joining garden walks that lead to bathhouses and a terraced array of ponds. Beside the largest pool, there was a huge fountain with water gushing out of a spire in the center. There were ornate wrought-iron benches along every path and in most corners.

A drawbridge stretched over a sizable moat operated by a complex series of weights and chains to raise it instantly at the first sound of an alarm. The front door alone was built from enough wood to properly construct a comfortable, sturdy home.

Autumn slid off the back of Trader Jack's horse and stood staring at the house, her mouth hanging open. Her nose savored the wonderful smell of roasting meat on the afternoon breeze.

Trader Jack left his horse with the men who had accompanied them and went with Autumn across the bridge to the door where a still, clean-shaven old man in a black gown greeted them.

"Greetings, Jack. Miss Autumn, I presume? Welcome to Winterthur House. My name is Gerald. I am pleased to meet you. Thank you for coming so quickly. You are, of course, expected. Please follow me."

They followed Gerald up several grand staircases and down a long, clean hallway with oil paintings hung on both sides. Gerald showed them into a plain office with two men and a woman in ornate robes and new leather shoes. The woman wore an entire town's worth of jewelry, all gold. Gerald left without a word and closed the door.

Jack walked across the room, extended his hand to the men, and said,

"Lord Bilston, Doctor Watkins, it is a pleasure to see you again, though I wish it was under better circumstances. Please allow me to introduce Miss Autumn. Autumn, this is Lord Bilston and Doctor Watkins."

"Thank you for coming so quickly," Lord Bilston said as they shook hands.

Autumn said, "I was told the situation was urgent. How can I be of service?"

Doctor Watkins said, "Not at all, I expect.", snippily.

"Excuse me?"

Bilston intervened, "Please excuse the Doctor. I have requested your help over his strenuous objections. He feels certain that there is nothing to be done about this terrible situation."

Autumn said, "I'm afraid that's often so. What's the situation?"

The bejeweled lady, who had been looking tearfully out a tall window, covered her face with her gloved hands and swished, weeping, toward the door. She raced out and slammed the door loudly.

Lord Bilston continued, "Well, that's a sensitive topic. I have to ask that you keep to yourself what you see and do here today. There has been a good deal of opposition to inviting you here—not just from the Doctor, but we have heard rumors of your skills and I felt there was no choice but to try. I must ask that you swear never to tell anyone what you see here."

Before the Trader Jack could respond, Autumn said, "We are Quakers. We do not swear. I only speak for myself in that I have no intention of ever speaking of the specifics of whatever the situation is here, no matter how it is resolved, so long as I live."

Lord Bilston nodded, one eyebrow raised.

Trader Jack nodded.

Lord Bilston hesitated, appraising Autumn.

She said, "There must be a trust between us in order for me to treat any sick person. If you trust me to give medicine and perform procedures, it stands to reason that you would trust my word that I will keep these facts to myself."

Lord Bilston nodded and said, "Agreed."

Doctor Watkins blurted, "It's a plague. All the children of the court have it. Fever, paralysis, black fingers, blue lips…there's nothing to be done about it. We've quarantined them, which is for the best. God have mercy on their souls."

"Children? How many are sick?"

The Doctor and Lord Bilston looked at each other.

Lord Bilston nodded to affirm his trust in Autumn.

The doctor said, "Eighteen."

Autumn went pale. She looked up at the ceiling and took a half-step back to regain her balance. After recovering, she asked, "Eighteen? That is not all of the children, is it?"

"All of the courtly children."

Confused, Autumn said, "I apologize, I don't know what that means. There are other children?"

Rolling his eyes, Watkins said, "These are all of the children of the families of the court."

Autumn asked again, "But there are other children?"

"Yes, of course, the workers and house people, but we are not concerned with them right now. They are not why you are here."

"I understand, but are they sick the same way?"

Watkins and Bilston looked to each other and shrugged.

Autumn said, "Well, there is not much benefit to keeping these sick children quarantined if whatever they have is, in fact, contagious and the rest of the children are sick in the same way, running about with their families."

Watkins said, "I'm sure they're fine. If there were a problem, we would know."

"The eighteen who are sick, can I see them?"

Watkins said, "You can see them through a window, but if you go in— if there's any kind of contact—we cannot let you out until we are sure you are not infected, which would take two weeks."

Autumn raised an eyebrow, shrugged and said, "Okay, I'll see them through the window."

Watkins said, "Just you, Miss, not the Trader."

Autumn planted her feet. "Where I go, he goes," she said.

Bilston agreed.

They left the office, turned right, and continued down a long hallway past many doors. At the end of the hall, on the left, was a heavy steel door with a diamond-shaped glass window in the center.

Watkins motioned for Autumn to step forward and look.

Autumn had to rise up on her toes a bit to see in. She gasped and stepped away. After a deep breath, she stepped forward again and looked longer, then she turned to Watkins, hot with anger. "What did you do, just pile them in there? This is disgraceful! Disgraceful! If this is how you treat your sick…you're savages. You're worse than savages. I don't care how rich you are. Mattresses on the floor? You left them in there alone!"

Doctor Watkins began to speak in defense of the conditions, but Autumn raised her hand to silence him. The sharpness of the gesture caught Watkins off guard, forcing him to stop talking out of shock.

Autumn looked intensely through the window again and asked for Trader Jack's binoculars. She looked though the window with the binoculars, adjusting the focus and bobbing up and down on her toes for several minutes.

The Doctor tried to interrupt her a few times, but she quickly silenced him with sharp, angry stares.

Eventually, she stepped back and said, "Okay, let's take things as they are and start with what we have. I was brought here to work. I came to work. I will do what I can, but, first, I need to talk to Lord Bilston, alone."

"Fine with me," Doctor Watkins huffed. "Jack, let me show you to the parlor. I am sure you have things to discuss with Trader Tom. He's looking forward to talking with you while you're here."

Trader Jack and Doctor Watkins walked down the hallway, leaving Autumn and Lord Bilston alone.

Autumn said, "Could we sit down and talk for a moment? I need to sit for a moment, please."

Lord Bilston said, "Of course, yes. Let us go to back my office. We will have privacy there."

They walked down several flights of plain stairs, through a pair of double wooden doors, through a short portico, and into a library with a ceiling so high that Autumn could not see it clearly.

One wall of the library was solid glass, held in place by thin metal bars. The other three sides were filled with wooden bookshelves from floor to ceiling. There were statues and works of art in each of a hundred alcoves and arches. Globes, framed copies of handwritten documents, and books stood majestically in ornate cases. Thousands and thousands of books of all colors and sizes were stacked neatly in each of a thousand shelves.

Lord Bilston sat in a massive oak chair with dark red leather padding and lion's heads carved into the armrests. He showed Autumn to a simpler chair at the edge of his desk. "Have a seat. Take a moment. Would you like something to drink?"

Autumn nodded, "Yes, please. Anything would be fine. Thank you."

Lord Bilston reached under the desk and pulled a rope. "Someone will be in shortly."

Although her thoughts whirled around her rapidly, Autumn took a deep breath, held the arms of her chair and said, "Lord Bilston, I am afraid that it is likely your doctor is right, there may be nothing I can do for them. It is probable that those beautiful children are already lost to us, no matter what."

Lord Bilston shook his head gravely, and Autumn caught the beginnings of a tear forming in his right eye, but there was a quick knock from somewhere behind her.

"Come in," Bilston called, collecting himself quickly.

A young girl in a light green smock came through a wooden panel that Autumn would never have guessed was a door.

Bilston said, "Refreshments for two."

The girl left, silently.

Autumn continued, "However, it is also possible that I may be able to save them, or at least some of them."

Bilston's face brightened as he looked to Autumn for hope.

"In order to find out if I can help, I would have to risk my own life by going in there. As you can imagine, as much as I would like to try to help, I am obliged to prevent myself from getting sick as well."

"Of course. I understand," Bilston agreed.

"Let me be clear. There are situations in which I would go through that door and do everything in my power to help your children."

"There are? What do you mean?"

"I would require two things from you. First, help and supplies. I need someone to send for my nurse at Arden House. She must be brought here immediately and safely, so I can begin my work. Also, I will need extra rooms along the hallway where the children are. Three rooms at least, in addition to the room the children are already in. We must expand the quarantine area to include the long hallway at the top of the stairs."

"Of course," said Bilston.

"Also, we will need a steady supply of boiling water, fresh linens, food, lanterns, and such, all to be delivered to a point outside the quarantine. My nurse and I will carry everything into the hallway ourselves. Nothing leaves until the sickness is over."

"All of that can be easily provided."

"I did not see a fireplace in the room where the children are. How is it heated?"

"Hot water runs through the radiator on the wall."

"How is it controlled?"

"By a switch on the wall."

"Are all of the rooms on that hallway heated?"

"They can be. There are knobs on the radiators; open them to heat the room. I apologize for the conditions the children were left in. You were right to take issue. Our people are absolutely beside themselves with fear, of course. The contagious—"

Bilston was interrupted by the girl in the green frock knocking twice on the wooden panel.

"Come," said Bilston.

She swept across the library in one silent motion, left a silver tray on a side table next to Bilston's desk, and exited the library without looking at anything except the ground in front of her.

The silver platter held a glass pitcher of apple cider, a pot of fresh tea, a plate of shortbread cookies, a loaf of bread with steam rising from it, a bunch of grapes, a wedge of cheese, and a half-carafe of red wine.

Autumn looked at the food and her stomach rumbled. She was unable to hide her appetite.

"Please help yourself, don't be polite; eat. I know you must be hungry," Bilston said, handing Autumn a glistening china plate.

She tried not to be greedy, but took a little of everything from the platter and poured herself a generous glass of cider.

"Do you really think you can save them, some of them?" Bilston asked after giving Autumn time to eat.

"Lord Bilston, I am afraid that some of them may have already passed away. If there is anything I can do to help the ones that are left, it must be done quickly—today, this afternoon. That is the one thing I am absolutely sure of."

Bilston nodded and said, "Agreed. I will send riders to Arden House to get your nurse and have those other rooms cleared so that you can use them immediately. Thank you for trying to help."

Bilston reached under the desk to pull on a rope, but Autumn stopped him by saying sharply, "I have not agreed to do anything yet. I said that I required two agreements. The first was for supplies. I am confident that you will provide what is required."

Bilston sat back in his chair, "I suppose the second agreement has to do with payment?"

Autumn nodded, swallowed, and said, "I have not yet decided if this attempt to help is worth risking my own life. This may bring a pointless end to my lifetime of training and medical experience, while providing no value at all to me or to Arden House."

Lord Bilston looked irritated and confused. He said, "As you can see, there is considerable wealth here. Winterthur House is well stocked. We have more than enough influence to reach equitable terms after this issue is resolved."

"Oh, I respect that, I do. But, before I step in that room, I must insist that we agree on fair terms of compensation, in writing."

"In writing?"

"In writing, yes. A verbal contract would be acceptable with multiple witnesses, but considering your desire to keep this matter secret, I expect you would prefer a written contract?"

Lord Bilston nodded in disbelief, then stood. "No. Absolutely not. That is out of the question. I will not enter into a written contract with..."

Autumn stood to leave, saying, "Very well. I will go now. Thank you for the refreshments. If you ever change your mind and decide you want an expertly trained doctor in an emergency, and you are willing to agree to fair terms, please feel free to send for me again and I will not hold this decision against you."

Lord Bilston let Autumn get all the way to the library door before he stopped her.

"Wait, wait. Please, a moment. Sit?" His voice shook a little as he spoke.

Autumn came back and stood before the chair beside the desk. After she sat, he sat. Bilston opened a drawer and pulled out a clean, white square of paper and a large black fountain pen. He dipped the pen in the inkwell and wrote, "Contract," across the top in large, clear letters.

He looked across the desk at Autumn, "I expect you have specific terms in mind?"

"Those cows I saw on the way in, those are amazing animals."

"You want cows?"

"No. I am not the Arden House Trader, so I cannot speak for us in the matter of trades. Only our Trader does that, as you know. He has a reputation as a fair dealer and he is entrusted to speak for Arden House on trade issues. I will not do anything to risk his reputation or get in the way of him doing his job. What we need, you and I, is some currency. We need some way to transfer bargaining power to Trader Jack so that he can work with your Trader to exchange the things Arden House needs and Winterthur House has."

Bilston looked impressed, if not a bit challenged. He said, "Why don't we use gold? That would be simple enough."

Without pause, Autumn said, "Because gold is of no use to Arden House without an agreement about a specific quantity of value that Winterthur House would be willing to part with in exchange for that gold. Gold doesn't help us, so let's talk about cows."

"Cows can help us?"

"Yes, ten healthy cows, delivered safely to the Arden House barn. That's a helpful value, isn't it? If you and I were to agree, between us, in secret, that Winterthur House were to owe Arden House ten healthy cows, delivered, and we agree to that in writing, then we can let our traders do their work."

"How?"

"Without disclosing our terms, we can let our traders know that Winterthur House owes Arden House ten imaginary cows. They can barter and work out whatever deals make sense at the time. We get our value in return for my work, and, if my trader, at any point, is not satisfied with the progress of the bartering, he can fall back on the original terms that we put in writing here and demand delivery of ten healthy, real cows. Although, the terms of the agreement, of course, would no longer be secret."

Lord Bilston hesitated.

"Don't worry, Lord Bilston, you have my word that I will never let the terms of this agreement be known to anyone except Trader Jack, and you already trust him. You can write it into the contract. If I ever disclose the terms, our contract becomes void."

Lord Bilston thought for some time. He stared out the wall of windows, looking over the fountains, sculptures, and emerald ferns. "I've never drawn up this type of contract before. This feels crooked, but I'm not sure how. And besides, ten cows a hefty price. We have had whole barns raised for less than that."

Autumn nodded. "Yes, it is a considerable sum. I expect the terms of the contract seem strange to you because they provide equal leverage on both sides, and you are probably accustomed to having all of the leverage."

Lord Bilston's face flashed angrily for the first time. He said, "You know, I don't appreciate your taking advantage of us like this. This is a disgusting time to come to me with a sharp trade like this. I don't feel comfortable negotiating these terms while those children are up there getting sicker. It's like you're preying on sick children!"

Coldly and completely without anger, Autumn nodded in agreement. "Yes. You are right about that. This is a squalid, seedy business. It is uncomfortable for us both. I apologize."

Lord Bilston stood, took a deep breath, then poured himself a glass of wine. After a drink, he said, "How do I know that this is not a trick, that you will not take the contract, do nothing to help the children, forget about bartering, and collect your cows on the way out?"

Autumn, expecting this exact question, replied, "Because the terms I propose are this: if my nurse and I catch what the children have and we all die, you owe Arden House nothing, but please feel free to give whatever you choose to as a donation in our honor. If all your sick children die, we get nothing. You owe Arden House nothing. I want that written into the contract. There is no payment due unless lives are saved. However, for every child that walks out of that room on their own, you owe Arden House the trade equivalent of ten healthy, delivered cows."

Lord Bilston was stunned. He sat down out of a fear that he might pass out and fall. "Ten cows per child? If you manage to save them all, that would be half of our herd! That's far too much. Far, far too much. That could take us years to pay back in trade. Each one of those cows is worth a year's field labor, at least. That's preposterous! Walk out if you like; I'll never agree to that. You can go."

Autumn did not move. Bilston's anger was genuine, but she knew it would subside.

Lord Bilston got up and lit his pipe, pacing around the library. The more he walked and smoked, the more nervous he became. Autumn didn't say a word, letting him stew. Finally, Bilston said, "Eight."

Autumn raised an eyebrow. "Eight?"

"Eight."

Autumn said, "Ten. It's ten. Also, I will honor my promise not to discuss with Lady Bilston the fact that you tried to barter with the lives of your family's children. Remember, if I cannot save them, the terms of our agreement will never be known. If I can save them, you look generous. I will never reveal that we agreed to terms ahead of time. Only the traders will know. To everyone else, you will look like a thankful, generous father."

Lord Bilston let out an enormous, exasperated sigh, then sat at his desk and wrote on the paper for several minutes. When finished, he handed the paper to Autumn and said, "Where are you from? Where did you get your training? Were you born into a prestigious family? Did you attend some formal school far away?"

Autumn did not respond, but focused on reading the contract.

When she finished, she asked for the pen, signed the contract under Bilston's signature, folded it, and handed it back to Bilston. "Do you have a seal?" she asked.

Bilston lit a candle and drew an ancient wooden handle with one brass end from the lowest drawer of his great desk. He dripped a puddle of red wax from the candle onto the fold in the contract and mashed the brass seal into it, making a sharp, clear script "W" in the wax. Autumn blew twice on the seal, shook hands with Bilston, and slipped the contract into the breast pocket of her vest.

"I need to get to work, your Lordship. Please send for my nurse as fast as you can. I'll need those beds delivered as quickly as possible, with linens, washcloths, towels, and soap. If you give me a pad of paper, I will leave notes at the end of the hall for the other things we'll need."

"Very well. I will see to it that you have everything you need."

CHAPTER 41

Autumn took a long look through the diamond-shaped window. "I'm not sure I'm up to this," she said to herself before she put her hand on the door, took a deep breath, and went inside.

The smell and heat were overwhelming. Autumn started to wretch and back out of the room, but she stopped herself, covered her mouth and nose, and leaned forward, pressing in. She staggered past the children on the floor and went directly to the window and opened it. After several deep breaths of clean air, she turned to the children.

Some were semi-conscious; their eyes were open, but their faces were stiff and their eyes were drooping. They were paralyzed, drooling, and their fingers had turned black, but they did not have fevers. Autumn propped the door open with her backpack.

Their lips and eyelids were blue, although some were worse than others. "You poor little things, you poor little things," Autumn kept muttering under her breath.

Hearing noise out in the hallway, she went to oversee the arrival of beds and supplies. A line of young men dressed in the working clothes of Winterthur servants approached her slowly down the hallway, each carrying a canvas mattress. They stopped fifteen feet up the hallway, and Autumn said, "Come on, come on, they go in these rooms here."

The first boy in line nodded and pointed at the open door where the sick children were.

Rolling her eyes, Autumn closed the door. "Okay? Now please come open these other rooms up and put those mattresses down, four in each room? Thank you."

The working boys all looked healthy. They worked quickly and left.

Autumn saw a pair of young girls setting up a table and pile of supplies at the far end of the hallway. After they were done, she went down and got an armload of towels, a bar of soap, and a kettle of hot water.

Autumn started cleaning and examining the smaller children and carrying them into the other rooms with mattresses of their own, clean sheets, blankets, and pillows. As she moved the children, she gave each one a number, which she wrote on the backs of their hands with a charcoal pencil. She made notes in her notebook about the condition of each child by number. She set up three rooms for children and one room for a combination of supplies and dirty linens, soiled clothes, and wash buckets.

Autumn had never seen anything remotely like their symptoms. The first ten were all breathing shallowly and had stiff muscles, drooping eyes, black fingers, and pale skin, but no rashes or spots or bumps of any kind. A few had soiled themselves, and there was a little vomit, but nothing she couldn't clean up with hot water and towels.

As she wrote an 11 on a little boy's hand, Autumn felt that his arm was not stiff, and her heart sank. When she checked, her fear was confirmed; the little boy was dead. She carried him into the room with the supplies and dirty linens and covered him with a sheet. She crossed the 11 off his hand and wrote the letter A. She stood over him for a moment. When tears started to well up in her eyes, she turned away and went back into the first room. She wiped her eyes with the back of her arm and wrote 11 on the hand of the next child, a four-year-old red-haired girl. Autumn examined her and went back to making notes.

Autumn shook her head in disbelief every time she wrote, No fever. "How can they be this sick without a fever?" she asked herself. "Their doctor said there was fever. Maybe they had fevers before, but not now? More likely their doctor never got within ten feet of them out of fear of getting sick himself."

As she scurried about, moving and cleaning, her mind raced, gathering information, noting symptoms, wondering what might be causing this illness, and forming guesses about what might be done to help the poor children.

She left a note on the table at the top of the stairs requesting lye soap, clear alcohol, boiling water, chicken soup, tea, bread, cheese, eggs, and apples.

"Autumn, where are you? It's Susan. Are you here? What's going on?"

"Yes, oh, Susan, I'm so glad you're here; come on back."

"Is it safe?"

"I think so, but to be honest, I'm not entirely sure."

"There are supplies and food out here on a table at the top of the stairs, should I bring them?"

"Yes please, bring whatever you can carry. Hang on, I'll come help."

Autumn and Susan hugged. Susan was shaking with fear. "What's going on?" she asked.

"Seventeen sick kids. I don't know what they have. One has died already, and I fear there's not much to be done. I have some ideas, though. Bring the hot water, and I'll explain."

"Is it contagious?"

"I don't think so. They don't have fevers and they all got sick at exactly the same time, which means they probably didn't spread it between themselves. Plus, there are other kids in town who are not sick and none of the adults are sick."

"That's strange."

"There's a lot about this that's strange."

"Chicken soup, bread, hard-boiled eggs, and cheese? What symptoms do those treat?"

"Hunger. That's for us. Do you have any idea how well they eat around here?"

"Really? This is for us?"

"Yes, really. Dig in, eat up. I'm going to order steaks later. How do you like yours cooked?"

"Autumn?"

"I'm sorry. I don't want to complain, but, Susan, I'm hungry. I've been hungry for weeks. I know you've been hungry much longer than that. They have food here, tons of it. Enjoy."

While they stood in the hallway eating, Autumn looked at her notes and said, "I've given the children numbers on their hands. When we're done eating, I want to shuffle them around." Pointing in sequence, Autumn said, "This is Room 1, that's Room 2, and this is Room 3. The supply room is there—just be careful, I put the dead little boy in there under a sheet." Autumn checked her notebook. "After we've eaten, I'd like to put numbers 1, 2, 7, 9, and 13 in Room 1. Room 2 will get 3, 8, 10, 14, 16, and 17, and 4, 5, 6, 8, 11, 12, and 15 go in Room 3."

Susan raised an eyebrow, "Why?"

Autumn finished chewing a large roll with butter, took a sip of tea, and explained, "I think that will give us the best cross section of symptom progression, age, and gender."

"Why? What does that matter?"

"Well, since I really have no idea what is making these kids sick, I don't know what I can do to help them. If we only had one sick kid with these strange symptoms, I would have to take a guess, give that kid some kind of medicine, and hope it works."

"More sick kids is a good thing?"

"Well, no, but we have to deal with the situation that's in front of us, and with seventeen sick kids, we can try different things on each one. Then, we watch them all. If any of them starts to get better, we look at our notes, and maybe switch all the others to whatever we were doing for the ones that got better."

Susan finished her soup. "That's clever," she said.

"Not my idea of course, this approach is thousands of years old."

"Still, pretty clever."

"Let's hope it works. Are you ready, ready to get to it?"

"I am. After we shuffle them around, what's the plan?" Susan asked, finishing her tea.

Autumn flipped through the pages of her notebook. "I have three working theories, so I'll treat each room with one theory. In Room 1, we'll treat as if they all share a common parasite in their nervous systems. I don't know which specific one might cause these symptoms, but the paralysis without a fever and the black fingers make me think it might be a parasite. It's a guess. They could have gotten it from bad water or something else, although those kinds of things would probably affect more than this group. But it's one of the best guesses I have so far. The good news for the Room 1 kids is that I have a lot of medicine for them. My mother and I have a successful treatment, proven against all kinds of parasites. We make it from wormwood, cloves, and black walnut. It takes almost a full week to make a single batch, but we had just made some this winter and I brought a lot of it with me. It's an injection, which means we'll spend a lot of time sterilizing the needle kit between kids, but that's something we can do together. Dandelion leaf tea, made extremely strong, also helps with parasites, sometimes, and I have some dried Dandelion leaf in my kit. Of the six kids in Room 1, we'll try the injection on two of them. Two will get the dandelion tea, and two we'll give both the tea and the injection."

"Have you ever done both at the same time before?"

"No, and we're not going to give tentative doses, either. They'll get full adult doses because we must see results that are immediate and obvious. If we need to reduce dosages later, we can."

"Okay, what about Room 2?"

"We're going to treat Room 2 for poisoning. I don't know if these symptoms could be caused by some kind of bad food, but we'll try. For poisoning, the main treatments are usually ipecac to make them vomit and charcoal to help absorb whatever is left in their stomachs. They tell me these poor kids have been sick for several days, so I don't think there's any benefit to making them vomit at this point, but we can certainly give them charcoal. We also have an effective antitoxin, Queening Oil, that we can prepare in a tea. I'm not sure how we'll get them to drink that just yet, as their faces are mostly paralyzed, but we'll figure something out. The charcoal would work against the tea, so there's no need to give anyone both of them. We'll divide Room 2 in half and give half charcoal and half the Queening Oil tea."

"Got it. Room 3?"

"Those five are going to be our outliers. Each one of them is going to get a shot-in-the-dark, unlikely-but-possible treatment, just in case neither of my two main theories work out. Most of these will come from the medicines we inherited from Lady. I'll see to the patients in Room 3 myself and have you tend Rooms 1 and 2. I'll make notes of exactly what kinds of medicines and treatments each kid gets and when. I'll put a piece of paper on the door of each room where we can keep track of what we've already given them and how they're responding."

"Let's get to work, then?"

"Oh, and there's also Patient A."

"A?"

"In the supply room, under the sheet. He died before I started. If anyone else dies, we'll change them from their number to the letter B, so we don't get confused. I'm considering opening him up and looking at his organs to see if I can learn anything that might help us better treat the others."

"Oh my goodness," Susan gasped, pale.

"I know, it's difficult to think about, but there might be something helpful in there. He might be able to teach us something."

"I know, but still, I would not want to have to explain to that little boy's parents why his body is all cut up."

"That's true, but I also don't want to explain to any other parents that their children are dead if I didn't do everything I could to save them because I was unwilling to do an unseemly or uncomfortable task that might have helped. That would be selfish of me."

"I don't know. Perhaps you're right?"

"Okay, this food will do us good. Let's get to work. I'll write the instructions for each number. You drag or carry the kids where they need to go. We'll move the big ones together. Once that's done, I'll get to work on Patient A and Room 3 while you work in Rooms 1 and 2."

CHAPTER 42

"Paul, can I ask you a question?"

"Sure, Latin."

"I sprained my wrist yesterday. It's no big deal, but I need to take it easy today or it'll get worse."

"Sorry to hear that. Put yourself on light duty as long as you need."

"Actually, I was wondering…I know we're not all the way done, but we've made a lot of progress and it looks like we're going to be at our goal soon. I wonder if it would be okay for me to take the day to fire up the big forge? If it works, we could be working with lighter splitting mauls in two days, which would make us all more efficient and less prone to injury."

"Yeah, go."

"Really?"

"Sure, you're not going to be any use around here with a sprained wrist."

Latin got David to take the day off from the Craft Gild and help him with the forge. They carefully selected the best looking bits of scrap metal and started the fire with kindling, twigs, sticks and logs before converting to charcoal. Latin regulated the airflow with their newly designed ports, getting the fire hotter and hotter, gradually and evenly.

The molds sat off to the side, ready for pouring. The forge looked impressive, and the rising sound of air being sucked in through the side ports gave Latin confidence that his new ventilation system was working as expected.

While waiting for the forge to heat, Latin and David carved finishing touches on the wooden handles they had made in anticipation of their new axe heads.

CHAPTER 43

Susan was working back and forth between Rooms 1 and 2 when Autumn stepped out of the supply room with a pale and desperate look in her eyes.

"What is it?"

"I've examined Patient A."

"Oh? Come sit. Here, there's tea. Drink tea? Is it bad news? What did you see?"

"Where is the alcohol?"

"It's on the table in Room 2."

"Could you get it for me, please?" Autumn asked, leaning against the wall in the hallway.

When Susan handed the bottle to Autumn, she said, "Here you go, is there something I can help disinfect?"

"No," Autumn said, drinking directly from the bottle. "I need air. Do those doors open out onto the balcony?"

"I don't know; I didn't try them."

"Let's go."

Susan forced the balcony doors open, and they sat on the floor outside in the cool night.

"Oh, that's better, the smells were starting to get to me," Autumn said, drinking from the bottle again, then offering it to Susan.

"It only bothers me a little," she said, taking a sip.

"How is the tube working to get the oil down their throats?"

"It works well now. I had a difficult time with the first few, but I figured out how to get it in there without making a mess."

"Are any of them looking different? Better?"

"Not better. Not yet. They all look like they're getting worse still, but it's only been a few hours."

"Do you want more of this?" Autumn said, offering the bottle to Susan again.

"Maybe a little," she said, taking another sip.

"His liver was enlarged, Patient A. That doesn't change my thinking much. I suppose his liver would be enlarged with parasites or poison or a thousand other things."

"So I should not change any of the instructions for Rooms 1 or 2?"

"No, keep them the same. If any of those are going to work, we'll probably know by morning."

"Are you going back to work in Room 3?"

"I am. Are you feeling okay? I mean, besides tired? No numbness, no tingling, no changes to your vision, no symptoms?"

"I could use sleep, like you, but, no, I feel fine."

"Good, me too. Let me know if anything changes. I'll send a note that we'll need a new pot of tea."

"Autumn?"

"Yes?"

"Could I ask a favor?"

"Sure, Susan, what?"

"Could you ask for coffee?"

"Coffee? They have coffee?"

"I've heard rumors that they do. Tea would be fine, but if they have coffee—oh, I would be so thankful. I've only had it a few times, but I do love the taste of coffee. That's not wrong of me, is it, to ask? I feel silly asking for something like that with all these children so deathly sick."

Autumn nodded, saying, "There's nothing wrong with it. I'll put coffee on the list, for sure, as well as cream and sugar. We'll see if they have it."

Hours later, just before dawn, while they were savoring their first sips of hot coffee in the supply room by lantern light, Autumn said, "Room 3 is a mess. They're all getting much worse. I think poor 12 is almost gone.

How are yours?"

"Room 2 is bad; their breathing is getting shallower and shorter, and their lips are getting blue. But Room 1 is not so bad. I think 2 and 3 might actually be getting better some, but that could be wishful thinking and the lack of sleep affecting my judgment."

"Can you remind me, what are 2 and 3 on?"

Before Susan could answer, they heard a cough and a groaning voice call out, "Water?"

"What is that?"

"It's in Room 1."

"Someone's getting better."

CHAPTER 44

A few curious Friends gathered in the back yard of the Craft Shop late in the morning as Latin and David heated up the forge. The rush of air through the ventilation ducts made a hollow roar.

Just as Latin was reaching in with long tongs to open the side door and take out the crucible, there was a deep, crunching pop.

The entire forge structure slid and fell in on itself, shaking the ground. The crucible shattered under the weight of the bricks and cinder blocks, and liquid, molten metal spurted out in three directions, spraying wings of fire into the dry grass.

Latin, David, and a few others scurried into the chaos with what little water they had on hand in buckets and water bottles. They sent others rushing off to the well for more water, but managed to stamp the fire out before the first bucket arrived.

The only lasting damage was that Latin had caught one of his moccasins on fire.

After the crowd had left, David and Latin were cleaning up the mess when Arthur walked into the yard, slightly out of breath.

"My goodness," he said.

"We had a minor…Well, actually quite a major—um, it fell in."

"I see. Was anyone injured?"

"No, only Latin's pride," David joked.

"We're fine. Well, my moccasins, they're likely ruined."

"Latin, I have news."

"Is it Autumn? Have we heard from Winterthur?"

"No, not a word since Susan left. I'm sure they're fine. The news is that you have a visitor."

"A visitor?"

"Yes, for you, waiting in the Peace Room."

Latin left the rest of the cleaning to David and went back toward Arden House with Arthur at an eager pace.

CHAPTER 45

Trader Jack rode into town alone, stopping along the way to ask those working in the fields to please go to Arden House to help unload incoming wagons.

"All of us?"

"Yes."

"Incoming trade?"

"Yes, incoming trade to unload."

Trader Jack found Constable Pete along the Stile Path and said, "Pete, we're coming in with a big load of trade goods from Winterthur, and four of the big Bellevue wagons are about five minutes behind me. Along the way, we saw a mob of Skullers down in the hollow of Beaver Valley. Could you take a crew out to the intersection of Miller and Marsh to make sure they didn't follow us?"

"Of course. I'll round up the men and get out there."

"Maybe send a scout up to Naamans? I don't think they followed us, but we want to be sure."

"Did they attack the wagons?"

"No, in fact it looked like we caught them off guard."

"What were they doing? How many of them were there?"

"A lot, like thirty-five, and it was all men, no women or children."

"That's not good."

"You know, my gut told me when I saw them that they were lining up to make an attack on Granola House."

"Really?"

"I know it doesn't make any sense, but that's what it looked like."

"Okay, I'll watch behind the caravan and post two men overnight out there."

Word spread quickly through town and a large crowd had already gathered in the front yard of Arden House when a heavy wagon from Bellevue turned the corner from Miller Road. An excited ripple spread through the crowd. As the first huge wagon came around the corner, Autumn was sitting up on the bench with the driver of the four-horse rig. A second rig turned the corner with Susan beside its driver.

Latin burst into the Peace Room. There was a pretty lady dressed in black standing there, smiling at him. She looked familiar. Latin was confused for several seconds, then said, "Mrs. Murphy?"

"Yes, it's me, Latin. It's good to see you."

"What? How? I don't understand," Latin stammered.

Arthur explained, "Well, Latin, Mrs. Murphy has been a Friend of Arden House for many years. We have not seen her in a while, but she was visiting Longwood House and heard news of our new Healer being sent to Winterthur…"

"I knew at once that it was Autumn, of course, so I came to say hello and bring news from home. You still have the three razors you sharpened for me?"

"I do, yes, of course. Not with me, but back where I…in the…"

"Well, good. After we have time to catch up, I wonder if we might talk alone."

"Your letter! You gave me a letter to deliver to Miss Turner that night Autumn and I left. I completely forgot about it, oh no."

"Don't worry, it got there fine. She got the letter. Your grandmother must have found it in your things."

"My grandparents? Are they…?"

"Latin, they're perfectly well and healthy, or at least they were when I saw them last. Much has changed back home since you left. We'll talk about that later."

As Latin relaxed slightly, there was a tremendous cheer from out in the yard. Arthur went to the window. "Oh my goodness," he said. "Come look at this."

Everyone in Arden House was gathered around four big carriages in the street.

"We better go down and see what's happening," Arthur said.

Without ceremony, Autumn jumped down from the riding bench atop the first wagon and leaned over to whisper in Ruth's ear.

"These four wagons are filled with trade for Arden House from Winterthur House. Lord Bilston sends his thanks for our assistance in helping them with a medical emergency."

Ruth stammered, "What?"

Autumn said, "These wagons are filled with food. All four of them. Cheese, lentils, nuts, jerky, wheat flour, cooking oil, eggs, bacon, salted fish, and such. We'll pull those around and unload them directly into the Gild Hall, that will make it easier to stock the pantry."

Ruth said, "Are you serious?"

Autumn nodded.

"Guess what else?" Autumn said.

Ruth said, "I can't imagine."

"Coffee and tea. At least a hundred pounds of each."

"A hundred pounds of tea?"

Autumn nodded.

"And we don't owe them anything in return?"

"No, in fact, they owe us. Trust me, Lord Bilston is most pleased with this trade."

"What did we give him?"

Autumn said, "A miracle."

Ruth hugged her.

Autumn said, "Winterthur House has paid the men from Bellevue House to make this delivery, and I've taken the liberty of contributing a modest token or our appreciation to Bellevue House by letting the captain and a few of his men take their pick of gifts from the shipment. I hope that's okay."

Ruth nodded emphatically, "Oh yes, yes, of course."

Autumn continued, "I've also agreed that the Friends of Arden House will unload the wagons, so we'll need to make an announcement and get that started so these men can be on their way. Can I help you up on the carriage to make an announcement?"

Ruth said, "Oh no, you do it. You tell them. It's your news, you tell them."

"Are you sure?"

"Yes, go."

Latin, Arthur, and Mrs. Murphy came out to see Autumn climb up onto the top of the first carriage.

She spoke loudly so that everyone could hear, "Friends of Arden House, I have been asked to share this news with you and ask for your help. The news is that our hungry times are over. These four wagons are filled with food."

A wave of questioning excitement radiated out from the carriage.

"There is enough beef jerky, eggs, beans, peas, cheese, and lentils in these four carriages to see us through until our own crops are ready for harvest."

The news did not settle in immediately. Autumn saw puzzled looks.

"Arden House, starting tonight will have enough food for every one of us to have meat and cheese at every meal. Tomorrow morning, we'll have tea with breakfast. The children will have all they can eat, three times a day."

Cheers, clapping, and joyous yells went on for several minutes. Every mother cried.

As soon as she could shout loud enough to be heard, Autumn said, "Friends, Friends...We need to unload all of this and take it into the storage rooms, the kitchen, and the pantry. I'm sure many hands will make light work of that task, but before we start, I want us to..."

Autumn welled up with tears and struggled to choke back sobs that caught her unexpectedly. Overwhelmed, she could not speak, and reached back for the carriage to steady herself.

Ruth leapt up quickly, steadied Autumn, then held her while she cried. Everyone looked away and gave her time.

When she could, Autumn took a deep breath and blew her nose into her handkerchief.

Her voice still shaking, she said, "Before we unload our provisions, I ask that we all Hold in the Light those Friends no longer with us. Our survival comes at the staggering cost of the loving spirits recently lost to us, as well as those Friends whose journeys ended long before ours. May we follow a path to invest this great bounty to provide solid footing for those Friends who come after us."

End of Book Two

Mr. Bryan lives and writes in Arden, Delaware. Before dawn on his porch, late nights by the wood stove and evenings at Pendle Hill, he works on *Arden House: Book Three*.

Look for news about Book Three in the *Arden House* series on
www.rmbryan.com